A Hell Called Ohio

By John M. Hamilton

Originally published as Hell Called Ohio, 2013, by Dark Coast Press

ISBN-13: 9780991337941

RIP DCP

for my wife

I could pick my nose with a magnet.

BOOK ONE

1

Mario tried to close the cut above my eye with a butterfly bandage but it wouldn't stick. For a second time, he cleaned my forehead with an alcohol wipe causing a mixture of blood, sweat and oil to run into my eye. "None of this would have happened if production schedules were pushed back half a day." I squinted up to Mario as he worked on my wound. "You know? Parts from the previous day could be rattled first thing in the morning by the press monkeys." I was full of brilliant ideas that would make the plant run smoother. Someday, I thought, I might be in a position to act on them.

The second bandage fell to the floor. "Stop sweating," Mario demanded. He tore a new alcohol swab open with his teeth and started over. The heat caused everything to pour out. We were supposed to rotate fifteen-minute shifts loading and unloading the rattlers. These machines violently deburred and deoiled small parts by throwing them against each other or gravel or sawdust. Ten straight days of 103 degree afternoons had chased away the press operators who normally manned them. And so Mario and I were called up from the pen because we were healthy. I hadn't been touched by another human being for three weeks. It felt nice to be cared for as I sat on a box of parts beneath the first-aid locker. Machines thumped and banged their mechanical songs from the press room. Behind Mario opaque plastic screens concealed robotic welders that joined steel. Sparks bounced across the floor. A forklift passed in reverse, its alarm muffled with a rag. It was the third quarter and everyone was concentrated on making their numbers. As Mario pressed one thumb on my forehead and the other in my eye socket we discussed how I had been skulled. I lost my grip on a full shovel of parts and the handle came round with a clean knockout punch. "You were unconscious for at least ten minutes, maybe more." It worried him. But I couldn't report it to the safety office. It was too embarrassing. I had kicked my own ass with a shovel. I talked again about staggering production schedules and Mario squeezed my head a bit harder than needed. I wanted to make decisions, to improve our lot, but foremen slots were rare and unless your last name was Bullough no one wanted your opinion.

The afternoon pressroom temperature was over 110. The hot room made the floor seem cool. Someone had tied a Cleveland Indians thermometer to the rafter above the horizontal barrel deoiler that had been my downfall. The needle was pegged well past Chief Yahoo's foot at 120. Briefly I wondered at what temperature men die. The hot room wasn't hot because of the rattlers but because of the compressors that ran almost most the machines. The compressors created heat. The rattlers were in the hot room because they were noisy. In a factory where everything was hot and noisy the hot room was brutal. Life is gradations. Rich, working, poor. Beautiful, sexy, slutty...

"There, that should hold," Mario said with one last squeeze of my skull. "You could have used a couple stitches but this way you'll have a cool scar. It'll make a man out of you." Marines make the best medics. Mario noted what supplies he had used on the list inside the door of the first-aid locker. That was why he made foreman, that and he was an excellent welder. I thanked him and contemplated my tougher looking future.

2

I clocked out and walked to my truck through the gravel lot. The smell of the river hung in the burnt brown August heat.

Cars left their spaces. Their dust clouds carried through the nearby neighborhood. They would bottleneck at the light. I sat in my truck with the windows down. I might be too tired for anything productive, I thought. I waited five minutes for the light to clear, started the truck and left work.

Looking in the mirror as I drove to the library, I was happy with my cut. The brow had swollen and gave me a fighter's look. Obviously, I had been the better boxer to come away so clean. I ran my tongue over my teeth. They were still tight. I was lucky, but my hands ached and my knuckles felt like they were still full of sand. It hurt to hold the wheel.

Our library is a Carnegie library built on the old site of Fort Defiance, the fort that gave the town and county its name. It was here at the confluence of the Maumee and Auglaize rivers that General "Mad" Anthony Wayne defied all the savages to hell. It was a strategic place for trade and expansion. Only two cannons and a plaque are there now to remind us. Above the doors of the sandstone Tudor the engraving "Carnegie Free Public Library" announced the rich man's legacy. For maybe two years, this bothered me. It bothered me that someone could buy their way into the pantheon of famous American names. What did Washington, Jefferson and Hamilton think? What did Ruth, Cobb or DiMaggio?

It bothered me that someone could trade some trains or steel mills for hospitals or libraries and forever be seen as benevolent. People, The People, had no sense of history. "Read Franz Fanon and Ortega y Gassett," I used to think. But that faded and as I grew older I became more fond of deathbed conversions. Augustine's "not yet" seemed my ultimate ideal. In hell, as the captains of industry gather around their oversized boardroom table, Mr. Carnegie must have a good laugh on the many others who lacked true foresight while still on top. Poor Mr. Gould, someone should have told him.

It is the end of the day that counts. The library matters more than a thousand wronged workers. Its existence is an example of the unpopular notion of the greater good and if someone has to die in order to have buildings filled with books then I am for that too. I would just prefer the death not be mine.

3

As I walked up the stairs I was thankful for the building, thankful for the books and especially thankful for the air conditioning. I pulled the door open and stepped onto the cool dark landing. I turned toward the bulletin board, waiting for my eyes to adjust. I wanted the librarian, Mrs. White, to notice my cut, but she wasn't behind the counter. Some days I wouldn't see anyone else there and if I wanted to take something home I would leave a note on her desk. I preferred the library empty.

I pulled a Theodore Roethke biography off the shelf in the history section. Me and Roethke shared Saginaw, the town of my first ten years. My family had started there and stayed until my father was laid off from the foundries and went to work in Northern Michigan at the East Jordan Iron Works. My memories of that time are not long or vivid. They're mostly of the woods next to farm fields outside of the township. A few grandparents and a dog died then. Other than that it was a youth of bicycles and fishing holes and kind nuns at the Catholic school.

I was leafing through a dog-eared Norton Anthology looking for the names of poets I knew and learning the ones I didn't. Roethke was at the end of this book surrounded by trash. I recognized his name from the field where I played little league, Roethke Park. Then I discovered it was the same man and he was of the same town. It was under his sign that I grasped the fundamentals of base running and the double play. In all his poems I looked for the familiar, a poor tactic for appreciating anyone else's thought.

I wanted to make a note about Roethke's greenhouse on Gratiot road but I needed my notebook. Over the years of daily library visits I had developed a relationship with the building and with Mrs. White. We evolved our own language that was almost all baseball and we talked about life by talking about baseball. She appreciated that I knew who Hart Crane was, but she liked me because I was consistent and loyal. As the years passed and she grew older I think she took comfort that I lurked around, not young, not old, in uniform smelling of burnt steel and oil.

When light bulbs needed changing I changed them and when batteries died I jumped them and when hooligans needed quieting I did that, too. In return, I reshelved books according to my tastes and claimed one of the tables as my own. Of course it wasn't a prime real estate window seat, but I didn't come to the library to be distracted. My table was an odd one-seater in the History nook. Beneath the counter at the circulation desk, she let me keep a banker's file box full of my study materials. It was the closest thing I had to a safe deposit.

And now I wanted to make a note about Roethke's greenhouse. I went behind the counter and took a knee to retrieve my box. Mrs. White would often put a newspaper article, a magazine clipping, a bit of local history, or a baseball diatribe that she wanted me to see on top of the box. Sometimes it would be covered over with junk when I didn't get to it for a week.

Today there was a small two-paragraph biography of James Wright. I stood and read it in the better light and wondered where she found such things. I stuffed it in my pocket and grabbed my box and was halfway back to my table when I heard a new voice.

"Excuse me, can I help you?" a young female voice asked. Shoes clopped across the wooden floor. "Sir?"

I set the box down on my table. It was swathed in afternoon sunlight. A stripe of dust ran through the library air.

"Can I help you?" The tone was hesitant, unsure.

The library usually staffed students from the local college. They were always teachers-in-training who needed to fill course requirements in applied Dewey systems. Her attempt at seriousness exposed her for what she was—a child's face on a woman's body. But everyone has to work and everyone has their own uniform. She stood in bland shoes, nylons, knee length black skirt, and a white silk blouse. A little gold cross hung from a thin chain around her neck. Her hair was piled up in a red mass and her hands were clasped in front of her rather large breasts. Her authority made her nervous, which was the opposite for me. I sat down, looked at her, and decided then and there not to like her although she was much more attractive than the usual chapel mouse. But my convictions are often false or overturned.

"No, I'm alright. Thanks for asking." I think she suspected me of pilfering the petty cash but I didn't feel obligated to help her out. Had she watched me the entire time I was behind the counter? Had she crouched in the periodicals section? I could hear her shifting her weight from foot to foot behind my back. I took my time lifting the lid off the box so as not to give her an easy out. I stroked the top and side of the box as if it was a great treasure at the conclusion of a long quest. I opened it and rifled through until I found my naked lady pen, an odd graduation gift from a long dead uncle. I lifted the pen to eye level and turned it over. It malfunctioned. It was old. The dress fell half way, exposing only her tits. I tapped it with my finger nail like a syringe. The dress fell to her ankles. I turned in my chair and looked at the apprentice librarian.

"Can I help you?" I said in return.

She pushed her brows together. They almost touched. You could tell she wasn't used to being confused. She hid it poorly. Aloofness is the best camouflage for ignorance but she hadn't learned that yet. "No, I thought… never mind," she said and wandered off.

I opened a composition book and noted the date and the fact that a new intern was present. I piled everything back in the box and put the lid on it. In a life empty of substantial victories I had learned how to appreciate even the smallest ones. Run, hide, savor was my technique. I considered it a blessing and a talent to recognize these little triumphs whether over nature or man. It was something that should be taught and nurtured especially in boys and girls who show no great promise of future skill or will. Beat the contestants in a TV quiz show from your easy chair? Snap off the power, sit in silence and revel. These things help free your diet of shotgun shells.

4

Happy in high gear with the windows down I rounded the final curve on the Maumee's north bank and saw the too-familiar sight of my English Setter choking herself. She looked like a white ghost against the giant willow and river scrub. But I knew she was standing on her hind paws, chain taught, only gravity's inflexible bad angle keeping her from hanging. I pulled in the gravel lot and set her loose. She tore a long circle around the old service station scenting for anything new. I walked out to the road and put a coin in the paper box and bought the evening Crescent-News. Upstairs, I changed out of my dirty greens and pulled on a pair of shorts and clean socks and traded my work boots for soft walkers.

At the bottom of the stairs I whistled Ginger up from the bank half wet and happy. We crossed the highway and headed into the wood. Through the oaks and maples the air became cooler and darker and every hundred feet I stopped to listen. Deer flies and mosquitoes filled the lower air. The crows sat in noisy, civilized groups along the edge of the forest. A long shadow passed through a gap in the canopy. I thought it might have been a turkey vulture high overhead. We moved into a small fold that once was and would someday again be a stream and followed it north for another quarter mile. Ginger circled round hoping to walk field edge but I led with purpose through the center of the green. Finally a wide swale formed and the canopy lowered under shorter trees. It was my birch stand, where I came to think or hide.

5

I sat on a log. Mosquitoes circled my head but they didn't bother me because I wore some potent bug dope. I thought about work, books, and about the wood thrush that walked past me overturning old leaves looking for a snack and how odd was it that I had never seen a whip-poor-will? Their call had been with me throughout my life and once gave my heart great comfort on a night march in the hills of Virginia. Their song played in my head over and over until again I thought of nothing.

A bell woke me. The light had changed. It was past supper time. Ginger was scratching her neck and had turned her spinning choke chain into a chime. I stood on sore knees and walked out of the woods to the west skirting the green soybeans. It was silent but for a lone plane high above the flatness. We pressed for home and walking the ditch tops my boots pushed clouds of dust like waves off the bow of a boat.

6

When night came it was down to the middle nineties without a breeze. I stuck a box fan in the doorway and cooked myself dinner, a can of chicken noodle soup. It was the lightest thing I could think of. I sat at the kitchen table in boxers and sweated.

A small air-conditioner in my bedroom window ran full blast but it couldn't keep up. The heat just radiated off the countryside. It was too hot to read or watch TV. I thought I'd go to a movie. I put on shorts, sandals and a threadbare t-shirt. Ginger beat me down the steps and I was half way to town before I realized I brought the dog. I looked at her and she looked at me and I groaned. I couldn't leave her in the truck and I loathed any public displays of white trashiness and wasn't going to tie her to the bumper so she could hide in the shade of the truck.

As I passed the theater I realized my idea wasn't very

original. The lot was full. I drove past without even glancing at the reader board to see what was playing. I didn't want to sit next to someone and have arms or legs touch, even in air-conditioning.

I kept driving and pulled into the video store parking lot. The store had good AC and I took longer than necessary browsing the titles. I ended up with Where Eagle's Dare because of the snow scenes. When I pushed the door open to leave I almost broke Rochelle's hand. She must have seen my truck and might have even planned to jam her fingers in the door. I don't know. She is capable of such things. Rochelle danced and waved the wounded hand. I watched her dance, appreciating. She was thin and muscular and a little greasy. She worked in a restaurant and it left its mark just as the factory had claimed me. Her hair smelled of cheeseburgers. It was there, not obvious, but if you pressed your face into her hair. It was there.

"Oh, sorry sweetie. I wasn't looking," I said.

"Asshole," she moaned and then punched me square in the chest with her unslighted hand.

Rochelle was my love. I should say she was my ex but we hadn't quite figured out the terms. You could say our love had reached an Armistice. She shook her hand and hopped from foot to foot, running back and forth before finally coming to a halt.

"Shithead!" she assailed again.

I shrugged. "Come on. It wasn't intentional." I looked around, up and down the street. "Man, it's hot out here. Come inside." I opened the door for her and she entered.

"That's going to blood blister. I better not loose these nails, Warrell." Rochelle was still looking at her hand. "What did you get?" she pulled the tape from my hands.

"I thought the snow scenes would be soothing," I said. It was a standard. We had seen it many times before.

"Yeah, maybe," she said, turning her attention back to her hand. Rochelle was wearing a tank top, shorts and sandals. We looked like a couple of tourists. Looking at her collarbones and shoulders I wished I had thicker clothes on.

Rochelle looked up at me and her gaze settled on my eyebrow. She reached her hand for my face and I watched her collarbone disappear as her breast rose. Rochelle fingered just beyond the cut. "What happened?" she asked.

"I hit myself with a shovel?" I said.

"Really?"

"No. I fell. Why don't you come watch this with me?" I said holding up the tape.

Rochelle looked up at me for an uncomfortable few seconds and then frowned before agreeing. We walked out into the parking lot and I was glad that she had her own car. If she rode with me there was the uncomfortable decision of seating. The old order: driver, girl, dog would had to have been revised to the newer: driver, dog, girl.

7

I parked under the awning of the old service station to

give Rochelle space to pull in. Ginger looped around the house with her nose down scenting for any new development since we'd left. Rochelle pulled in and Ginger gave her two barks. I waited at the bottom of the stairs. She walked up looking very serious. Ginger followed.

"Listen," she shot pointing a marmish finger, "it's too hot to fuck so don't even try." But then she broke into a bright, girlish laughter and spun around at the dog. "Don't!" she laughed. Ginger had licked her calf. I went upstairs.

As I set up the movie Rochelle got me a water and made herself a gin and tonic. She was still completely comfortable rummaging through my cupboards and liquor cabinet. We settled on the couch and watched the otherness of the Alps unfold. As the movie picked up we settled back arm to arm. Rochelle picked up my wrist and put it around her shoulder. It was more comfortable. We watched or at least pretended to watch. I looked down my cheek at Rochelle without turning my head. She had sweat trickling down her forehead, upper lip and chest. Her hand was on the inside of my thigh and despite my desperate concentration on the snowy subterfuge I was getting hard. My dick had almost reached the end of my shorts, within an inch of her forearm. I tried to content myself with the restrained ecstasy of closeness. I tried to concentrate on the film. I wondered what it would be like to ride a tram. It might be enjoyable if no one shot at you.

"I'm scared of heights," Rochelle said and turned to smile at me. Her forearm pressed against me and she frowned. I raised my eyebrows, helpless. Rochelle's frown softened and then her left hand reached in and held me as we kissed. I regretted and possibly she did too. We had made it three weeks without touching, with only the civil politeness of shared space and barbeque. We stopped kissing and she turned back to the screen releasing her grip on me. My heart thumped painfully and my dick absolutely ached for her touch.

I gave in. I turned again and kissed her temple. Rochelle recoiled but I continued to her ear and she softened. Rochelle looked into my eyes and it was a look I knew very well. She was right about one thing. It was too hot to fuck. We couldn't get it done on the couch. We went in my bedroom and even with the air-conditioner we slid against each other's sweat. Stomachs stuck and it became impossible to know if the liquid came from her or me or both. Afterward I went to the bathroom and brought a towel back. I wiped Rochelle's whole body down like brushing a horse after a ride. She did an inferior job on me ignoring the really sweaty nooks out of politeness. But it was enough to return the blood and we had a second, slower go. After that I was too tired for wiping so we fell asleep with wet bodies and wet sheets.

8

I woke at 4:10 and after a quick cup of coffee was out for my morning walk with Ginger. Rochelle hadn't stirred when I left the bed. She was used to our early departures. It wasn't quite light as we crossed the road and followed the edge of the corn. When we returned a little more than an hour later Rochelle's car was gone. Rochelle was naturally a late sleeper and didn't need to be to work until eleven, so I was concerned.

9

I am not of Ohio. After a decade I might concede from but definitely not of. It was my grandmother who brought me here. She was dying and I left school to be with her. It was during the fall of my third year at Michigan State. I had just returned from my second summer of Marine Corps Platoon Leader Course, their equivalent of ROTC, and had something resembling a breakdown. I hid my condition from my friends, teachers and the Marines. It wasn't difficult. I was in good shape physically. My girly arms had finally filled out and my acne had gone into retreat. My temple looked solid. The problem was my brain. I was reading Hegel and having a tough go. The words stopped having any meaning. Then all words stopped having any meaning, even the words spoken by friends and teachers. I started to sneak away to my room to read Sherwood Anderson and Carl Sandburg, which just made me cry out loud. Only by rousing myself with my 'command voice' was I able to leave the dark apartment and face the world. Even my chess skills unraveled. I perceived opening moves as affronts, insults and threw away games on useless sideshows. I feared that with a gold bar on my collar I might do the same with the fruit of Texas and Georgia.

But then my grandmother called and said, "it's cancer" and I was rescued. After I hung up the phone, I looked out my basement window for the first time in months and discovered the sun. The day was crisp with the sound of leaves and the smell of wood smoke. I cleaned out my rented room. Everything I owned fit in a couple of sea bags and driving South away from school I was confident that I wouldn't return. Two days later from Ohio I called my recruiter, Lieutenant Moore, and told him that I quit. To my surprise, he didn't yell. He only asked I think hard about what I was about to do. That the decision would ban me forever from the officer corps. He said leaving would break my contract, and it was then that I knew the wisdom of a phone. He couldn't see me smile.

10

There was no real reason for my coming to Ohio. I didn't do anything for my grandmother more than stand around. But I was there and that was something of a comfort. Her husband and I drank beer and played euchre in the afternoons. By fate he was a Marine vet of the Pacific and this could have been very uncomfortable. He could have seen me as a quitter or worse, a deserter, but Fred literally got half his ass shot off on the 'Canal and viewed the Corps as a slavery machine. Fred was a freedom-freedom Republican and thought every man should own himself understanding all possibilities and hazards. He didn't "kill nips by the bushel so some big black mamie could sit on her fat ass collecting government checks." In a time lacking great wars or noble causes he didn't mind my semi-desertion as much as he minded my unemployment. Fred called his friend Zachary Bullough and got me on at the factory. It wasn't supposed to be forever, just until my grandmother died. But I stayed on until Fred died. And then I stayed on after that.

Years passed. My parents tried to rally me out of my Ohio sojourn. I know my father was disappointed. I think he was most disappointed in the fact that he no longer had good stories to tell his fishing buddies. I shrugged it off though, as fathers and sons are natural adversaries. My mother's quiet disappointment was much more painful. To avoid it I reeled in my contact and finally she refrained from asking the wrong questions during her calls.

Fred set me up with my house, too. He was a big wheel in Defiance County and owned a lot of properties, including a string of service stations from which mine fell out of use. The county wouldn't re-permit the underground tanks so close to the river. That made Fred furious and he bought two elections but was never able to swing the science. It sat empty for fifteen years before I moved in. I brought my dog down from northern Michigan and got back into small game hunting. I made a couple of friends but for the most part stayed to myself out by the river. I had a nice life going.

11

Four years passed without touching a woman. My desires were strong, but I knew the odds of meeting someone were so slim that it was hardly worth thought. Subscriptions to nudie mags helped. I have always believed that too much sperm is bad for the health, especially mental. An apple a day… same theory.

Once when I traveled down river to Toledo to visit the art museum I was propositioned by a man. He was nice. We shared a beer while I listened to his pitch. "You can just lay there," he told me. "I'll do everything and you can see if you like it." A very convincing argument, but in the end I told him that it just wasn't my bag. He was disappointed and I almost let him fuck me out of sympathy. As I drove home I felt the joy of being desired. In the end he had given me much more happiness than an ejaculation could. I felt human. And later I felt like a tease.

12

Rochelle only came into my life by an act of malice. She was working as the lunch waitress at our local hangout but had always been involved with a long hauler named Tim. When Tim wasn't on the road he bellied up to the bar both to spend time with Rochelle and remind all the other men that he existed. I liked Tim. We played pool when he was around and he had a quick wit. But Tim decided that he was in love with another waitress somewhere in Louisiana and we never saw him again. It was then that Sean McClelland, a jackass from work, started circling Rochelle. He tipped too much and complemented her on everything. He was like an animal with slobbery jaws. I think Sean was scared of rushing in too soon on the heels of Tim but I don't know. My dislike for Sean was deep, deep enough to screw him out of love.

One day after our dinner break I waited for everyone to clear out of the bar and head back to work. Sean may have noticed me still seated as the crew slid back their chairs but he left with the others. Sean was terrified of tardiness. When the door finally swung closed I walked over to Rochelle as she cleared a table.

"Do you want to get a beer after work?" I asked with all the confidence that disinterest and malice could muster. Rochelle smiled and said sure. I got her address and we set a time and then I walked out the door. I wasn't even late punching back in.

I didn't think of her much during the second half of work but as I waited for that final bell I grew excited. Who knew? Maybe she was a saint and needed only to be discovered. The error of my thought would later be laughable.

When I got to her apartment that night Rochelle was already drunk. The long red dress she had on was completely impractical for anywhere we might have wanted to go. She told me she had picked it up in a second hand store. I thought it looked like something my grandmother might have worn. My grandmother was kind of sexy in a dark way. Obviously Rochelle had been steeling herself up for something with vodka and cigarettes. I was uncomfortable. Warning buzzers were going off in my head. Closing the door didn't seem like a good idea but I closed it. Disaster hung heavy. Rochelle didn't say much as she brought me a beer from the fridge. She turned the music louder before going into a sad dance. This was the Ohio I never wanted. It was just like Michigan but uglier. Rochelle didn't seem concerned about me at all and I drank my beer as fast as I could. If Ohio was a river I was about to go dick deep. I grabbed Rochelle by her thin arms and kissed her. She dropped her drink to the floor and wrapped both her arms around me, attacking me with kisses. Minutes later, at the most, she was on her knees popping my belt buckle and swallowing me with incomprehensible enthusiasm. She was looking up at me as I came and I saw tears in her eyes. I put my hands around her upper arms and pulled her to her feet. I picked her up, she was light, and we made the awkward walk to her bedroom with my pants still around my knees. We fell onto her bed and I kissed her face until the tears were gone. When she smiled I pulled up her dress, no underwear, and returned the favor. She pinched her nipples between her thumbs and forefingers and then came loudly. We spent the rest of that night fucking away every demon we could conjure.

13

Three years later as I crossed the highway returning from my morning walk I was disgusted with myself. I knew why Rochelle had left. She must have woken with the same regret. I knew she would blame me, although she hadn't fought very hard. I got another cup of coffee and went down by the river. I sat on the bank and watched the brown Maumee trudge by in the morning light. My Father would never have let himself get into this position, this half-world between no and yes. It seemed my whole life had been spent in that country. Success had been all accidental and failure was the result of misstep. I preferred fate to make my decisions and would have made a lousy officer. I looked west, upriver, where around two bends the Auglaize joined the Maumee, and a job waited for me on the opposite side of the river.

14

For the last year I had been working as a rover. I was free to show up at the plant any time between six and nine. I filled in for anyone who was sick or on vacation or when the order was too much for the normal crew. I spent weeks in welding, a day in maintenance, four at a press, another week in shipping. I could do every job in the factory. Some were better than others but I was thankful for the change. Every morning I would search out the General Foreman, Turnbull, and ask him for my assignment. Turnbull's real name was Bob Reuther but everyone called him Turnbull. I had no idea why. Because I was a stopgap Turnbull liked for me to show up a little later but I could always switch tasks and a little accrued overtime didn't ruffle too many feathers.

15

My relationship to the time clock progressed in phases like everything else. Some months I was ruled by its iron schedule, arriving and departing exactly along the long vertical arms of the clock. And at other times I merely picked a quarter hour to arrive, checked my watch and figured a departure eight and a half hours in the future.

16

It was Friday and I knew where I would be assigned. Octavio Romero, who had a wonderful name but was forever tagged as "Number Eight", was on vacation out of grinding and I had been there all week. So I didn't worry about arriving at work before seven. I bought the morning Toledo Blade from the other box before I left. On the way in I stopped at the drive through for doughnuts and more coffee. I read the scores in the gravel parking lot before clocking in. The Tigers lost again. The first half went well and I thought about the nature of everything. Close to our dinner break Mario drifted into grinding holding a freshly welded part. The adult hall pass. It seemed more than a bit ridiculous that we even pretended. But we did.

Before Mario spoke he pointed to the part.

"Want to go to Mae's?"

I knew what he was going to ask and knew that since it was Friday, our mandatory dine out day, he would be searching me out. I could have thought of an excuse instead of contemplating the nature of all things. So I produced some noncommittal sounds.

Mario again pointed at the part. "I want to go to Mae's," he said.

"I don't want to see Rochelle," I said.

"Move on. Your love life is ruining my diet."

"I saw her last night," I said, pulling off my gloves. The break bell would ring in ten minutes.

"Saw her?"

"She spent the night," I admitted.

Then it was Mario's turn to make noises although I knew the meaning of his. He turned and walked away but stopped after a few steps and returned. "I still want to go," he said.

"If I go you have to agree to have beers tonight. Moral support."

"Deal," Mario said.

17

Mario returned to his zone and I policed my area. Mario didn't deserve my craziness. He had been a good friend for years. We did many things together, at lunch and after work. We played on the same softball team, the company team. He was a hell of a third base. Granted he had never liked Rochelle. No, that's not true. He did like Rochelle until his wife Jill didn't. Jill and Rochelle shared a mutual animosity. It started at a company picnic four summers ago. All the men labored attention on Rochelle. She was well known by all that took dinner at Mae's. I don't know if Jill saw this as some manifestation of sluttiness or was just peeved but the two had words and cemented their relationship. Rochelle would only say that she "didn't like the bitch." Jill would hardly use Rochelle's name when I dined at their house, always unaccompanied. Jill would only ask if I was still seeing "that girl" and my answers would consistently disappoint her. Visits to the Lopez household were rare. It wasn't only my relationship with Rochelle that chilled the waters. I was drinking with Jill's brother Sam the night he died. Of course it wasn't my fault, but nonetheless, I was there.

I put a fresh belt on one of the bench grinders and tried

to remember Sam. I couldn't picture him clearly. I thought of slouched shoulders but nothing concrete. The truth is, I never liked Sam and that made me uncomfortable. I suppose it is correct to hate the dead if they deserve it but a petty dislike seemed ungenerous. I was still alive. Sam had been a failure at everything except being a failure. He was brilliant at that. Who falls asleep on railroad tracks and then doesn't wake up when the train comes? I couldn't beat those thoughts away so I went looking for Mario. He was at his desk working on the afternoon's job list and held up a finger for me to give him silence. His foreman duties still had to be attended even though we would spend the final part of the day in the hot room. The welders were being shut down one by one and the operators walked past us on their way out. They would line up at the clock and we would lose a couple of minutes waiting for our turn to punch out.

Mario put his pencil down and looked up at me, "you got to find someone else." How many thousands of times had he said this to me? Maybe it was a mark of true friendship. "You should come to church with me and Jill. It sounds silly, but it's a good place to meet women. It worked for me."

I protested that the single women at church were single after the fact. They all had children and pasts with messy presents and needy futures. If I didn't want my own children why should I want someone else's? Anyway, Jill was just moved to town when Mario pounced on her.

"Well, it worked for me, and that's all I'm saying." Mario headed for the main building and the time clock.

We took my truck the three blocks to Mae's. We passed all the small white houses. I often thought it would be nice to buy one of these houses and have neighbors who know your name and the details of your life. Then I think, it's too many rooms for me and the dog. One of the bedrooms could serve as an office or den. I had always wanted the den of a country gentleman, a library. It went back to my attempt at officerdom. More than being an officer of Marines I wanted to have been an officer of Marines. Retiring to a nice house in the country would have been my sole purpose in taking up arms. I don't know exactly the origins of this fantasy. Besides the impossible economics, it was a very non-Midwestern concept, rather English or Southern. No, these little white houses wouldn't work for me. The empty rooms would grow with junk and I would collect spare cars and motorcycle parts until my life reeked of gasoline to the bed sheets. It wasn't a good direction. Better to stay in my little apartment with the clean wood floors and a view of the river passing. Better to have some open fields for Ginger to run. Better to keep my earnings at the Savings & Loan. This growing wealth (not wealth in any real worldly sense but the wealth of a single man who earns a solid hourly wage and refuses to stuff it down the throats of others) was my magic lamp and someday I would rub it and demand a new life. Maybe I would return home to Northern Michigan and start up that life of gentlemanly farming without all the accoutrements of honor and experience. Eventually my parents would fall ill and I would have to take care of them in their final winter as I had my grandmother. But who would spend time with me, I thought, in my last days when I am wheezing, incoherent and bitter at the turn of fate that laid me down?

"Are you alright?" Mario asked.

"What?" I had forgotten that I was driving. Luckily we lived in a very slow town.

"You just sighed like… like you lost a hand at poker."

"Just thinking." I steered the old truck into Mae's parking lot. "When did you start talking in metaphors?"

"I did that just for you," Mario smiled.

18

Rochelle's car was parked outside. We walked into the small restaurant that serves as a sort of clubhouse for the industrial workers of the world, or at least of Northwest Ohio. The two TV's hanging at either end of the bar played a day game between the Indians and Boston. The game was at Fenway. We both stopped at the first TV and glanced up getting our bearings, the score and inning.

"Looks like a nice day in Boston," Mario said.

"I can't figure out what all those people do. None of them have to be at work?"

This made Mario laugh. "I'm sure a lot of them are supposed to be at work."

We sat at a table with a view of the far TV. Mario picked up a menu from the center of the table where it was nestled between salt and pepper shakers, the assorted hot sauces and a napkin dispenser. He knew what he wanted but still looked to be polite.

Rochelle was at the order window by the kitchen laughing with the cook, Jake. Jealousy had at one time made me suspicious of their relationship but not now, I told myself. She was wearing a denim skirt, a Mae's tee shirt and running shoes. It was her standard work outfit, but it made me vividly remember pulling that skirt up as we drove around the neighborhood on one of her breaks.

Rochelle looked toward our table and frowned like the neighbor's dog was shitting on her lawn.

"This ought to be pleasant," I told Mario.

"Buck up little bro." I was always "little bro" to Mario even though I was two years older. It had to do with size. There had to be benefits to being small, I just hadn't found them yet.

Rochelle walked over to our table. Two small bruises spoiled her otherwise smooth legs. As I said before she wasn't attractive in a traditional sense. If tits and ass make a woman then I had been fucking a teenage boy for the last three years. Her lines were almost straight. She was sinew and muscle. But more than anything she had a true humanity, an unmanufactured knife like live music. No doctor put her together. Her tears were always real, and her sexuality oozed from every pore, leading a man to believe that she'd hold you through the night when you needed it and fuck you into submission when you needed that. She was a beautiful adversary and my balls ached to look at her.

Rochelle faked a smile and put one hand on Mario's shoulder. "Couldn't you give it, no…" She took her hand away and reinforced something in her mind with a stamp of her left foot. Rochelle then looked at me, talking quietly and direct. "No, I don't care." Then she turned a smile to Mario. "Sweetie, what do you want?"

We ordered and Rochelle walked back to the kitchen

window.

"I think that went pretty good," Mario said.

Rochelle's tactics confused me. She was not the type to be subtle. Her style was frontal and all at once. Her style was that of wolverines and minks, all screams and claws until the opponent ran in confusion and fear. But was she really done with me? Was last night the last time? True, it was what I hoped for, but the possibility of succeeding frightened me.

The rest of lunch went in the same vein, all smiles and politeness. Mario got her standard dose of flirtation, which she withheld from me. That mild sexual innuendo was the reason she made almost as much as I did and didn't have to pay taxes on it.

We watched the end of the second inning and then went back to work. Of course we tipped well. Mario and I worked the third quarter in the hot room and prepared the day's load of brackets for shipping. And I survived without another conflict with a shovel.

19

During the last hours of the workweek our factory was like every other school and business in America, distracted. Thoughts went to leisure and glances went to windows and doors. Sean left his post on the pressroom floor and toured the factory reminding the company softball team of our game on Sunday afternoon. The fall league was starting and every other Sunday for the next two months we would have a game against a rival business or civic club. The season always ended with a final game against the cops, which usually decided the champion. Last year we won.

"What? When... Are you sure?" I liked to fuck with Sean any chance I got.

By 3:15 I had cleaned my area and put new belts and discs on all the grinders as a welcome back present for Number Eight. Hand trucks were in short supply at the end of the day when all the smaller sections began to push the day's work towards shipping or quality control. I had hid one in the back of my zone just after dinner break. I realized that was petty but the world is run by pettiness and personal advantage. Just look at the tax code. The bigger sections had their own lift trucks, welding had one, as did materials and the pressroom. Shipping had two but they didn't like to cross the gap and come over to the production side. And it wasn't hidden that well. The forks were under the four by four box of parts and the handle was pushed to the floor. If someone had come looking for it I might have given it up. I worked the handle, raised the box off the floor and pushed it towards shipping. After turning in my parts I went to look at the river.

The shipping building ran perpendicular to the river whereas the factory ran parallel. The loading bays faced the river and trucks had to drive almost to the bank before backing in. From the loading docks I looked at the Maumee through one hundred degrees of relative cool. Heat waves danced in the strip of burnt grass lining the bank but the brown river moved on. Soon that water would spill into the big pond, Erie. I was in the shade leaning against one of the posts supporting the overhang when Turnbull came up behind me. His voice startled me. His words confused me.

"How you doing Swanson?" he asked.

"What?" I removed my earplugs.

"I asked how you were doing?"

I unleaned myself and unfolded my arms. "Fine," I said. "Good." I wondered what he was asking about. Did he know about Rochelle? Probably. Turnbull knew everything that happened in the factory and most of what happened outside it. I looked up at this giant's eyes through his thick glasses. They looked oddly human, concerned. I wanted to ask why he asked but I didn't. I turned back to the river but didn't lean against the pole and didn't fold my arms.

"I don't get it." I had to say something. Foolishly, I said what I was thinking. "You can hardly spill a glass of water in this heat. Yet the river… I don't get it." I knew about springs and tributaries but at that moment, in that blast furnace, I couldn't fathom the whole. Maybe a spilt glass is part of the river and maybe I'm part of my culture.

"Friday," I said.

"You thinking you're going to stay around here?" he asked.

I became a bit more worried and wondered why he would ask me that? I provided the standard answer we both knew was bullshit. It was the 'yes sir' that couldn't be anything else. "As long as there's work," I said.

"What about a real house and a family?" he asked.

I was a touch offended. I shrugged my shoulders and didn't answer. That was a personal question, something that could be asked by a friend but not by a boss. Turnbull and I had talked often over the past ten years but always about work or war but never about love or life. I respected him as my superior and I expected him to remain there. I didn't want a chatty boss full of false concern for the welfare of his machines. I looked at him sideways but he was looking out toward the river. This giant of a man, what was he up to? What did he care about my domestic yearns? What if I lived in an abandoned gas station? A mystery. A six foot six, two-hundred-and-fifty-pound mystery, too honest to be an enigma. Just a mystery.

"I have a dog," I stammered.

Turnbull seemed disappointed by this answer. He frowned and turned to leave but then looked down on me once more. "In or out Swanson. You're either in or you're out," he said, and then walked away.

It was my turn to be disappointed. Fuck you, Turnbull. If I wanted to look at the river for the last ten minutes of my day that was fine. I had my numbers and I worked harder than most. Fuck you Turnbull, I thought. Of course I didn't know anything.

20

Mario was gone by the time I reached my truck in the gravel lot. I didn't need to remind him that we were going to meet for beers. We always met at the same place. As the truck warmed up I fumbled for a pair of sunglasses from the glove box in the stale afternoon heat and thought about Turnbull's words. In or out. A quarter of the workforce was questionable to show each day. I was always there. I didn't even need the money. Frugality of wallet and spirit meant my bank account was full. I showed up every day because that was what I did, work. It was what I needed. Vacations and even weekends made me nervous, unrooted. As I pulled out of the lot I left with the last of my indifference. The change was coming and I was the last to know.

21

I drove past Mae's. Rochelle's car was gone. I knew it would be but I drove past anyway. Then I drove by the cop shop and counted the cruisers. One was on the prowl. I drove out of town, out past Rochelle's apartment, a one story L of four units. Her car wasn't there. Her neighbor, old gimlet-eye Ed, was searching the ditch for cans. I hard stared him and wished he would have waved so I could burn him with my eyes. But he didn't wave. He saw my truck and went back to searching for cans. Ed was a wife beater with no wife to beat. He beat his wife even when she had cancer. Afterward, Rochelle had found a sympathy for him and brought him leftovers and items from the store but I couldn't find it. No sympathy for wife beaters. I turned in the cemetery gates and drove the little asphalt paths in first gear. The devil's face which in the daylight was only a marble stump stared up at me. Farther past it was my grand-mother's grave and Fred's grave. Every few days I liked to give them a drive by, make sure everything was in order. I drove back to town, to the river and to the library. I trudged up the worn steps and pulled open the heavy wood door. Mrs. White smiled down at me from the circulation desk. I braced myself and adjusted to the relative darkness.

"Looks like the tribe is on quite a tear. They won again today. 7-3."

22

I worked for an hour. I walked into the history section and pulled volumes. I was in no mood for poetry. I needed concrete. A stack of hard books grew in front of me. I made notes. Piper was killed in the Alsace-Lorraine. Why would he move there? No one was ever charged. The Mossad? Possibly, but a little off target. I closed my books and left the land between France and Germany. On the way out I chided Mrs. White about the miraculous powers of Sparky Anderson but she only waved both hands at me in frustration. I did not have any new arguments. There were none. As I turned to leave, the red-haired student stumbled on the first step and shot up when she realized two people were watching her.

Mrs. White said, "Warrell, this is Emily. Our new intern. Have you two met?"

"Yes," I said.

"No," she said.

"It helps if you wait for your eyes to adjust. I'm Warrell," I said.

"Hello," she said and then walked past me. I left.

23

I was lacing my boots when Ginger came and sat next to my legs, laying her weight against me. I scratched her neck and behind her ears and felt the loneliness that Rochelle's leaving created. No longer were these quiet moments in my house a lull before her gathering storm. All of the sudden a painful emptiness filled my chest and tears welled in my eyes. More than a lover, I felt that I was losing a friend. I kissed the dog on the head and cleared my throat. There was still a half hour before I had to meet Mario at the bar so I pulled a beer from the fridge. I thought of Rochelle and wondered where she was and who she was with. The possibility of another crushed me. I truly couldn't fathom the thought and this saved me from some more pain.

I worked my way through a second beer and dug through a pile of boots in the closet. Hunting, fishing, cowboy, combat. Beneath that pile was solid row of old retired work boots. It's hard to throw away a pair of boots so long as they still lace up. I dug out the back left pair. From one of the toes I pulled a wad of cash wrapped with a rubber band and peeled off five one-hundred dollar bills. Thieves never steal old boots. I reburied the boots and put the money in my front pocket, separate from my wallet. I turned off all the lights except the kitchen overhead and held the door open for Ginger. Before locking the door I reached in the corner and picked an old twelve gauge double barrel. I had shells in the toolbox of my truck. Ginger rode in the cab next to me and we headed for town.

24

Mario lived a few blocks from the plant and a block further was The Dead Bull Oasis, one of the worst bars in town. It wasn't bad in the way of reputation or clientele, The Bull just couldn't figure out what it wanted to be. It had once tried to feign a cowboy theme which devolved into a strange railroad motif. Dust and cobwebs settled on everything- bottles, the model train, the steer horns. It's recent aspiration towards sports bar reached its pinnacle of two TVs and a deflating beer logo blimp. But Mario and I liked it because it was always empty. It was our secret, the kind of secret that didn't help the owners pay the rent.

The proprietors lived in the upstairs apartment and it was an even money bet if one would be downstairs when I came entered. Heavy footsteps descended behind the jukebox in the corner and I knew we would be favored with the presence of the man of the house, Bill Gentry. Bill and his wife Honey ran the Dead Bull. Honey failed to live up to her name. She would cluck her tongue at Mario and me if we swore too much or became too vulgar when telling stories. But Bill didn't care about anything, not even the bar. Whatever you were drinking Bill would drink. Possibly he was keeping an eye on quality. It was the reason he owned a bar yet wasn't a drunk. I had never seen him drunk. That fact, I'm sure was related to his size. A three hundred pound man with a thick nose and full jowls he was as constant as a boulder.

"Evening Bill," I greeted him as he circled around the bar.

"Warrell."

"I'll start with a pitcher please. My Mexican friend should be joining me."

Bill nodded as he pulled out a plastic pitcher from under the counter. He filled it then poured himself a glass of beer.

"Can I have a glass too Bill?" I asked.

He grunted. I poured one myself and raised it towards him in a cheers. Bill was already finished with his. We continued drinking in silence.

"I saw Rochelle at Mae's today. She looked good," he said.

It was my turn to drain the glass. "We are not together anymore, haven't been for three weeks," I told him. I didn't need to give my bartender the messy details.

"That's too bad," Bill said. "She always been nice to me."

"Well I'm trying to forget so can we please drop it?" I was stabbed by a new pain.

Bill nodded and returned to silence.

After a while, he spoke. "A good woman's hard to find," he said. "Honey's not so good."

I didn't say anything. We sat in silence alternating pulls from our glasses until Mario saved us from that uncomfortable purgatory.

"Let me guess, Bill. He's been crying on your shoulder about women." Mario was laughing out loud as he said this and instantly cured the mood. Bill smiled at Mario and shrugged his shoulders before reaching under the counter and handing him a glass.

"Thank you," Mario said.

"Sure."

I poured one for Mario and told him I didn't want to talk about Rochelle. We could talk about anything else- religion, politics, my latent homosexuality, anything but her. Mario agreed but told me to lighten up.

"I put that old gun you had in your window underneath

your bench seat. Some highschooler would have come by and stole it before you even set your beer down. You got to be careful. The shits keep breaking into my garage looking for beer," Mario said.

"Ginger's in the truck."

"She's no guard dog. She licked my arm as I reached in."

"She knows you," I said.

"Not really."

Mario put some quarters in the jukebox and we played shuffleboard. We talked about work and baseball and softball. Mario wasn't much of a baseball fan despite being a sensational third base. The hot corner took natural talent. At second I could get by with hard work. We started betting on shuffleboard and I started losing money because I took too much pleasure being the spoiler. I didn't play for the win and thus didn't.

To avenge my losing I began talking shit. That's the reason I play any sport, really. I made a couple amazing shots which I followed with hoots and taunts, but mostly I lost. Mario became annoyed and told me to pipe down or he would pipe me down. I told him that that didn't even make sense and he said I knew what he meant. I asked him if he might want to check something in the alley and he said "sure," setting down his beer.

"We'll be right back," I said to Bill as I pushed open the door.

As I turned the corner into the little alley Mario gave me a push in the back that almost sent me to the ground. "Oh, I see how it's going to be."

"I'll show you what pipe down means," Mario said.

Mario and I had similar builds although he had a good four inches on me. We paced around each other like grapplers before grabbing the upper shirtsleeves. We Indian wrestled, no punching or slapping. All lower body. Mario tried pushing me straight back and I kept pulling him lower to the ground upsetting his balance. We both took knees several times. I laughed through the whole fight. It's a nervous condition that has plagued me since grade school. Principals and Drill Instructors were rarely amused. Mario liked to call me a little girl. I countered that he would know. The fight was ended when Mario turned his hip on me and sent me flying over him. I skidded to a halt in the gravel and mud.

"Fuck you bastard," I moaned. "You win."

Mario was laughing and he helped me up. That is the reason I only fight friends. They don't stomp your skull when you're on the ground. I picked up some glass on my slide and was bleeding from my elbow. We examined the wound and agreed that wasn't worth stitching. We returned to the bar. Bill didn't ask what had happened but kept drinking with us. I felt especially tough drinking my beer with blood trickling down to the end of my pinkie finger.

We drank some more but my thoughts returned to Rochelle. Mario would be going home to his wife but what would I do? I moaned my sad song some more. Mario listened. Eventually we got ready to leave and I paid the tab. Mario put his hand on my shoulder as we walked toward the door.

"You'll miss her for the rest of your life. You'll think of her when you're an old man sitting on some porch wishing you could get your dick hard." He advised me to move on but to never forget her. "She's a part of your life, just like your mom or your little league days. Don't forget the bad stuff though, otherwise you'll kick yourself for ever letting her go. You'll end up regretting a lie, which is doubly stupid."

25

Mario offered me his couch but I told him I was going to drive north to Michigan. Mario doubted the sageness of my plan but didn't argue. I waved goodbye and he walked down the street towards his house. He returned a one-fingered salute. And climbing in the cab I realized that I indeed felt better. That was what I had driven over there for- a little booze, a little sympathy and a little pain. I felt I could inhale fully for the first time in two weeks.

I headed north and made it all the way past Ludington where I turned off on a side road in the Manistee National Forest and dozed off at four in the morning. I pushed Ginger to the floor of the cab and opened the driver's door so I could stretch flat across the bench. The blood of my elbow dried to the fabric of the seat and I woke with a scream when I tried to roll over. It was 5:53 and the sky was bright. I pushed Ginger from the cab, pulled my gun from under the seat and loaded two shells. I didn't have a Michigan hunting license but I didn't expect to run across a game warden. We went into the pines and within two hundred yards Ginger found a stream to drink from. I set my gun down and washed my face with the cold water and then washed the dried blood from my arm. I realized that we were both too hungry to do any good in the woods so we went back to the truck and headed north again. I had coffee, eggs and corned beef hash in a roadside cafe outside of Bear Lake. I ordered a second helping of the hash and walked outside and gave it to the dog. She loved me for that. At least that's how I viewed it.

26

The land rose up and pine alternated with hardwood and pasture with orchard. This sandy land wasn't good for much except fruit trees. I continued navigating secondary roads past empty stores at far-flung crossroads long replaced by asphalt and supermarket chains. Wood barns caved in on themselves and deserted implements sunken into the tall grass of forgotten fields. It's easier to notice the effects of time on other people or on land than to see the change in the mirror. Every face I shave seems to be the same one as yesterday.

27

I skirted East Jordan. The foundry was just over the hill but I had seen it before and knew that it sat idle on this Saturday. I turned down a dirt two track and drove past the sign that designated it a "Seasonal Road- Not Maintained by County in Winter." As a young man I prided myself for being able to navigate from Mackinaw City to Charlevoix never touching pavement. This is handy for avoiding cops, wardens, or in the case of guerrilla warfare. Four miles later I turned left on the faintest of trails, less than a two track. Ginger was fully awake to the smells and sight of the woods. She knew this area and strained to escape the cab. I had to scold her several times.

Deep in these woods I finally parked my truck. I had come to a ravine cut through by a stream and carpeted by dead leaves. The forest canopy was high above and very little under brush grew. It was a perfect spot to shoot a deer, clear avenues of fire. I opened my door and stepped out pushing Ginger's head back in the cab so I could close the door. I rustled through the toolbox until I found a long piece of yellow nylon rope. Ginger never wore a collar proper so she only had a choke chain to tie the rope to. She eyed me with malevolence unused to being bound in any fashion. "Tough titties," I told her. She jumped down out of the cab and sniffed the leafy floor preliminarily before tugging at the rope twice to confirm her suspicions. I pulled my gun from under the seat and put two shells in my front pocket.

We walked the base of the ravine for several hundred yards before I turned and started up a steep hill towards the edge of the wood. I tied Ginger to a tree and she protested with a whine that I shushed away. Where the tree line ended an open field began and the hot afternoon sun tried to penetrate this curtain. Nearing the edge I could feel the temperature rise as if I was approaching a hot griddle. I crouched down eventually working myself into a low crawl. I used a tree trunk to break my silhouette and peered into the open land. A small yellow farmhouse sat neatly between a car garage and a tool shed. My father walked through the mowed yard carrying a shovel. He was heading towards my Mother's garden but stopped and returned to the back of the house entering through the screened porch. He probably had to re-ask what she exactly wanted done again. After a few minutes he returned and went to the garden and began digging.

28

Satisfied, I shimmied backward down the crest and turned just in time to see Ginger pull herself free of the rope and collar bondage. She kept pulling in reverse even after the collar slid past her soft ears. I stood slowly and dropped my gun, opening my arms wide. But Ginger knew she was free and hit a full gallop in two strides. She passed me and my slow reacting body and raced into the meadow. Ginger lowered her head and looped through the grass. I went to the edge of the wood and looked toward my father. He was still digging, still bent to the task, still staring at the soil. But he noticed things. My father could sense a hammer left in the dirt at four hundred yards. I put my fingers in my mouth and let out a sharp whistle. Ginger raised her head and came straight for me. I dove on her when she was close enough. She squealed but I grabbed a solid handful of nape and then standing I kicked her in the ass and called her, "stupid shitbird" in a hushed, angry voice. After throwing her in the truck I went back and gathered her collar and the rope and then up the hill my dropped gun. It was empty but I checked it again before stowing it under the seat.

29

I sat in the cab with the windows open and waited for the amount of time I figured it would take my father to cross the open space with his purposeful stride. I looked in the mirror and was disgusted by my unshaven and bloody slovenness. I licked my hand and tried to remove a black smudge from my cheek. I watched the wall where the sunlight defused, but his figure never appeared in the tree line. I waited some more and then started the truck and backed down the trail.

I drove west until I got 131 and headed south. It was a pleasant day. We drove with the windows down and listened to the Tigers on AM radio. By eight we were in Ohio. Climbing the back stairs I felt dirty and tired but not assuaged of any of my doubts or loneliness. I had found temporary focus away from myself but now I returned to familiar ground. Inside, I showered and shaved and wished it was Monday, but it was only Saturday night.

BOOK TWO

1

The floor and the dishes were already clean as was most of my laundry, so I gave the dog a bath and combed her long white and rust hair until she looked like a show toy and trotted around the kitchen. Unfortunately I smelled like a dog and had to take another shower. So, both clean and soft, we climbed into bed and I battled with sleep while Ginger snored.

Sometime during the night the rain came. I woke to the soft sound of drops on the roof. It was 4:07 and I knew that I was done sleeping. I put my feet on the bare wood floor and could feel the dampness in the air. Horrible purposeless Sundays. Make coffee. Just make coffee and then everything comes from that.

Ginger walked out of the bedroom with sleep still in her eyes. She was all fuzz and curls from her bath the night before. When I opened the screened door for her she just stood in the doorway and looked at the rain. I nudged her butt with my foot and slowly she made her way down the stairs into the mud.

2

I poured a cup of coffee and went back to the landing at the top of the stairs. The clouds hadn't cleared and they hung low. More rain to come. The brown river water worked its way east. Rochelle was somewhere on that southern bank. So was the factory, the library and the cemetery. I considered going to church. It was Sunday after all. I wanted to go to church. I wanted something to believe in that was more than myself. But I never could get past the notion that it made no sense, choosing one God over another. History and geography explained too much and I'd rather be a lonely man than a liar. There would never be a leap of faith for me and that was my own fault. I lacked the imagination for such a move.

Instead, I would do something I understood. I bought both Sunday editions and drove out to the cemetery in the early heat and humidity. If the church couldn't soothe me I would sit next to my dead grandmother. Her stone comforted me. Her stone located me. It was the original untied shoelace, the prime mover. Sometimes I would read. Other times I would nap. I never talked to her because I didn't believe in such things. Okay, sometimes I talked to myself but that's as much as I'll admit.

3

Turning into the drive I locked my front brakes. The gates were still locked. Almost seven and still locked. I looked toward the caretakers shop but his car wasn't there. I opened the gates. I did his job for him. The chain lifted like a necklace off the two inner staves. This was common knowledge to teenagers, adulterers and the occasional graveyard aficionado.

The groundskeeper was not my friend. We would nod toward each other if we crossed paths but I didn't know his name, where he lived or if he had people. He was an old black man with wine stained lips and a bent back. He always knew where his shoes were. He could be late opening the gate on a Tuesday or a Thursday but not on a Sunday. Sunday was the day old people came out to change flowers and contemplate the future. I was worried that some jackass would notice and complain. You can't count on the understanding of your fellows. Even the man at the next machine may be plotting against you. I worried for his job. Worse than death I had this fear of unemployment. Death was known. Death didn't create worry, it ended it.

I pushed the gates into their catches then drove the asphalt trail around the little knoll and stopped on an old oil stain. I was in line with the devil and it was a good place to acclimatize. I pushed the brake and killed the engine. It was hot under the low sky. I stared at the devil but he was only a woodcutter's grave in the daylight. He was a vision in headlights only. In the dark, from where I was parked, a face would appear on the marble stump. It was the devil's face. He had horns and a pointy beard. He was a vaguely Spanish looking devil. And I had seen him.

Mario first brought me here. When I started at the plant I was cutting my welding teeth and Mario was my teacher. We started taking dinner breaks together and then would have beers into the night. Mario was showing me the things I needed to know to have a full life in Defiance. He showed me the train bridge, the island, the dam and the devil. The other places I found on my own; the birch stand and the library. But the devil could never be found on accident. Untrained headlights would flash over the monument and his face would hide. The marble needed to be warmed. The beams had to settle on the stump and slowly his face appeared. I can't imagine that the carver had this intention when he created it. How would he know its position in relation to the curving trail? I think the devil appeared of his own will. At first I found it odd that the devil should live in a marble stump in Northwest Ohio. But after a couple of years I figured, why not? Why shouldn't he? Defiance made as much sense as Paris or Moscow. And maybe the Devil wasn't there when not looked at. Maybe he only appeared at night, in the headlights. Maybe there were many devils. Maybe each town had one. Some might be hidden in a parking curb or mailbox. Only chance could reveal his face, our little Ohio Lourdes.

4

I grabbed the two papers and walked down the trail to my grandmother's grave. She was to Fred's left. His first wife, killed by a train at an unmarked crossing, was on his right. I admired my grandmother's strength. She went into the ground before Fred and took her place next to his first love. I don't think I could have admitted the obvious, that others existed. Throw me in the river before qualifying my love. Some men are petty and selfish. I am one of those. But then Fred went into the ground and he might hold both of their hands.

Reading the papers with my elbow in the grass was pleasant. I read the stories about the towns and the world and felt helpless in their matters. I don't know why but that was okay. An ant crawled up the back of my shirt and I had to stand to shake him out. I left the papers and walked back to the truck. No one else had yet entered the cemetery but I knew my peace was fleeting. I opened the toolbox and rooted around, past the tools and the dog's food and water. An old tall boy lay dented and dirty in the bottom and I fished it out. I folded the top over and foam came seeping up. It was warm and skunked and exactly the thing I needed to perfect the morning.

I went back to reading the papers.

5

"You can't sleep here." A black man against a darkened sky.

"What?" I said. I had fallen into deep visions more real than sleep. I was confused. Sitting up, I brushed some cut grass from my cheek and looked around. A page had drifted off and rested against a stone. A couple other cars had parked and an old woman was treading through the monuments carrying plastic flowers.

"You can't sleep here," he said again.

"I had to open the gates," I said looking at my watch. Damn, past eleven. I wanted him to understand that I had saved his job. He should be grateful. But the low clouds passed through my head and I felt more stupid than normal. I just sat there and blinked, trying to figure out what was what. I wasn't still dreaming. I was pretty sure of that.

"You can't be drunk and sleep here," he said without looking at me. Great, I thought, a drunk thinks I'm a drunk. He was probably drunk himself. Walking away he looked headless because of his hunch and the keys on his belt and the chain on his wallet chimed like bells.

I stood and gathered the papers and the beer can. My jaw hurt from sleeping on my face. Odd to be sleeping above your forever-sleeping family. But it wasn't the first time. I looked at my watch again and it was 11:21. That made me smile. An embarrassing but substantial nap.

6

The clouds had not cleared from the night before and they were growing dark again. I felt the electricity building into a thunderstorm. Very different than what would happen in the fall. I still enjoyed these little artillery barrages. In Ohio we have no waves to watch or mountains to ponder. In Ohio nature's wrath comes from the sky. A drop landed on my shoulder and I made my way for the truck. By the time I crossed the river the first lightning struck. Again, unrecognized portents. I pushed the thin pedal down and four barrels drank deep, fishtailing around corners in that first dampness that brings up the oil and fuel.

7

I skidded in the gravel and ran up the stairs to find Ginger in the depths of an insane fear. Her eyes were wide and her legs splayed. "It's alright," I said calmly, glancing around for signs of new chewing, possibly the windowsill on the river side. "It's alright girl." I spread my arms out to herd her towards my bedroom and the closet. She accepted and turned. Ginger would sit out the storm in the darkness of the closet trembling on my dirty clothes and shoes. The other occasion that caused such a retreat gave me a regretful pause. If Ginger sensed that Rochelle was hurting me she would circle the bed growling. This can damper certain amorous feeling and dogs can't understand therapeutic pain. I would scold her and she would sulk off to wait out the cries of desperation in the closet. It was my secret pride, that the dog should equate our sex with the ripping of the sky.

8

I turned on the TV but the Tiger game scheduled for 12:05 was already on rain delay at Cominsky so I read Manchester's Goodbye Darkness as a cure for self-pity.

When my mother phoned for our Sunday chat she asked how things were and I told her I had just gotten back from church. "Really?" she asked, disbelieving my half lie. We talked about the weather and work and my sister and nieces. She told me my father had seen a dog that looked like Ginger in the yard yesterday and I assured her Ginger couldn't roam that far in a day and she turned from the phone and told my father.

The rain slackened and then finally quit in time for the softball game, which we won 17-8. I went five for six with three doubles. Sean and Mario had four homers each. I made some good catches but fumbled the ball twice as I tried to switch from glove to hand. Rochelle wasn't there to call me an idiot and calm me down after I got flustered. But we won.

9

Monday morning broke clear and cool. I woke at 4:12 and the sky was just beginning to show intentions of change. I felt good and threw the sheet back. Making coffee, I regretted ever driving north without stopping to see my parents. That was just stupid, I told myself. I looked at my elbow and realized that was also stupid.

After a shower, I looked in the mirror and discovered a few more scrapes I had missed earlier. There was an abrasion over the right eye and the cut over my left had scabbed over, so I finally pulled off the small dirty bandage Mario had affixed. I shaved up and with a little gel in my hair looked serviceable. I examined my elbow and washed it again. Infection had started in around the pebbles and dirt and the washcloth wouldn't bring them to the surface. I went to the laundry sink and got a scrub brush. Opening old wounds wasn't as painful as you would think. I knew the stones and dirt had to come out and this made it tolerable. After the surgery I spread a sheen of antibiotic and covered the largest raw patch with a gauze pad and fastened it with cloth tape.

Before work Ginger and I walked in the woods. The robins and blue jays were battling for control of the hardwoods and the crows were bouncing up and down in the beans. We kicked up two rabbits but no shootable birds. As we walked back towards the road and the house the morning crispness was gone. The air got thicker as the first whiffs of humidity came in. It's a shame to leave sweat marks in your shirt at 6:30 in the morning.

I tied Ginger to the willow and gave her food and water to last the day. If it rained she could take shelter under the steps. Driving to work I invented little three note songs with words like, "it's going to be a hot, hot day and still four more till pay." I drove through the party store and got two plain donuts.

The factory was loping along like an old tractor as I punched in but by 7:10 all the presses were pounding out their steady rhythm. Turnbull was nowhere to be found so I donned my leather apron and went to grinding. Number eight waved a thank you to me and I shouted, "How was your vacation?" Too short, he sighed and I nodded my head. I pulled up an overturned milk crate next to a 4x4 box of parts and started in with a little die grinder. The brackets had an interior hole cut by the plasma press and I took off the burr around its edge. It was boring and tedious but I tried unsuccessfully to turn it into art. How ugly the burr, how beautiful that smoothed edge…

Is this earthly heaven? With hands busy and mind content to drift from subject to subject exploring all meaning and substance? Have I found my perfect place? Certainly not! As I spun my die grinder around the cut steel I knew my very short and supposedly precious life was passing on the hands of the time clock. Yet this was what was. For many small reasons this was my life.

I thought about that burr coming off and I thought about my life. Just as there was a box that held parts there was a box that held my thoughts. As I sat on an overturned milk crate working my way through one box I danced around the other like a fighter. I recognized outlines and backed away. Over the years I had gotten better at controlling my thoughts. Fewer and fewer days were spent on regret. Some thoughts were surly and could push me to the ground in doubt and defeat. I avoided those. Some were bright rockets, fantastic and short. Naked women running wet and wanting. I avoided those, too. I deburred another part and looked at another thought that might have been the box. Not wanting to break things, I thought about thought and I realized that this is how my life was passing. The time clock eating my life piece by piece. Each part that I ran my die grinder over was a piece of my life never to be seen again. Those sparks flying were bright bits of my life burning and then gone. I'll never see yesterday or today again. What was accomplished? What steps were taken? What soil was turned? Was work done? Was I happy?

Happiness! The word itself made me angry. Emotion as a goal. I snorted under my shield and fogged the lens. I couldn't fathom why the founding fathers had included its pursuit. Why not honor, contentment, or dignity in death? I blamed Jefferson, the hippie. Happiness achieves nothing, creates nothing, not even its own permanence. Happiness never laid a brick or poured a wall. Happiness never founded iron or joined metal. Happiness never felled a tree or won a battle. Happiness was not in John Glenn's heart as he circled us.

If not happiness, what then? I was really up to speed now, tearing through my pile of parts. I hardly looked at each one. They jumped through my hands. Burning metal showered around me. The finished pile grew. There was progression. Progress? Progress towards the grave. We build. We do. We want and we suffer. But progress entails a belief in something outside, something bigger, a culture, a society, a civilization.

I finished the last part in the box, stretched and checked my watch. 9:08. Perfect timing for the morning break. I felt satisfied with my internal dialogue. Nothing was resolved, but points were made and refuted and most importantly time was passed. I looked down at the finished box and marveled at my ability to work two jobs simultaneously. I was a production machine and I deserved a break.

10

Quality Control was filled with hangers on, people like myself who came to this air-conditioned office just before break time armed with spurious questions. "Is the tolerance .01 or .015? Twenty gauge, right? You want welds here and here right? Not on the outside?" I didn't bother premeditating anything. With my floating status I could always be looking for someone, someone there or not. I went to the corner and poured some coffee in a Styrofoam cup. I fished a quarter out of my pocket and dropped it in the can, making sure it made noise. Parts lay scattered on the granite table painted machinist blue and scratched with measurements. I leaned against the wall waiting for these men who belonged among the calipers and gauges to officially go on their break. They never left the room. Why would you go to a steamy and crowded break room when your work station is the most comfortable corner on the floor?

Jeff Krager was writing on a part with a yellow paint marker. I watched without saying anything. I didn't want to bother him while he worked. He looked at his watch and pushed his stool back.

"Mr. Swanson. How goes things?"

I stepped up from the wall and leaned against the table. "Can't complain. How goes it in paradise?"

"I'll tell you. Air conditioning isn't all it's cracked up to be. It makes my knees ache."

I expressed my condolences and asked about home life. Krager was something of a big brother to the few of us younger guys. He hadn't married until thirty-five and now described a version of domestic bliss that couldn't be all truth but it was nice to hear. When prodded he went on to tell of a drink or a joint waiting for him when he walked through the door and of a wife who was insatiable and obsessive in her love for him. The facts tended to give credibility to his tales. When they were married after a two month courtship he took on her two kids as his own and six years later he still brought her flowers and they acted like teenagers full of lust and abandon. I looked to her for this happiness. After the shit she was formerly married to, Krager must have seemed the savior with a wicked sense of humor. Her ex was a drunk and a bully. I knew him. He was one of those grown children who aren't whipped because of the glandular conditions that turned them into giants.

It was refreshing to hear a man talk well of his life. It was rare. Some give positive estimations based on religion or economics but few because of emotion. And Krager talked graphically of their sex life. Which I enjoyed. You may think him crass or base but I consider his tales as true as Whitman, as beautiful as ditch daisies.

Turnbull walked into the room and I stood straight out of reflex. Damnit, you were never in the military so quit acting like it, I chided myself.

"Swanson. You're here early." He passed from QC to the side office of Bob Thomas, the purchaser, and closed the door.

"Always!" I said, another reflex, and then turned to Krager. "Early for what?"

"The meeting."

"What meeting?"

"About the new line. It's at 9:30. I thought that's why you're here."

I didn't know where to begin so I condensed my stupidity and merely said, "what?"

"The new line. I heard it was going to be your show." Krager looked at me then continued on. "Don't worry you're here on time, that's more than half the battle."

"But I'm here to fuck off. No one told me about any of this. What if I went out to an early lunch?"

"Well, that wouldn't be good. But you're not and the results are the same, so just act like you meant everything."

I slowly returned to my spot against the wall, masking my terror and panic. I considered running out of the room but I was kept there by the eyes of my peers. My mind examined the past few weeks and everything became clear as river water. There had been more meetings than usual. Groups of engineers and toolmakers had toured the floor with some unknown party a couple of weeks ago. But this could have been any new customer. I didn't know what anyone was talking about. I wasn't exactly an observant student of nature. You could sneak an elephant led by a hundred drag queens past me. I admitted this all to myself and decided the best course was to keep silent.

Sean walked through the door. If this was to be my show why was he at the meeting? Sean was, officially, the pressroom foreman, which is not as impressive as it sounds. It meant he was anchored to a press everyday and also took every matter of complaint from his compadres. I had a little bitterness suppressed because I felt the position should have been mine. We were both up for it three years ago but Sean won out due to seniority. After that I took the girl he had been wanting and didn't hide the joy she gave me. Since then he had been dating cows but that wasn't my fault. That's how I squared it in my head, anyway.

After Sean had made his way around the room talking a little with everyone he came over to me. "Mornin' slugger." It was his usual taunt. He chided me for my lack of a long ball on the company team. I didn't protest that grounders were more effective in moving base runners and the point of the game is to score runs, not to always be the hero. Produce something more than praise you ass, I thought. I nodded back his greeting.

When the door opened again in walked the toolmakers Mike Goetz and Paul Brown, old men who hoarded their knowledge. They were worried for the day when a machine not only drew the pattern but spit out the tool. That day was coming and that machine did exist but not for small operations like ours.

They wanted to make it another six or seven years until they could retire. The dogs of progress were hunting them but hadn't yet found their scent.

Before the door closed Justin Bullough stormed in. He didn't walk. He attacked. Almost the size of Turnbull (they had played college ball together) he moved his factory with the strength of his will. Good idea or bad, we rushed to fulfill his thought. It was his birthright. His father, Zachary Bullough, had started this factory in 1936 from a car garage. From mechanic to industrialist, it was the American dream. I tried and tried to dislike the man and his father for the power they held over me, but the facts didn't help. The Bulloughs' paid me a fair wage and I had a doctor when I needed one.

"Where's Turnbull?" Bullough asked out loud. Everyone pointed to the closed door. Bullough crossed the floor directly for me. He came right up to me his face only a foot away, looking down more that across. I was glad I had removed the butterfly bandage. I tried to press into the wall. "What the hell happened to you, Warrell?" I followed his eyes to the gauze pad on my elbow and then looked back up at him. He was staring into my eyes.

"I… fell."

"You fell, my ass. You fell on your face, too. What were you, drunk? I hope you at least got a punch in."

Turnbull saved me by walking into the room. Justin spun around and instantly forgot about me and my scabs. "OK. OK. Well, OK. Now it looks like we got the contract. We start the new line in a week, right?" He turned and questioned the toolers.

They nodded that they would be ready. "The only thing left is to get the government thumbs up. Friday some defense inspectors are going to take a tour and make sure we are up to standards. Fire extinguishers and minimum wage. Things like that. No sweat. Still I want to get all A's. There is always more milk from that cow. Her teats are freakin' huge!" everyone laughed genuinely, not even a boss laugh. "So we'll have a general clean up and polish. Swanson you'll be doing most of it since this will be your show. That is if you can stay off the gravel." Everyone laughed again, except me. "Well, that's about it. You know what has to be done, right Turnbull?" He nodded.

Justin Bullough left the room followed by his engineers and toolmakers. QC slowly went back to work. Turnbull pointed at Sean and myself with two fingers on one hand. "You two, follow me."

11

We followed him out the door into the heat and humidity and the noise of the factory floor. The humidity washed over us like a wet sponge. Turnbull walked fast in long strides and the two of us were at a trot to keep up. He spoke over his shoulder in the loud factory voice. "Just use your heads. Clean all the presses and paint new lines on the floor. You'll have to paint after everyone leaves. Tomorrow or Wednesday night. That's overtime. I'm sorry if you had plans but they just got changed." I didn't have any and I doubted Sean did. "We get a new eye wash station Thursday and it'll have to be bolted to the floor and plumbed. Easy stuff." Turnbull stopped and spun pointing one finger at both of us. "Don't be stupid. Don't fuck this up. Don't waste your time being bitches to each other. Understood?" We both nodded and Turnbull left us slack jawed and sweaty.

I turned to Sean. "Would you mind telling me what this is all about?"

"Yes." Sean walked away.

"Bitch," I said.

12

Back in QC I asked Krager to explain everything to me. It was a standard request. I felt like asking him how life worked but that's what he was telling me all along. Compliment your wife, fuck her real good and often, show up to work on time, do more than you're asked, and finally, call your Mom now and again.

"Sean is such a little bitch. He just walked away and went back to his press."

"He feels chafed because you got this instead of him. He thought he was next in line." Krager put his calipers down.

"Him next… that's idiotic, I'm next." I was so flustered I spit.

"I don't see why either of you deserve it. Why not Paul Anderson? He's been on the floor for ten."

"Paul? He's not management material." I regretted that stupid phrase before it even escaped my mouth.

Krager frowned. "Is that what you think? You guys are 'management material' because of a couple of years of college? Any idiot can fail out. Not finishing something is worse than not starting." Krager had thrown the annoying quotes around my stupidity with his fingers.

"Sorry, that's not what I meant. I don't know why me and Sean are next in line for foreman. It's probably because we're younger than everyone else and Turnbull and Bullough like us or something."

"Yeah, you're a couple of prom queens."

"I'm sorry, Jeff. You know I'm not that big of an ass. I'm just confused about all this."

Krager smiled at my retreat and then told me everything I had missed. Bullough Metal had been trying for a contract with United Tracked Truck in Indianapolis to make aluminum frame supports for the new army jeeps. The aluminum was a special grade and would later be coated in Kevlar for bullet resistance. Everything was coming together. Parts had to be kept separate from the rest of our operation, at U.T.T.'s request. That had something to do with military specs. The parts would also be shipped daily in special boxes to Indy. Cutting, pressing, washing and shipping would all be in the same area. No inventory would build up. That had to do with material cost and also it was in line with United Tracked Truck's business plan.

Krager picked up his part again. "So you two idiots better pass muster. Be thankful for your luck and know that you're stepping on more than one toe."

In the pressroom Sean was working at his press. He had bypassed one of the two triggers, holding it down with a C-clamp. That allowed him to close the press with one hand. His other hand was free to oil the next sheet of metal or scratch his ass. It was how people lost hands and arms. One hand still loading a piece when the other hits the trigger. Then crunch. You now have a hand shaped like an oil pan.

I watched Sean pass sheets through the press. I could see why Sean might be disappointed. His job was terribly boring. He probably made one or two decisions a day- who would work what press and what job. Whenever I came into the pressroom I always knew it was temporary. The day or two was an experience not a lifestyle. I enjoyed the thumping sounds and imagined music, a giant engine working, or a battle. But Sean was stuck here. This could be his life. Oil and metal and jaws that never grew tired.

"Sean," I shouted over the noise. He looked back and pushed his safety glasses up his nose with the back of his free wrist. "How do you want to do this?"

Sean frowned but gave in to the reality of the job. "You clean. I'll mount the eye wash and help you paint the lines Wednesday after everyone is gone." His plan made sense and he still had to run his press where as I could be cut loose anytime. "OK," I shouted back. I finished the rest of the day in grinding.

13

As I punched in Tuesday morning I had yet to realize the opportunity in front of me, to realize the door that had been opened. Quickly I obtained a tilt dumpster. It might have belonged to some other station but I passed by with a pallet jack and it was gone. I had no time for proprietorship. Possibly the whole future of the plant depended on me. I was working for everyone's advancement, not just my own. I pushed it into the pressroom and emptied all the trashcans. Then I swept the whole pressroom floor, from ears to asshole, from one corner in a widening arc until I once again found the distant corner pushing a pile of rags, paper and metal scrap. I followed my broom into the next room. I swept through grinding and around the robotic welders, taking burns on my scalp without a flinch. I pushed through the staging area outside Quality Control and then looped back into the pressroom. Sweat dripped from my nose in a steady rhythm and it was not entirely due to the high nineties. I was working, pushing harder than a boss could ask, spurred by myself and my dreams. When I looked up I noticed that almost everyone was gone. A few stragglers still wandered toward the clock. It was rare that I wasn't able to approximate the time within ten minutes. I smiled, this was good. I borrowed a forklift and dumped my trash.

14

After clocking out I looked for Mario's truck but he was already gone. Tuesdays he usually took dinner with Jill at home. She didn't work on Tuesdays. I went to Mae's, took a table by myself and read the Fort Wayne paper. Rochelle looked tired but I hardly noticed. My life was moving in new directions and new possibilities were appearing. I only had to recognize them.

"Mornin' Sweetie. How's life?" she asked, possibly not even noticing who I was.

"Lonely, but encouraging," I said. Her eyes opened a little but quickly faded to the previous sleepwalking stare.

"The usual?" she asked. I nodded.

Next to me an eight top was filled with my coworkers but

I didn't say anything. I don't think there was any animosity but I may have come off smug. I left a little early, eager to get back at it. With the sweeping done I set to cleaning the presses and their control boxes with an artist's eye. I knew it would be impossible to clean a factory, to make it shine. So I cleaned what would be seen to the naked eye. I practiced walking through the plant. The foreground needed attention but the back could fade with the natural oily patina. I needed the inspectors to see a competent workforce that produced according to a system that involved quality checks and assurances not the anarchy of a Guatemalan street fair. I cleaned the press sides and control boxes with my rags and solvent. I tried to make small talk, to joke with the operators, but they had to keep working. "Housekeeping," I would shout over the noise. That got a couple of laughs but Deborah Barnes ruined the tactic. "What?" she asked again and again until I explained the joke and explained that the joke was a joke but then she looked at me like I was trash. I felt self-conscious, an intruder in the soot. I didn't like it, feeling like an outsider. I couldn't muster the distance it took to be a boss.

15

Maybe it wasn't me. The atmosphere of the pressroom had a death row permanence. An operator could work the same press for ten, fifteen years. There was less joking, less camaraderie than the other sections. It was solitary work in a room of solitary workers. Sean kept everyone supplied with blanks and the parts kept dropping into trays destined for rattlers or parts washers or QC. It was the picture that burned in a Ludditte's eye-dark, dreary industry without the row houses and squalor. The work never bothered me, it was their resignation and I looked for the strength of Epictetus or a pleasant enabling ignorance but then maybe I was thinking too much.

16

I had made it through the smallest presses, the widget makers, and was progressing toward the giants. Through my journey I had removed artless porn and left family pictures infinitely more disturbing. Homicidal spouses and criminal offspring pushed the operators on like personal Stalins, reminding them of what they had to look forward to. It's what made this voluntary Ohio gulag possible. Better were the pictures of cars, fish and deer. Even the impossible airbrushed bodies were better. But the sex had to go. The government was coming and for some reason they had outlawed sex. Possibly it was a consolation to the religious for outlawing God. Probably not. My cleaning journey was near its end and I feared to ask Dale Wierenga to remove his pictures.

Against the far wall, like an altar to the pews of the smaller presses, Dale worked a 600-ton monster made by our brothers down in Minster. All day he threw blanks and parts that grew in thickness from sheet to near plate. His strength and size seemed complimentary to the press. His neck was constrained with two buttons open and even with a total of seven fingers he was a hand crusher. Dale was Korea not Vietnam and only the older Bullough had been around longer. I doubted Sean ever told him to do anything and now I was about to rid him of his women? I could always blame the faceless government, a coward's retreat.

But as I came closer I noticed something else. Quality, an almost artistic quality, more suggestive than explicit. An arched back. Clawing fingers. I studied the pictures more. Two were printed on nice heavy paper. One was a laminated postcard and the last had been razored out of a book.

"Nice, eh?" Dale stopped working.

"Yes, very." I continued looking, absolutely free of embarrassment. "Where'd?" I asked.

"Amsterdam," he moved closer and pointed with his ring finger. "That one's French and the postcard is Norwegian but I got them all in Amsterdam. I go back every five years or so, visit my mother's people. They still live there. You should go there. You can get anything… anything." He pushed my shoulder with his vise like fist for emphasis. I had to reset my feet.

"I need to…"

"Yeah, I know. Just be careful and put them in my locker when you're done." With that Dale went back to work, taking it for granted that I knew which locker was his, which I did.

17

Wednesday I worked in shipping and at 3:30 I crossed the breezeway. The line painter was kept in the maintenance bay. I looked at the floor and the shadow of the old lines. They wouldn't be difficult to repaint. It was just tracing. Too bad I couldn't get the floor really clean, down to the concrete. The whole factory floor was covered with a black gum made of oil, dirt, metal and whatever other raw materials circulated in the air. I could press my fingernail into it yet the forklifts left no tracks.

"What the fuck are you doing?" Jack asked.

I stood. "Afternoon, Jack."

"What's so fucking good about it? This place is fucked-it's all politics and cliques. But you'd know about that. You're all buddy buddy with Turnbull." Jack went to his toolbox and started putting the day's tools away. Jack seemed to hate everything-the job, the workers, the air. I accepted that he hated me.

"Oh, I don't know about that."

"What, are you stupid? Don't you see what goes on? If they had a chance they'd can us all and fill the place with Mexicans. The Bulloughs only care about money." Jack threw some wrenches in a drawer and then slammed it shut. "But fuck 'em at the pay window, right?" He was wiping his hands on a shop rag.

Overtime. Neither Jack nor I needed our overtime approved. Maintenance worked until their jobs were complete and only they knew that schedule. Everyone knew maintenance padded their hours, went on parts runs that took half the day. And I hadn't been under a foreman in two years. There was no one to check my time card. I was on overtime poking my fingers in the dirt.

I shrugged my shoulders. "Maybe," I said.

"Maybe. Yeah right, maybe. Play it both ways. You and that pretty boy Sean." Jack walked past me. "Just don't fuck anything up. Last time Sean painted lines I had to dip the whole trolley in thinner." He walked away throwing the rag in the trash. It should have gone in the laundry.

18

I had never thought of Sean as a pretty boy. Jack made me tired. I didn't like talking to him. The line painter was in the corner, loaded with a fresh can of paint and two more at the ready. I was hoping for a little instruction from Jack but I didn't want to ask. It wasn't too hard to figure out and within ten minutes I was tracing right along. A little while later Sean came by.

"You don't really need my help, do you?" he asked.

"No," I said and then he walked away. It took me two hours to repaint every line in the old buildings. When I was done I cleaned my tools then clocked out. I noticed what cars and trucks remained in the lot. Turnbull was still working, as were the engineers and toolmakers. I drove home.

At home I changed into a t-shirt and a pair of shorts and sat on the top step and listened to the Tigers game with one ear. A gentle breeze blew the willow's long arms and the summer heat seemed to be dissipating. The days would still be hot but there might be some relief. It was 2-3 in the 5th. Detroit had a runner on third with two outs. I fetched a beer from the fridge and sat on the top step. The batter looked at two fastballs and then struck out swinging at a curve. The inning ended. I looked out over the river and wondered what it would be like to play on a team so outside the running that the games mattered only to the players and statisticians. The players could be motivated by pride, respect for the game and a sense of professionalism but most likely they were spurred by fear, the worst whip. There was no job security in baseball. You either produced or went away and sitting above the river watching the slow brown flow by that seemed cruel. Our society had no compassion for the almosts and as a man of no great talent I could root for the winners but too often identified with the losers.

19

Thursday passed quickly. I ran a shear press all day. I was away from the pressroom and my cleaning efforts. No one walked to materials to express either displeasure or satisfaction. At lunch Mario said the lines looked straight and I thanked him for that. At the end of the day I again swept the pressroom and emptied the trash bins. The lines had been scuffed in the traffic areas but this gave them a natural look.

20

After work I washed the bugs off my truck. My rambles through northern Michigan had covered the window and grill with a film of insect death. I let Ginger run loose and she sniffed along the river's edge and then tore across the highway into the field and looped back. Whenever she came within range I squirted her with the hose. That just motivated her to run some more. Stupid and happy was a good way to go through life.

I was washing my tires when I noticed a bicycle coming up the road over the hot black asphalt. People often rode this way, even some laden with camping gear and flying their little orange flags of health. I went back to my work but as the lone bicycle came closer I noticed it was being ridden by a girl and this demanded one of my eyes attention. I felt no shame in that. In this monochromatic land beauty stood out garish and rude. The lone train bridge or old silo figure as triumphs but most Midwestern architecture stirs sympathy instead of awe. The lack of the natural and cultural force you to expand your criteria to the human. I'm merely a student of aesthetics I always told myself after ogling some innocent. And there is a thin line between aesthetic appreciation and a leer. I walk that line.

I returned to washing my grill which was pointed toward the road and looked down toward the girl on the bike. It looked like... but no it couldn't be. Two hundred yards out I was pretty sure it was. The bicyclist coming across the hot asphalt, out of the mirage of heat waves, was the librarian Emily.

Ginger tore off down the road toward her. My sponge was stuck in the open grill but I couldn't get my arm to move. I looked again at a hundred yards and reconfirmed my sight. Why? I was confused. I couldn't understand progression, cause and effect, action and reaction. I started to scrub feverishly on the hood, too feverishly. I looked again at Emily, it truly was her, and she was talking to Ginger as the dog trotted along her side. I stood up straight and tried not to smile so wide. The librarian was only thirty feet away from me. She was in the one place where I could do anything, where I felt comfortable, where I was myself and not an employee or a buddy or a brother or a son. Emily looked at me standing next to my truck wet with washing in the midst of a desert of Ohio nothingness. Her face screwed up tight like she couldn't place me. I thought that was bad.

"Hi," I said with a forearm wave.

Emily swerved a little then smiled, finally placing me in her mind.

"I don't have that many overdue fines do I?" I could have hugged myself. I wanted to run around the yard and spin cartwheels. Never had I been so witty. Her smile was proof and her tiny hands pressed on the brake levers.

"Hi," she said back.

I wiped my hand on my pants and stuck it out toward

her, “I’m Warrell.” She smiled and said she remembered and I regretted my lack of style. Sometimes honesty isn’t enough.

“What are you doing here?” I was still confused.

“Riding my bike. Not now, but I was.”

A blue jay barked and the willow shook its sad arms. Then a car passed. Still, I didn’t know what to say. I wanted to walk away and jump in the river.

“It’s a nice day and I wanted some exercise. So here I am.”

She was wearing shorts and an old gray tee shirt wet from sweat. Her forehead sparkled with the dewdrops of perspiration and her long red hair ran in a braid all the way down to the small of her back. I loved its length. She radiated health and beauty and I basked in that warmth.

She wiped the sweat from her upper lip with the back of her hand and looked at me.

“Would you like a glass of water?”

“Sure. That would be nice.” She dismounted her bike and pushed it by her side as we turned in off the road.

“I see you’ve already met Ginger.”

“Who?”

“Ginger, my dog.”

Emily looked down at the shadow of a canine and said,

"Oh, yes, she met me down the road and led me here."

I wanted to give Ginger a treat, maybe a side of beef.

"You live here?" Emily was looking at the River House incredulously. "In a gas station?"

Right then, as if commanded, a wind blew some flaked yellow paint off the old wood building and floated down toward the river. The awning sagged toward the metal plates that covered the hole where the pumps had been. Behind the dirty first floor window-yellowed newspaper clung out of habit. I had read all the stories and ads. Cars were very cheap in '72 but inflation is a difficult concept.

"I live upstairs. It's pretty nice, actually. The place was owned by my Grandmother's husband but he's dead."

"Your grandfather?"

"No. Just her husband."

"Where's your Grandmother?"

"She's dead, too. They're all dead, that generation."

"I'm sorry," she said.

"Yeah, it happens. That's why I'm here. Ohio. I'm really from Michigan." We were at the foot of the back stairs. My rusted lawn mover and an old bicycle lay decrepit under the steps. I didn't know if I should invite her upstairs, so I looked out at the muddy river.

Silence fell upon us, a silence she probably thought was

regret for the dead but was actually the stupidity of the living. "I sure could use a drink of water." She smiled at me.

"I'll get you one." I started up the stairs.

"Actually… can I see your house?" She put her small smooth hand on the old railing. My hand was a foot away on that same railing and I could almost feel its touch.

"Sure, come on up." She followed me in. Ginger followed the two of us.

"Wow," Emily said once inside. "I didn't expect it to be like this. I mean the color." She looked around at each wall. The living room was painted a dark wine color and kitchen next to it was a bright yellow.

I walked to the fridge and pulled out the water jug. "A few years ago I went through a phase of reading about artists. I call this Van Gogh yellow." I swept my hand around the kitchen like some game show. "I couldn't draw a straight line so I painted my walls. Rollers are like crayons. My bedroom is a dark blue. That's supposed to be soothing." I regretted mentioning my bedroom. It seemed too forward.

She walked over and looked through the open door at the blue. "I like it," she said. I followed and handed her the water. I was glad my bed was made and all the clothes were off the floor. Looking in the bathroom I noticed that my towel was crooked on its rail.

"I couldn't decide on a color for the bathroom."

But Emily was back in the living room looking at the

bookshelves that ran the length of the west wall.

"I like books," I said.

She continued reading the spines. I hoped she wouldn't be disturbed by any of them. I had a few histories of the SS and quite a bit of classic erotica. But she just glanced over it all.

"I don't understand."

"What's that?"

"You have copies of the same books that you hid in the World War Two section."

"Well, I didn't want to search all over for them."

"But if you own them, why do you even go to the library?" she asked.

I didn't want to tell her of loneliness out here in my bachelor perch. "I only buy books that I know I'll want to look at twice."

"Yes, but Sandburg, Whitman. You have copies of all these here," she said with what I thought was professional curiosity.

"Well I can't carry them around with me," I said.

She stood and smoothed the hair from her forehead. "May I use your bathroom?"

"Sure." I pointed the way but there was no other option. When the door closed I hurried over and tried to see my books with her eyes. A redundant section of guidebooks had never taught me the difference between firs and pines. There were definitely some questionable titles. Genet next to Nin next to Sajer. She must have thought I was a rapist. I was infinitely glad I had put my half finished model of the Bismarck in the closet. At least the bathroom was clean.

Emily came out of the bathroom, smiled and resurveyed my house. "I didn't expect you to have a TV."

"How would I watch baseball and movies then?"

"You like baseball?"

"Oh fuck yeah," I said. There was some silence. What did she mean by expect? Did she ride out here to see me? I suspected the machinations of Mrs. White, but a glance at my library record would have revealed my address.

"I should get riding," she said.

"Alright," I said, immediately regretful of her leaving. I missed a woman I didn't know before she'd even left. We walked to the screen door and I held it open for her. She thanked me for the water again and said goodbye. Emily patted Ginger on the head and I had to hold the dog's collar to keep her from following after the woman. I stayed upstairs and watched Emily ride her bicycle off toward town. Outside the water was still running.

BOOK THREE

1

I watched from the kitchen window until she disappeared around the curve. I turned to the dog. "What the fuck was that?" She didn't know either. I inhaled deeply and thought I could still smell the slightest hint of perfume and sweat. It may have only been my imagination, but the result was the same- sheer and boundless ecstasy. I hurried to close the door and windows, trapping her essence. I put on some music and danced until I was sweaty and laughing. Ginger lay on the couch wondering if I had lost my mind. I thought I should go out and hit the bars but knew other people would deflate me.

Then, the phone rang. I answered.

"What are you doing?" Rochelle asked.

"Dancing, hang on a minute." I put the phone down and turned the music off. "What were you saying?"

"Who are you dancing with?"

"No one. Why?"

"I just wanted to know what you were doing. I wondered if you wanted to do something. We could watch a movie?" Her voice was soft and sad.

I put the phone down and paced in a circle. Damn this woman. My good mood was gone and my cock had stiffened. I didn't want her. I wanted Emily, and not in the same way. I wanted to hold Emily's hand. I wanted to smell her again. I wanted to buy her things. I picked up the phone. "Sorry, I had some water boiling over."

"What are you cooking?"

"Nothing."

"Then what…"

"Look," I cut her off, "if we're really split we shouldn't be hanging out together." I patted myself on the back for the courage it took to say that but I felt ill.

"I had a bad day at work. I don't want to be alone…" Her voice trailed off in a plead for friendship.

"Alright, come on out. Pick up a movie, though."

"OK, I'll see you in a little." She hung up.

I felt as if I had sullied my afternoon, soiled the memory of it. I walked around the house opening windows and doors. I sat on the couch, head in my hands. I knew what would transpire and honestly I didn't regret inviting Rochelle out. I smiled and looked at Ginger. "Well shit. Isn't life odd?" She didn't respond. Then I remembered the half finished wash job in the driveway.

2

Outside I picked up the hose and scrubbed off the dried soap. I was just finishing up when Rochelle pulled in the driveway. I asked her what tape she picked up. Something new, stupid and appropriate. As we walked up the stairs I asked Rochelle what happened at work, but truthfully I didn't care. Now that she was here her presence made me angry. I didn't like the power she held over me. She talked and I didn't listen. I told her I still needed to take a shower and to make a drink if she wanted one.

She knew where everything was, everything.

In the bathroom, I took off my clothes and stood under the water angry and defeated. Rochelle's voice was far off as I let the water run over my head and thought of Emily.

"I asked if you had seen this."

When I opened my eyes Rochelle's face appeared at the far end of the shower. She looked me up and down, smiling. I said, "Get!" like I commanded the dog.

Most of my negativity went down the drain with the soap and sweat. I was thinking of Emily as I came out of the bathroom and found Rochelle lying on the couch covered with the camouflage poncho liner that I used as a blanket. She got up to fix us a couple of drinks and I slid underneath the blanket without any clothes. Rochelle saw me do this and smiled. She walked over with two drinks held high like she was serving at the bar and handed me mine. The drinks were pretext. I took a sip and put it on the floor. She placed hers on the end table and asked, "shall I?" I nodded. She unbuttoned her shirt, not in a slow teasing way, but with a confidence and poise. Then off came her bra and finally she slid out of her jeans. Rochelle rarely wore underwear.

I told her how beautiful she was and it wasn't completely a lie. What she lacked in artistic form she more than made up for in style. Her movements made her beautiful. Her self-assuredness knowledge of her own body made you fear its power. From ass to armpit, she was in control.

As we settled in for the movie, Rochelle lay on my chest between my legs while I rested on some pillows. The movie was not funny but I couldn't help but laugh at every joke. I don't know if I laughed out of pity or of embarrassment but nonetheless I laughed. About forty-five minutes in Rochelle grew bored and started to stir. She had been holding me but her hands grew animated. Then her head disappeared under the blanket. I tried not to laugh at any of the stupid punch lines but I shook the couch once or twice. To Rochelle's credit she stayed on target and I thought it had turned out to be a pretty good day.

3

The moment I asked Rochelle if she wanted to stay the night I realized it was not the smartest thing to do. We made love the old fashion way and Rochelle came in her usual boisterous and violent manner. I was having difficulty concentrating. My thoughts were wandering between the librarian, work and Rochelle's body. This was an unusual problem for me. Rochelle noticed my consternation when she regained her sanity and she flipped me over in an attempt to ride me home.

"It's no good," I said, holding her waist.

"Why? What's wrong?" There was hurt in her voice.

"I don't know. I think I'm thinking about work."

She slid down next to me. "Oh baby," she paused, "don't you want me anymore?"

"You're all I want. There's nothing in the world like being inside you." I lied, although I didn't know to what extent. Even now it is hard to tell.

She laid her head on my chest and warm tears fell from her eyes. She continued to stroke me and I stared at the ceiling, wondering if it was all over.

Rochelle slid up to my ear and whispered, "I can go some more if you can." As soon as I nodded she had her beautiful ass pointed toward the moon and the river. I thought it might really be the last time and that thought spurred me to enjoy her depths, her smells and sounds. When I finally came it wasn't momentous or memorable... more like slipping off a moss covered rock. Neither of us was tired but we feigned sleep so as not to talk.

4

I woke up early, 4:05, and snuck off to the shower. I shaved carefully and combed down my hair. Sitting at the kitchen table drinking coffee my mind was on the inspection. I imagined stern government officials with a military escort were going to measure and note everything then judge if we really were a superior enough operation to be awarded a contract. If so, then everyone smiles and the sound of corks popping rises above the factory din and it's all handshakes and backslaps for me. The fantasy vaguely resembled a successful NASA mission.

At a little past five I decided to drive into town for a couple of donuts. I bought the Toledo paper and read it while the truck warmed. I knew Rochelle would sleep until I woke her. Ginger got in the cab beside me and we drove with the windows down toward town. The sky was losing its last touches of pink. The air was cool and moist but it was going to be hot. I thought it might be a good idea to take a spare set of work clothes in to the plant so I could have fresh creases.

The drive through was open. It was always open. I bought my doughnuts. It was 5:30 and I could have driven straight to work. I would have if not for the naked woman in my bed. In days past Rochelle would sleep until she was satisfied and lock my door on her way out. It was nice to be at work and think of her slowly stirring and then walking across my bare wood floors, her naked body giving grace to my home.

I drove east again along the river. Ginger tried to eat the donuts and I slapped her twice on the nose. I quietly shut the screen door behind me and peeked in at the sleeping woman. Her hair was wild and matted and beautiful and in that moment I regretted that we could never seem to make it work. We were free to turn away from this and look for something else that may never be found. That was our reward for keeping sperm and egg separate. I read the rest of the paper and ate one of the donuts. At 6:20 I went into the bedroom. Rochelle lay on her stomach with her face toward the wall. I rubbed her shoulders and tried to whisper her awake. My hand grazed her back, exploring the skin it had visited so many thousands of times and finally stopped to tickle her ass. She woke and spun an angry look up to my eyes. I didn't know what she initially saw in her half sleep but her eyes found my smile and her face softened and arms reached toward the heavens hands clasping open and shut.

"You're all ready for work." Her voice was broken by stretches and sleep as we embraced.

"Big day today," I said.

She frowned as I pulled away and checked the clock on my bed stand, 6:24.

"What time are you going in?"

"By seven."

"Why don't you lay down next to me for a little?" She opened the blankets, exposing one beautiful flank.

I told her I couldn't and instinctively looked at the clock again.

"You always have time," she pouted. "Get out of those clothes and come down here with me."

"I can't…"

"You know you're going to regret this." She tossed the sheets completely off her and rubbed her sides and hips with open palms. I wondered how she could wake up so together and truthful. I would regret not climbing into bed next to her and it wasn't because of the power of suggestion. She pushed her lower lip at me in a mock pout. I began unbuttoning my shirt and she clapped her hands like she had just won a gamble. I had to sit on the edge of the bed to take off my boots. Rochelle rolled from side to side, giggling, taunting me.

A proper regret would be for my weakness or for the power this little woman held over me. But that regret would be as false as my belief in the power of sweat. It worked for us then. It worked better than most other times. Possibly because we were fresh in the morning and not yet weighed down by the reality of our emotion.

After our embrace slackened I realized that I would not make it to the time clock by seven. Rochelle rolled out of bed and skipped off to the bathroom. But I just sat on the edge of the bed rubbing my shaved face, then regretfully put my clothes back on over a chest and back coated with sweat and loins still wet with the juices of weakness.

I didn't rush. I sat down and enjoyed another cup of coffee with Rochelle. She refused her donut so I ate it too. We talked about my work and it was peaceful.

In the driveway, I gave Rochelle a kiss goodbye like we were parting for ten minutes. It was a quick meeting of the lips not filled with the mournful passion our situation warranted.

5

A little late for a job that never had a fixed start time I drifted through the old plant picking up rags and straightening anything not bolted to the floor. Even with my paranoid and overly interested eye what I saw was straight and true to an aging factory on the banks of the Maumee because no amount of paint would turn the wood and tin into steel and concrete.

Yet I wanted to do more. I wanted to be asked to do more. I wanted to jump out of an airplane and storm a machine gun nest. I wanted my own personal Normandy. Such little effort, such little concentration could only pay off accordingly. There were no ten to one odds. Here it was even money. Maybe I hadn't done enough. Doubt filled my chest like expanding foam. I stumbled towards Turnbull's office convinced of my failure. I stuck my head in and he muttered "welding" without looking up from his paperwork.

Ignoring his command I lingered, leaning on the doorjamb, as my heart slowed to its normal gait. The fearful moment had passed. Next to me a small widget press hit fifteen times to the three strikes from one of the large plate benders. I listened to the building factory noise.

The robotic welder behind me was saying something in

morse. It made one short tack and then ran two beads. Again, the same pattern and then a break as the arm swung to a new position. Over and over again these two letters: dot-dash-dash, dot-dash-dash. I tried to remember my morse but couldn't get past SOS. Unfortunately my Boy Scout troop had proved more adept at hockey than deciphering code. I wondered how many messages throughout life I had missed. Burning bushes were in short supply. But what of the rustle of leaves, the pattern of wind swept waves and the staccato sound of factory machines?

"Welding," Turnbull said again and I unleaned myself.

6

Mario was at his desk in the next building over doing paperwork. I sat on the edge of his desk and he quickly said, "don't," so I stood again. He continued entering numbers into his calculator and then noting the results. "Are you here for a reason?" he asked.

"I'm working with you today."

Mario looked up with pain. "No shit? This is what I get for being on top of my game, huh?"

I shrugged and sat on the edge of his desk. Mario was upset because he was good at his job, both as a welder and a foreman. Mike Johnson was out for three days because of a vasectomy and Mario had already planned for the missing man. Being saddled with an extra man when one wasn't needed was considered babysitting. It was a game the section heads liked to play with each other. Whenever possible they passed their bad cards on to the next guy.

"Sean might need me," I said, thinking only of the inspection.

"No, Turnbull knows what he's doing. Maybe he wants you kept out of sight." Mario smiled, knowing he had cut me.

So I was put on a 10" grinder to smooth welds on tractor suspension hangers. The job wasn't too bad. At least I wasn't inhaling welding fumes. Grinding is nice because it's visually stimulating. The showers of sparks let you know that you are doing something. I invented games to soothe my mind. The pieces were 1/2 inch steel plate. Each one weighed fifty pounds and had three welds on each side. They were a little unruly and the temptation was to bend over at the waist and just flop them over and then on to the next pile using only your arm but I tried to move each one correctly, with my legs. This slowed me down a bit but it protected against a back injury. Too many men were chopped in half by bad backs. Once your back goes you might as well return to school and take up accounting because your active life is over.

The first quarter went fast and I tried not to think of the inspection. But when we went on break my feet ran over to QC and I just followed them. I asked if the inspectors had been through but no one had seen them. Second quarter went much the same and still, no tour. Mario had packed a full lunch, or Jill had packed it for him, so I went to the grocery store and bought some fried chicken out of the deli case.

Back on my grinder in the afternoon I tried to think of Rochelle or Emily or even of the job but my mind continued to go towards the pressroom and the inspection. I felt like a first time father waiting outside a delivery room. I tried to concentrate on the sparks coming off the grinding wheel. I wondered what the difference was between a spark, an asteroid and a comet. I thought an asteroid flew straight and a comet had an orbit but I may have had that backwards or completely wrong. A spark seemed similar to a comet because of the burning metal nature but this may have been wrong as well. I was complimenting myself on my powers of concentration when a large spark slash comet bounced off the concrete floor and came back up. It grazed my leather apron before flying under the shield on my helmet and finally burning itself out in my right eye.

7

My right hand shot up in an impromptu salute and with my arm fully extended I let go of the grinder. It fell the six feet to the floor and landed on the spinning disc, which broke and cartwheeled wildly past my leg. I bent over at the waist, my useless helmet falling off my head, and moaned and cursed toward the floor. My hands clutched at my eye socket. The commotion got the attention of other welders. Mario was by my side asking what was wrong but all I could manage was, "ah… fuck… my eye." Mario took my arm and led me outside, through the open breezeway into the main building. He led me the first aid station and the eyewash. But when he turned the faucet, nothing happened. Sean hadn't plumbed the new one. I was in too much pain to be angry. Mario smartly went to the first aid cabinet and grabbed two eyewash jugs. I was reluctant to release my grip on the offended eye but Mario pried my hands away. Then, holding my eyelids open, he doused the eyeball with a full bottle. I couldn't tell if anything good was coming of it but it was temporarily soothing. But once the solution stopped, the burning resumed.

"Yup. It's still in there," Mario told me.

"Fuck," was all I could manage.

8

Mario led me by the arm because I had both my eyes clamped shut. I don't know why but it was difficult to keep just one shut. I felt the air conditioning and knew we had entered QC. We went to Jim Steven's office, who was the head of purchasing and safety. I heard Krager's voice ask what happened from behind me.

Mario gave them my story as I stood by like I had been wounded in the mouth instead of the eye. My lids were spread open again and almost immediately Jim said, "come on, we're going to the hospital," which didn't make me feel any better.

We took a company pickup to the hospital. I rolled down the passenger window with my left hand, because my right was clutching my head, and Jim tried to soothe my fears.

"You'd be surprised how much this happens. It must have been a lot worse back before safety glasses. You were wearing yours right? There is always the possibility of an OSHA investigation but that's the same with any time loss injury. Back then I doubt there was anything to even do about an eye injury. Everyone probably went blind. Well just look at Dale for example, an old timer. How many fingers has he got? Three? Shit, things are a lot better now. The hospital has this all down. If Dr. Nadar is there, he's the best. You'll be all right, you just wait and see. That's a pretty big piece, but don't you worry."

My eye hurt too bad to think. The right side of my body

began to cramp. My shoulder and forearm and hand and even my foot all began to tighten. We pulled in to the driveway of the emergency room. Jim parked in front of the automatic doors and went in beside me. I sat in a chair while he talked to the nurse at the desk. I heard them talk about numbers and addresses and the nurse asked a few questions.

I lowered my hand and opened my good eye. The fluorescent light burned and my eye watered. I wiped the tears away and decided to address what I could. One by one I bent back the fingers on my right hand. I slowly tried to stretch each muscle that had cramped. After a few minutes, I felt better. Most of the muscle pain was gone, replaced with tiredness and hunger. I could have fallen asleep, a deep untroubled sleep, if my stomach wasn't trying to eat my other organs. A cracker was all I needed. I thought of asking the nurse.

Jim and the nurse laughed about something. He turned towards me and said he was going to park the truck. "Don't cry, Dr. Nadar is here," he said before laughing and patting me on the shoulder. My throat was too dry to respond. Jim walked out the doors and I began to doubt my injury. I opened the offended eye and my vision was blurred like after a long sickness but I couldn't even make out shapes. I moved the ball around, side to side and in circles, under the lid and felt only minor pain. Probably just a scratch, some dust even. A shame came over me. My eye went round and round searching for a pain worthy of all this attention. True, it hurt, but not enough. I had overreacted and was making a fuss over nothing. I didn't want the Doctor to look at me. I had to end this charade before it got out of control, too costly. I stood and looked around for an escape. The blood rushed from my head and I wobbled a bit. I had to reach for the back of the chair.

Jim came back. "It may take a little while. How you feeling?" Jim handed me a paper cup of water. I drank it and felt I could speak again.

"I'm alright. I don't know if anything is still in there. It doesn't feel like it," I said.

"Well, better safe than sorry, right? If you leave metal in the eye it rusts and then you're in big trouble. It's better to have the doctor check it out."

"I hate to pull you out on a day like this. You know, the inspection." I rotated my wrist around like there was much more involved, something complex not easily stated.

"Don't worry about it. Half the time the inspectors never get past the front office. It's just a government procedure. I'm sure whoever they've sent is totally incompetent. They wouldn't know why to turn us down so they always give the thumbs up. They just follow the last inspectors lead," Jim reassured me.

"Really?" I was feeling a little better, possibly it was the water.

"Oh, yeah. Why do you think we had those yellow lines repainted? Did you do those? They look good. That's the kind of thing they notice if the tour ever even gets to the floor. New lines, you get a good rating. It's a joke. We make sure all the nudie pictures are down in case the inspector is a woman, but other than that…"

It was time to go to an examination room. The nurse tried to make some small talk and I asked if she knew Mario's wife, Jill. She did and smiled and made like they were great friends.

Once in the white room I sat on the examination table and Jim sat on the stool in the corner. The counter was covered with the normal assortment of doctor gear, gloves, swabs, depressors.

9

"I forgot to clock out," I said.

"Don't worry about it. I'll take care of everything," Jim said.

The door opened and Dr. Nadar walked in. He was short and dark. I think he was south Indian and I know he was blacker than all the black folks I had ever known. I expected him to talk with a heavy accent and was disappointed when he didn't.

"Jim! What have you brought me today?" the doctor asked in plain, Ohio English.

"This is Warrell and he has something in his eye. You were welding right?" Jim was now standing next to me with his hand on my shoulder. I felt cooped in but explained that I was grinding.

"Let's have a look." Dr. Nadar moved in. His fingers pried my lids apart and if felt like my eyeball shrunk back in the socket. "You do have something in there" He let go of my face and I felt a shame and cowardice. "It doesn't look too bad." The doctor went to the counter and grabbed an oversized cotton swab. He moved back in and slid the swab over my eye. "That was easy," he said. I was mortified. He showed the end of the swab to Jim and then me. A black sliver about two millimeters long sat on the end of it.

"That's it?" I questioned.

The doctor nodded. Jim just grunted.

"But you probably scratched your cornea." This satisfied me a little. "I'll have to look at it under the light. Follow me." The doctor led us out.

"How's it feel?" Jim asked.

"Better," I said, secretly hoping for more injury.

We went down the hall into a side room that was little more than a closet. An optometrist's scope hung from the ceiling above a fixed chair and head frame. I sat down before the chin rest.

"I need to put some dye in your eye. Then I'll be able to see the scratches under the black light." As Dr. Nadar approached me with a bottle I thought of past experiences with black light and chuckled. He dropped some solution in my eye then we waited a couple of minutes. Jim and the doctor talked about grade school. They both had children attending and seemed to be involved in a parent group. Then he turned off the overhead light and switched on the black light. I put my chin on the rest and my forehead against the cool metal bar. Dr. Nadar slid up to my face behind the magnifying scope, a Rube Goldberg Halloween mask.

"Oh yeah," the doctor said. "You've scratched the cornea pretty bad."

I felt relieved and vindicated. The doctor slid around on his wheeled chair and looked at my eyeball from several different angles. I had to look up and down and from side to side.

Finally he slid back and turned the lights back on. "Well, the scratches aren't bad enough to warrant a stitch or anything that intrusive but you do have one small flap that I'm concerned about. It should heal by itself but I'm going to want to look at it again." I grew a little concerned. The doctor looked at his watch and continued. "It's Friday so I'd like to see you Wednesday and we'll go from there. I'll give you some salve to put on it three times a day. It's antibiotic. And you'll have to keep it closed. We'll set you up with a patch."

"Can I work?" There was a touch of panic in my voice.

The doctor chuckled a little. "Absolutely not. Not until Wednesday at the earliest."

Jim nodded and my spine felt like it melted. I wanted to cry and demand a second opinion. My eye didn't hurt that bad. What was the bid deal?

"The nurse will help you with the patch." The doctor got up to leave and Jim thanked him. Despite his condemnation I thanked him too.

"What do I do, Jim?"

"What the doctor said. Unfortunately L&I doesn't start until seven days. Do you have any vacation built up?" he asked.

I said I did but I wasn't in the room. I thought of work and already I desperately missed my job. I wanted nothing more than to return to the floor. I would work for free, just let me in. Why couldn't I have been injured last month when absolutely nothing was new or important? I hated Sean at that moment knowing he would try and weasel into my spot. Everything was dependent on this new position. I wanted to cry for real, not because of the bright light.

10

The nurse walked back into the room describing with an annoying pertness what needed to be done. She might have been making a pass at me. I don't know. I was too angry to pay attention to anyone else. The nurse taped a gauze pad over my eye and told me to leave it on for the night because the eye would "weep" in reaction to the wound and the drops.

"Tomorrow you can just wear this eye patch." She held a pale flesh colored patch with an elastic band in her hand. The covering piece was bigger than I expected. It was ugly. It wasn't what I had expected. When I was told eye patch I thought Moshe Dayan who ranked in my pantheon of soldierly looking men with Robert E. Lee and Otto Skorzeny. But this was the eye patch of someone who ran with scissors. It was disgraceful.

She held it out to me but I refused to touch it. "Don't you have anything in black?" I asked. Jim chuckled in the corner, obviously amused with my reaction.

"But this one is less noticeable," the nurse protested. She was a woman comfortable surrounded by beige walls, a woman who might allow you to make love to her but would never fuck.

"And terribly ugly. I'll take black if you have it."

She doubted if they had black and left the room to go check. I looked at Jim with my one eye. I could see the tape and gauze pad on the crest of my nose. "What do the black dudes wear?" I asked.

"That's the only patch I've ever seen. But I see your point. Why pretend?" Jim was pretty smart for a factory worker.

11

The nurse returned with a black eye patch. She held it with the tips of her fingers like it disgusted her. I smiled and thanked her. Once I had it over the gauze pad I checked the mirror and smiled at my image. Jim laughed again.

"Might as well have some fun with it, eh?" I said.

Jim patted me on the back and we left the examination room. As we drove back to the factory I pleaded with Jim that I felt fine and could work but he would not agree. "The doctor's word is like a contract. If he say's you can't work until Wednesday then you can't. If you got reinjured or walked in front of a lift truck because of the eye patch our ass would be grass as far as the government was concerned." I understood his point but knew those rules were made for the lowest common denominator and I didn't feel that they should apply to me. "All the same you've got some days off, so get used to it." The appeal process was over and we pulled into the parking lot.

12.

Inside QC I was the center of attention and the subject of endless pirate jokes. It was 2:35 and everyone was thinking of the end of the day. Krager told me that the government inspectors had done a quick trot through the factory floor and everything looked to be positive. "They had no idea what they were looking at. It was actually funny. One lady looked like she was being stabbed. The noise was too much for her. They couldn't run to the front office fast enough. Sensitive Souls. Bureaucrats!" Krager laughed. Still, I was sorry to have missed it.

I went out to the floor and looked for Turnbull. The heat was horrible and I could feel the tape start to lift off my face. Over in the northwest corner Trevor Daley, a lift truck driver, was moving things around. I hurried over.

"Hey, what's going on?" I asked.

Trevor stopped and then shut off his engine. It was late enough in the day where any break in the flow could signal the end. "Hey Warrell. What happened?" Trevor asked. I told him it was nothing, just a scratch from grinding. And then I asked again. "I'm moving all this shit over to shipping. Making room for the three presses they're bringing over here. I thought you knew about all this shit. I thought you were in charge?" Trevor asked.

"I am. I just didn't know it would happen so fast." The noise from the pressroom started to fade down. People were beginning to clean and end the day. We didn't have to shout at each other. "How long before we're able to work?" I asked Trevor knowing that he wasn't in on any of these decisions but often he knew more than any other man on the floor. Each section could run by their own plans but they needed one of the two forklift drivers to move every piece and tool.

"Maybe Wednesday afternoon but more likely Friday. Maintenance is really behind. It will probably take them a couple days to get the presses working. When are the first pieces supposed to go out?"

I opened my mouth but didn't say anything. I didn't know.

13

"Swanson!" Turnbull shouted. He was walking quickly toward me and I feared. "What the fuck are you still doing here?"

Turnbull didn't let me answer.

"Get the fuck out of here."

With a strength that only comes from fear, I didn't run away. "I just wanted to know what was happening," I said.

"Isn't that obvious." Turnbull was looking down at me. He always looked down at me because of our size difference.

I turned and looked at the opening space and couldn't think of an argument. I couldn't even think of a question.

"Don't worry. Everything's going to be here when you get back." Turnbull patted me on the shoulder and then pushed me towards the time clock. "And Sean can look after things for you." Turnbull smiled at his jab but I didn't know whether to laugh or fall at his feet and beg.

By the time I punched out I must have shrunk two inches. My back was curved with the defeat of old age. An on looker might have supposed that I was worrying over my eye but I had the fear of a parent over a sick child. Things were beyond what my hands could fix and I felt my own impotence. It had been years since I felt so meaningless to my own position.

Driving out of the lot I remembered my eye when I had to owl my neck in order to make a right turn. Looking right with my left eye only pissed me off. I drove through the heat talking to myself, arguing my position over and over again. It was obvious that I was right and should be allowed to work or to at least supervise the set up of the new section.

14

Walking up the library I was talking to myself, more or less still at work, when I heard Emily's voice.

"Warrell! Oh my God, what happened?" Her hand was over her mouth as she came from behind the counter.

I remember being shocked at the way she used my name. She put her left hand on the instep of my left elbow. It positively burned. I looked down at her hand and had not a clue as to where I was or even who I was. I'm sure my stupidity made my eyeball seem worse. My brain fog must have lent a shell-shocked aura to my purposeless steps.

"What happened?" Her voice located me and I looked again at her hand and smiled.

"Nothing." I pulled my arm away from her touch. Its warmth was painful. "I scratched my cornea a little. No big deal."

She forced me to tell her the whole ordeal. I told her of the hospital and the nurse and the eye patch, laughing at that point which she didn't seem to understand. Then I told her of the new section and being unable to head back to work until Wednesday but she didn't seem to understand that part either. After I told her of it a second time she only said, "doctors know best," and then I was sure she didn't understand. When I was done she merely said, "you poor thing," which made me feel like a sick dog. I wasn't sick, I was hurt and that was something completely different. I grew angry at the whole day.

"If you need anything just ask me," Emily said.

15

I sat at my table and tried to think of books I had wanted to read if I ever had the time but couldn't remember a single title. I could only think of work so I got up to leave. Emily came forward from her counter again. I thanked her for her concern and reassured her that I was truly fine and only upset because of the work issue that she didn't understand. "Think of it like a minor league player who struggles and struggles and then one day the call comes but as he gets ready to go he shuts his hand in the car door. One chance and it's gone." I looked at her to see if she understood but her head was cocked sideways like a confused puppy. "No, it's really not like that at all. I just hurt my eye and I'll go back to work on Wednesday. Thanks for your concern, but I'm alright, really." I reached out and patted her hand, the way you do with a child or an old woman. Outside, the heat was still oppressive.

16

At home, I lay down on the couch in front of the fan before calling my mother up in Michigan. I told her I had gotten hurt on the job. She didn't seem too concerned. "Bad?" she asked. Not really, I said, informing her of the doctor's orders. My mother had the normal respect and ignorant awe of doctors and their word. Sympathy, true sympathy, the understanding of what events meant, was as elusive as kind beauty. Behind her voice I could hear a soft pop, like knuckles cracking, and I knew she was snapping beans, moving them from one bowl to another with the phone cradled on her shoulder. I told her of the new line and she seemed slightly more interested, but that may have been a learned response from living all those years with my father.

"Why don't you come up here for a few days? It's been a while since we've seen you. You could help your father stack fire wood," she said.

I thought of my half drunk and scabbed recondo mission that was nearly blown by the overbred idiotess. I glared at Ginger but she was focused intently on a leg supporting the kitchen table. The three hundred miles that separated me from my parents seemed especially cruel and pointless. My petty migration hurt me more than the metal shard in my eye. It was cowardly to move from nowhere to a nowhere without design. I told my mother that I would consider making the drive but that I wanted to be close to the factory so I could drop by and see how things were progressing. At which she replied I was just like my father. My patience decreased after that and the conversation petered out into silence.

17

The evening was starting to cool so I laced up my walking boots and pulled an ancient .22 revolver from my desk drawer. I stuck the pistol in my back pocket and went down the stairs. Ginger tore across the asphalt and disappeared into the corn. I looked both ways before trotting over. Midway the pistol jumped out of my pants and crashed on the road. It was a single action gun so I wasn't worried it would fire, but it was embarrassing.

Although no one was watching I snatched the gun and hurried for the cover of the trees. I again put it in my back pocket- this time barrel up, weight down. It was ungraceful. If, somehow, it did manage to cock itself and fire, the gun would probably shoot me in the back of the head instead of the foot. I wondered how it would be ruled. Murder? Suicide? Stupidity?

I headed straight for the birch stand and had to whistle Ginger back in from the field. She looped in, working the forest floor in zigzags. Even though I had walked this route a thousand times it was difficult with one eye. I stumbled on a log and later on walked into a snag that almost speared my covered eye. It grazed my temple then ripped my ear. I swore and felt the blood come from the cartilage. Just a nick, really. Not like when I was a high school freshman and tackled a six foot by four foot, 300 pound senior lineman during a padless scrimmage. That time my ear had to be sewn on and taped to back to my head. It was a good way to learn that heart is not enough.

I reached the birch without any further injuries and crashed to the leafy ground. Leaning against the log I struggled to free the larger 50 cal. ammo box from my stash. Ginger came close and I tried to get her to lick my ear but she was too preoccupied with the squirrels and birds overhead. Disappointed, I pulled the mosquito netting from the bottom of the can and donned it over my much-battered head. Cross-legged and straight-backed I balanced the pistol on my right knee and balled my fists under my armpits. Thankfully, no thoughts came. I didn't think of work, of women or Democracy. I heard the bugs flying and Ginger's far off bell. Eventually I came to the image of the Chinese man blocking the battle tanks in Tiananmen Square. I didn't think of what it meant, only the image. After a while I felt better and walked back.

18

At home there was a message on the machine from Mario. "Brother! Jill and me were wondering if you could feed yourself with one eye. I suppose you can… Come over for dinner if you want. Pot Roast! Have a nice night… Fuck off!" Click. His obvious love made me smile. I sat on the edge of my bed and unlaced my boots. Oddly, I felt content. Other nights I would need beer or sex to quiet my mind. But the fear had gone somewhere. Half-blind and bloodied, I was ready for sleep.

19

That is the difference between morning and night. At night you pray for the cessation of thought and in the morning you wonder if you've lost the ability for it. But halfway through my first cup of coffee it was hard not to think of work. I spent the day trying not to think about it. Mostly I sat around and looked at half of my normal world. Reading was especially difficult. My one eye tired quickly. I went for two walks with the dog through the canopied shade of the woods. I sat in the cab of my truck two different times struggling against my own reason. The factory called but I never left the driveway.

The afternoon dragged. A hole had been torn in my life and I didn't know how to fill it. I was suffering from the early stages of Stockholm syndrome. I went to the closet and pulled out my model of the Bismarck. It was a gift from Rochelle and two years into construction only the hull was laid down. I spread some newspaper on the kitchen table and got to work. At first it was satisfying, putting down the little braces and supports, cutting off excess material. Detail and concentration. My mind drifted away from my hands. It was almost like work except that

I chose the task. I imagined a life of leisure, that this was my natural condition. An impossible wealth had to be assumed and its relation to Freedom was troubling but with one eye it was hard to see both sides. In this new state I traveled the world seeing all the great museums. That took some time and there were exotic women thrown in but they bogged me down as I had no references and therefore their likenesses were disturbingly close to Michigan and Ohio women I had known but with darker skin and accents. Eventually my day dream self returned to a large country estate and worked around the house, painting and gardening, before turning some fallow ground out back under the plow. And even though I worked from dawn to dusk in this Zhivago trance something was different. The sight of the trees and the smell of the soil were foreign, a bit removed. I was detached from the dirt. Somehow the work had become unreal. Unreal in the dream not unreal because of it. Something hovered around me and a terror was in my chest. I worked harder. I bought Belgians and sold the tractor. But still this gray cloud closed in until it was everywhere; in my bed, in my fridge, in my nose, in my mouth. It was a single word. Boredom. A word that has enraged me since I was sixteen and could read real books. It was the terror of a bloodless life. Boredom, the second worst word in my complete lexicon, surpassed only by ennui which, mercifully, was culturally impossible.

As I put another piece of deck platting down I knew why my dream mind would not idle. Why the sweat off my nose didn't touch the dirt in the same way. Fear. Boredom was the absence of fear and self-interest. In my dream fear had been removed and it had pulled the connection between action and meaning. Unfortunately fear made life palpable and fear in any form is a fear of death. And where did fear, the great motivator, exist daily? Was it nature's wrath or rolling war? No, it was work and the spectre of unemployment. Work and its fragile claim of meaning. Even bracket making, broom pushing, weld running. Even Sisyphus' rock pushing had meaning. Lament the death of craft and Ford's Great Sin but work always remained. Even my work. And like a junkie for metal in the nose I couldn't imagine it any different.

I'm not deaf. I could hear the poets at the cemetery gates rail against clean porcelain and repetition, of souls being eaten by jaws that never grew weary, that man wasn't made for this. But man wasn't made for anything. He wasn't made. He just is. No, no, that's not right. Too Buddhist. Too Nihilistic. Man is for man's purpose, to fulfill man's thoughts no matter how unsound or absurd.

"What the fuck!" I said and pushed my chair back from the table. This was the kind of shit that broke my brain in school. I stood and flashed my arms around. I went to my toes and threw punches. I shook my fingers out. "Fuck," I said again. Fear, that was fear. The fear of going nutty. I drank two glasses of water from the jug in the fridge and when I turned to the calendar I realized it was only Saturday.

20

I went outside with my slingshot sent rocks sailing from the gravel driveway into the brown river. It was hard to aim with my right eye covered but the river was a big target. Ginger watched the stones fly away and wanted very badly to chase them but she was wary of the water. Instead she bounced up and down on her forepaws whimpering with impotence. I laughed at her and her pain assuaged mine.

I cut limbs from the willow, stripped them of their leaves and then snapped them whip-like over my head. I had never whipped Ginger, but somewhere in her genes she knew it. She ran in circles around me at a safe distance of thirty feet and yelped with each whip crack. The dog was endlessly fascinating with all her phobias and mental aberrations. After the willow branch broke itself I returned to shooting rocks. It wasn't a bad way to spend an afternoon. I wanted a beer but was too lazy to walk up the stairs.

21

Cars and trucks passed regularly on the road and I only turned to notice when I heard wheels on the gravel. I didn't recognize the car. I rose from my one knee shooting stance and ridiculously stuck the slingshot in my back pocket. I walked towards the car convinced that it was some lost doctor from Columbus or Cleveland looking for Toledo. But a woman was driving and then I knew who had pulled into my driveway.

Emily tried to get out of the car but Ginger held her pinned with a happy nose and an eager butt. Emily gently pushed her aside and stood up.

"I don't know what you did to her but she sure likes you," I said.

"I'm glad she does. The opposite would be regrettable."

"What brings you out this way?" I asked.

"I came out to see how the eye was. And I brought you some dinner."

I didn't know what to say.

"Have you had any visitors today?" she asked.

"No."

"Good. Then I feel justified," she said.

"Was that a concern?" I asked.

"Well I wouldn't want to be a pain in the ass."

It was the first time I had heard her swear. It was nice. She seemed very relaxed and confident. Her hair was up and it made her face look very young and untouched.

"I know you like your privacy and I wouldn't want to bother you if other people had been stopping by all day. But if I'm first then I feel alright."

"How did you know that?" I asked referring to my privacy.

She wasn't confused and continued. "I can tell a lot about you by just looking at you."

"Am I that obvious?" I asked.

"No, I don't think so. You're just not secretive."

"Really?" I felt a little insulted but wasn't sure where the insult was.

Emily wasn't fazed and continued, "Do you like eggplant parmesan?"

"I don't know."

"Do you like eggplant?"

"I don't know."

"Well, we'll find out." She reached in and grabbed a casserole dish from the passenger seat along with a bottle of wine. "Do you at least like red wine?"

"Yes."

"Well, that's a start." She handed me the dish. "That needs to go in the oven for forty-five minutes on three-fifty."

I was amazed by her confidence. She was so young and beautiful and completely sure of herself. We went inside. I followed her up the stairs with the pretense of politeness but really I didn't want her to see the slingshot in my pocket, which I ditched as soon as I entered the door. I put the dish in the oven and then turned to her. Like a boxer working a weak side I had to keep her to my left. I shuffled and centered her in my vision. She was looking at my books again. I was glad I had put my model ship away. "Should we have some wine now?"

"We should save some for dinner," she said.

"I have more." I poured two glassed and walked toward the couch. She sat down on it first and I foolishly sat in my reading chair. I noticed the look on her face. It was suppressed amusement.

"I should at least ask about your eye," she said.

"It's alright. I just wish I could go to work."

"Really? Why's that?"

I didn't know how to answer this very simple question. It was like she had just asked me something in French and I couldn't understand. I thought of explaining it but knew eventually that would all happen. "I don't know. Habit, I guess."

"Are you a creature of habit?" she asked.

I didn't know how to answer that one either. I drank some of the wine.

"Did you have school today?" I asked.

"No. It's summer. I only have the library."

"But you don't work on Saturdays. Only Mrs. White works on Saturdays." Damn! Now I surely sounded like a stalker.

"That's right. Thanks for noticing." Emily smiled at me and instead of feeling creepy I felt embarrassed. "No today I just read and then went for a bike ride and then I made some food for you and came out here to visit."

"Thanks." I smiled again.

"Do you play guitar?" she asked pointing at the old acoustic that lay propped up in the corner next to my pile of guns.

"No."

"Then why do you have a guitar?"

"Sometimes I make up little songs but I don't know any real ones," I explained.

"Then you do play."

"Not really."

"I'd like to hear one of your songs someday."

"I wouldn't hold your breath," I said. When she said 'someday' I felt it in my stomach like a soft jab. Are we going to fall in love? Are we going to get married? Are we going to have a crop of children who though beautiful would never play guitar?

"You do have a lot of guns."

"Not really."

A silence entered the room and I knew it was my fault. I had felt put under the light. I felt that she was asking too many questions though she wasn't. That is how things are done. At first there is a lot of conversation, a lot of talking and a lot of words. That's because we both had to tell our stories. We needed to discover each other through the filters of our own teeth. I knew I had to try harder. She wasn't attacking me, just trying.

I walked over to the pile. "Mostly these are junk." I turned and looked back at her. She stood up and walked over. "Do you like guns?" I knew it was a stupid question and an ungraceful bait.

"No."

"Are you afraid of them?" I asked.

"No."

"OK. Well, most of these are junk. It seems whenever someone dies I get another crappy old shotgun. But what can you do? You can't sell them. That would be… ungrateful." I looked at Emily and she nodded back. "Anyway they're all shotguns except for that one. It's a deer rifle, 30.06. And that little one. It's a .22. They're a lot of fun for shooting cans and squirrels and such." I said that on purpose and I looked back at her face to watch her reaction. She screwed up her face beautifully. I laughed. "I don't do that much," I said.

"What do you hunt?" she asked.

"Birds and rabbits. I used to hunt deer with my dad up in Michigan but we don't get along and deer are a pain in the ass to clean. I'm kind of a sissy when it comes to guts."

Emily laughed at that. "Do you eat them, the birds and the bunnies?"

"As much as possible. It's good for you. I think it's good for you. I don't have any science to back that up though."

She laughed again and I smiled. We checked the dish in the oven and then I suggested we go for a walk and work up an appetite. She agreed and we were led down the stairs by the dog.

"What would you like to see, the woods or the river?" I asked.

"I think I can see them both from here but I'll choose the river."

22

The light was starting to soften and we walked to the bank. A small breeze running up river kept the mosquitoes at bay. The brown Maumee in all its majesty was twelve feet below. A path the size of a deer trail went down the bank and then followed the river's edge. Ginger and I scooted down quickly out of habit. Emily was more cautious. I watched her ankles as her canvas tennis shoes sought sure ground. They were nice. She stumbled the last few steps but caught herself before I could.

"I see people fish out here but I never do."

"Why not?" Emily asked.

"I don't like to fish and I don't like water that's too dirty to see through."

"When I was a child the Cuyahoga lit on fire."

"Is that where you're from, Cleveland?" I asked.

"Shaker Heights. It's the suburbs."

"How was it?"

"Growing up? Good. Happy. I guess that's unfashionable, but I had a happy childhood."

"I think I know what you mean. That's really a stupid way to think," I said.

"That's why I like you," she said.

My face was warm with blood as I smiled and looked out

over the river. We walked down the trail a little and then took turns throwing rocks. Her arm wasn't horrible for a girl. Softball must have been somewhere in her past. I suggested that we should go in and check on the oven. Emily had some difficulty coming back up the trail and I held out my hand to help her. She took it and when we crested the bank I regretted letting it go. Walking back to the house I had to look away twice because a smile came across my face that I couldn't control let alone suppress.

Dinner went well. It turned out that I did like eggplant and eggplant parmesan. We each told small stories about our past and laughed at the right moments. I thought Emily made a point to tell me that she was single but maybe it was just my ears.

After dinner we had one more glass of wine and then sat on the couch. I wanted to invite her to stay for a movie but thought better of it. It was turning dark as I walked her to her car. An awkward tension came between us and we both waited for a kiss that seemed inevitable. Instead, I choose to talk.

"Thanks for dinner."

"You're very welcome. I had a good time."

"What are you doing tomorrow?" I asked. Emily was going to visit a sick aunt in Toledo. I would stare at my dog and the river. I asked her about Monday.

"The library. Yourself?"

"Same," I said. She smiled at me. For once it felt like I didn't have to seize something, that a chance wasn't fleeting. I stood straight and we said our goodbyes and then waved at each other as Emily backed out of the driveway and headed toward town.

23

Happy and tired as if I had just completed a very long run I sat on the couch and gently fell asleep in the silence. The sound of tires on the gravel woke me. My heart leapt and I wondered if I was still lost in some happy dream. A car door slammed and then footsteps climbed the stairs. My heart leapt then it quickly sank. The feet were coming too fast. I sat up straight and looked at my pile of guns. This is how it happens, I thought.

"Hello." The voice came in through the screen. It was Rochelle. I hadn't thought of her. She opened the door and looked at me. "Oh sweetie. You poor thing." She came across the floor and kissed me on the cheek and then on the eye patch and then on the lips. My cock stirred and I became angry at my body again. "I heard you got hurt so I had to come out here. I'll nurse you." Rochelle straddled my legs and rubbed my chest.

"It took you long enough to get here. I got hurt yesterday," I complained.

"I just found out today and I had to go home after work and shower and do a couple of things. But I'm here now baby and that's what matters."

"You think so?"

"Don't be cross, baby. I'm the best medicine you could ever have."

"Hmph."

"Don't be that way or I'll leave you here all alone. Ginger can't do the things to you that I can. Who's the world's greatest lover?"

"Jenna Jameson?"

"Don't be that way." Rochelle stood and reached down and patted my crotch. "You can't lie or pretend."

I frowned. I wanted to tell her to go away.

"I need a drink and I think you do to." Rochelle went to the kitchen.

I smiled to myself but doubted that Rochelle was smart enough to figure such things. Ice cubes clinked into glasses. Then a silence came.

"Been drinking wine?" Rochelle asked.

"Yes." I grew a little worried.

"Out of two glasses?" Her voice had changed. It was quicker and louder. She mumbled something like 'lipstick' and then went to full volume. "Who the fuck have you been drinking with?"

"A friend," I said quietly.

"Friend my ass." The cocktail glasses crashed into the sink. Something broke, probably a wine glass. Rochelle walked over to me, her face red. "What were you going to do? Fuck me and then tell me? Or weren't you going to tell me at all?"

"I hadn't thought of it," I said.

"Bullshit!" she screamed. Rochelle grabbed her purse off my reading chair and moved toward the door. "Have your slut come out her and nurse you and suck your dick for all I care!"

I wanted to tell her only she was the slut but doubted I could dodge punches with one eye. Rochelle went out the door and down the steps. She stopped mid flight possibly waiting for a plea that didn't come. I put together a pained smile. It was better this way. I could never make a good break like Rochelle could.

As her car wheels spun I was very angry with Rochelle for extinguishing the warm fire that had been running over my skin. I tried to reconjure the sensation but it was difficult. I closed my eyes and repeated the name, "Emily" over and over again like a mantra. Her hand was almost in mine but it wouldn't become flesh and I couldn't make the leap of faith. I wished I had a picture of her. I gave up and went to bed.

24

Sunday passed like a normal Sunday because I realized it was Sunday. I was soothed that no one was working. But Monday was problematic. I woke at 4:30 and had nothing to do. I tried and tried to think of something that would be worthy of these free days. I thought of driving to the four hours to Chicago to watch a White Sox or Cubs game, the two and a half hours for a Tigers game or the two and a half hours for an Indians game. I even momentarily considered the Reds but I loathed heading south for any reason and I really didn't care for the National League. Say what you may against the DH but pitchers aren't serious hitters even if they want to think so.

At 6:10, showered and shaved, I left the house and headed to town for some different papers. In the drive through I bought a Detroit Free Press and a Cleveland Plain Dealer and then drove home. I had more coffee and read my two regular papers and the two specials. Unfortunately Cleveland was in New York, Detroit in Seattle, the Sox had the day off and the Cubs were in Kansas City. I had enough money in the bank to do anything I wanted. Why did I want to go to work?

25

Ginger and I went for a walk in the woods. I didn't take a gun and as expected all the squirrels and rabbits for a hundred miles came out to show themselves and chirp at us. Actually only the squirrels chirped. Rabbits rarely make sounds and when they do its terrible and unnerving. Ginger didn't mind that I wasn't shooting. She still pointed and flushed in her haphazard manner. I imagined I was a soldier home from the distant war not knowing what to do next. Life had been so real and purposeful until so recently. I needed an activity to fill my time. Nick Adams had found the town of Seney burned out but to me everything looked the same. I walked back to the house satisfied with my stroll.

But I knew somewhere men were working. Across that river machines were being moved and things were being readied. I didn't know what to do. The day passed terribly slow. Ginger and I went for another walk and then I lifted weights. I put the medicine in my eye, twice, once in the morning and once at lunch. I could see fair without the eye patch and I doubted the reasoning behind keeping it covered for a week but as science was always my worst subject I thought I would trust the doctor.

At one I drove into town. I wanted to stop into work and

check progress but I settled for a drive past. I tried to peer into the darkness of the overhead doors as I slowly drove through the parking lot but the midday brightness burned away my attempt. I drove on and ended up at the library.

26

Emily wasn't at the front deck when I walked in. Mrs. White was. I had to explain my eye patch and tell the whole story. I ended with the promise that I would use my free time well and Mrs. White liked that.

I selected the Sunday New York Times from the reading room and went to my desk. I read about the world and then the nation and was moving on to the arts but every third sentence I wondered where Emily was. I looked around again but she wasn't to be seen. I tried to read. Much was considered art by many and I didn't agree with their estimation. When craft is labeled art why couldn't anything requiring manual dexterity be thought of as such. Why couldn't my welding and grinding be considered art? It seemed more reflective of the human condition than the example in the article. There were a lot of clever people in the world and no one seemed to know the difference between artist and artisan.

27

Emily's voice shocked me out of my tirade. I looked up but her face wasn't warm. "You can't leave this in books." Emily was holding a post card from a Thomas Hart Benton show I had seen at the Toledo Art Museum. It was Persephone, a picture of a beautiful naked woman next to a river running through fertile Midwestern landscape. A farmer had stopped his wagon on the dirt road near the river and he peered around a tree to look on this beautiful body. I loved that painting and the postcard was one of my favorite bookmarks.

"That's my bookmark."

"You can't leave it in books where children could find it," she said.

"It was marking my spot." I reached for the postcard suddenly filled with an unlocalized fear. With the card in my hand and my heart slowing I asked, "why not?"

"It's not right," Emily said.

My defenses up, I attacked. "It's not pornography."

"No, it's just not right. Don't leave things in library books."

I looked up at her with my eye and wondered who she was. I didn't know. I agreed not to leave anything in library books, although deep in my chest I considered them my books. Satisfied, she left me. I got up to leave. Mrs. White commented that my visit was awfully short and I assured her that I would be back though at the time I wasn't sure if I would.

I walked down by the river and pulled a paperback copy of S.L.A. Marshall's fanciful Nightdrop from my back pocket. I sat down on the grass behind the library in the oppressive heat and read about the Screaming Eagles. Luckily I was drawn instantly into the Normandy countryside. I read until sweat ran down the inside of my arms. I wished I had sunglasses. My covered eye was sweating. At least that was what it felt like.

A small whistle came to my two ears. It was like that of a child. I turned and looked up the bank toward the library and Emily stood under a tree waving at me. My eyes burned from the brightness. Emily waved me over to her. I obeyed.

"Hi," she said as I closed the distance.

I didn't say anything but I couldn't suppress a smile.

"Do you want to go somewhere for lunch?" she asked. Emily looked back towards the windows of the library. She was talking in a low voice just above a whisper.

"What's wrong?" I asked.

"Nothing. Let's just go to lunch."

"Where do you want to go?" I asked.

"I don't know. It's your town. Where do you usually go?"

I couldn't take her there. I smiled, then lied. "Henry's. Across from the courthouse." I rarely went there. It catered to the business and government crowd.

28

Emily drove. I wanted to protest for her earlier coldness but I knew I didn't have the right to do so. Nothing existed between us that would have made it possible. She asked about my eye and I assured her that it was healing.

"Do you always wear your work outfit even when you're not going to work?" she asked.

I looked down and sure enough I was wearing my greens. I hadn't noticed. I hadn't even thought about it. Getting out of the shower I had gone through my usual routine and therefore was dressed for work. I laughed and told her I had no excuse for it.

At lunch I ordered a club sandwich and Emily had a BLT. Our waitress was Carol Penny and she provided the only unpleasantness. I had briefly dated this woman four years ago. She was clinically crazy and took medicine for it. Carol told me that she had heard that Rochelle and I had split for good and wondered if it were really true.

"It is," I said.

Carol grunted and delivered our orders to the kitchen. She didn't ask about the eye patch. It must have been normal.

"Sorry about that. She's crazy."

"I thought so," Emily said with a smile.

"No, really she is. It's her crutch. Anything she does wrong is blamed on her mind." I tapped my skull for effect. "Drunk driving, child neglect, forgetting to take birth control. It's all blamed on being crazy."

"Isn't she a character."

"Not really. She's just annoying."

We ate our lunch without any more rudeness from the wait staff and then drove back to the library. We were both smiling but as we turned the corner on First and neared the library

Emily became quiet and serious. I wondered if my comments about Baptists had offended her.

"You're not Baptist are you?" I asked.

"No, Lutheran."

She looked at the library and I looked at her.

"Are you coming back in?" she asked.

"No, I think I'll go by work and then home."

Emily smiled at me. I didn't want to leave her. Even her car smelled good. Everything about her was clean and well cared for. I felt like a child.

"Do you have any plans for tonight?" I asked.

"No," she smiled wider. "Why do you ask?"

"I thought you might want to come out to my house for dinner."

She agreed and asked if I would be cooking a meal from the woods. I explained it was too early for pheasant season, which was my specialty. So the best I could offer was a rabbit stew.

"I don't suppose you would like that would you?"

She locked her car door and turned to go into the library. "I don't know. I'll try anything once."

"Eight o'clock then?"

"I'll be there."

I waved goodbye as she climbed the sandstone steps. I wanted to blow her kisses. I wanted to lavish her with the real things.

Driving past the open factory doors I again tried to penetrate the darkness. I thought of parking and drifting inside but it had only been a couple of days since my injury and the pace of work was such that nothing would be noticeably different. That was what I supposed and of course I was wrong. But my thoughts of work were overpowered by my thoughts of a young woman with long red hair. Her scent was still in my nose and I cherished it. I drove on. I had much to do.

29

At the grocery store I bought onions, carrots, celery and some more white and red wine. I wished it was fall and that I was able to fix a nice pheasant meal for Emily but rabbit would have to do. A stew would be best because it would mellow the gaminess and I wasn't sure of Emily's fortitude. It was too hot to eat well. I wished for a cool night and a rich meal followed by apple brandy, followed by heavy bedding of flannel and down. I was sweating as I drove back out toward my house. Damn this heat, I thought.

Once home I stored the perishables and put on my canvas brush pants. I wore my hunting vest with no shirt on underneath. Never in the presence of other people would I do that but I knew I would have to walk and hunt hard today. There would be no easy quitting after a half hour of non-purposeful meandering through the countryside. I tried to think of a back up plan but none came.

Honestly I did consider poaching a pheasant or two- but only if they ambushed me, surprised me, startled me and I shot before considering the law, twice. But sadly I have always been fearful and incompetent at all levels of law breaking.

I needed to get some rabbits, and needed a certain crazy dog to perform uncharacteristically well. "You hear me?" I said to Ginger. She looked the same. It didn't matter if she had followed my thought or not. I pulled my very best gun from the pile. I loaded five number six shot shells into the sixteen gauge and put five more in my vest pocket. I realized to a purist, something I occasionally feigned, that this was terribly gauche but I had one eye and a beautiful woman to worry about. Style be damned. I was going to kill something.

30

I had barely crossed the road when sweat began running over my whole body. The tape holding the gauze pad over my eye finally gave way and I stuffed the soiled bandage in my pocket and continued with just the black eye patch. I thought of it as a good omen.

I tramped the rest of the day but we had little luck. My home stand of wood seemed to be void of rabbits. Had I killed them all? That wasn't possible. I had seen them the days before and everyone knew their breeding power. In any case I hadn't been hunting them for some time. I had grown tired of eating rabbit so I quit killing them. I have friends that swear by some mountainman oath that they eat everything they kill and only kill what they plan to eat but I can't claim that magnanimity. I occasionally vaporize chickadees out of boredom. I know this is morally reprehensible but there it is. I also never eat the squirrels I shoot but the foxes must take care of them because the corpses are never in the same place the next day.

The hunt didn't go well. Ginger only flushed one rabbit. She was working the far side of a brush pile that in the past had always treated us well. I was resigned to failure and stood with my gun across the opposite forearm and waited for the dog to get frustrated. But Ginger was not so fickle and sent one rabbit flying. It sprinted directly at me and as I fumbled with my gun it passed within two feet of my boots and continued past into the tall corn. When I finally got my gun to my shoulder I discovered blackness. I have always been a one eyed aimer and that eye was blacked out by my Israeli General patch. Too late to switch eyes, the rabbit was gone.

We followed a drainage ditch for a half-mile to another stand of woods. This was not public land nor secure in right like my own piece, but I was desperate. I occasionally came across the sea of corn and soy to hunt this area. During the rain of the spring and fall it was almost impassable. The farm mud, clay really, stuck to your boots until fifty pounds weighted each leg. The process of walking, scraping, walking became so tiresome that I soon gave up. I wasn't Maryweather Lewis and I was content with that.

But I wasn't poaching, just trespassing and it was a workday afternoon so I felt safe. Who has a Monday to walk around in the heat with a dog looking for the occasional rabbit hidden in the brush? Dentists maybe. This area of Ohio was devoid of landed gentry and that worked in my favor. We continued on. Law and man be damned.

We hunted one edge of the rectangular wood then pushed back to the far edge. Ginger was thirsty and drank some brown water stranded in the corrugations of a culvert. I yelled at her not to but she drank. That stale mosquito water was most likely half pesticides and fertilizer but she was thirsty and a follower of her instincts. Defeated we headed for home.

As we neared the ditch that crossed the open fields Ginger finally caught on to something. Her head went down and her tail went up. I readied my gun. I flipped my eye patch up like an infielder's glasses and opened my right eye. It was blurry and the light was painful so I closed it again but kept the patch up. Ginger's pace quickened to a gallop through the brush. She was cutting back and forth and I knew that she was chasing a rabbit. Running birds weren't that fast or agile. Insane and overbred or not, that dog was beautiful to watch in her element. Given the correct task she was perfection. I shouldered my gun and led Ginger by a safe fifteen feet. This was difficult because I had no idea where the next turn would happen. I would trace the wrong direction and then have to catch up and lead again only to be thrown again. Luckily both rabbit and dog finally broke for the cornfield. I sighted down the two track between wood and crop and waited for the creatures to cross. The rabbit was only visible for the smallest fraction of a second when I pulled the trigger and the gun barked. Ginger was hot on the chase and I worried about hitting her as I sent the rabbit's ass end spinning in front of his head. I hadn't led enough. In the clarity that only these moments provide I chastised myself. First and foremost, it was dangerous to the dog. If I had shot Ginger in the head I might as well eat the next shell because I sincerely doubted that I could have lived with the guilt. Secondly, the hindquarter shot would mess the meat and thirdly it wasn't a kill shot just a takedown.

The rabbit screamed and I rushed forward. Ginger had overrun the rabbit with momentum but had turned and was moving in for the final attack. Ginger had never figured out the gentle pass of game to master and I always had to keep up. I had to kill the rabbit, break its neck, which I did quickly to beat my rising squeamishness. I praised Ginger and pushed her away and stowed the dead rabbit in the game pouch in the back of my vest. The weight felt good. It felt like an accomplishment and I thought of Emily. My worry had passed. I petted the dog and lavished her with compliments. She nearly knocked herself over with an out of control tail when we started for home.

Passing through our own woods Ginger again picked up a scent. She flushed the rabbit and I made a good kill shot not even fully shouldering the gun. I barely even aimed. It's amazing what confidence can do to skill. I loaded the second rabbit into the pouch and unloaded the three remaining shells from my gun. Now there was enough meat for everyone including the idiot savant dog. We walked happy the rest of the way home.

I cleaned the rabbits at a table at the bottom of the stairs. Ginger begged for the scraps. I kept the hearts, kidneys and livers and threw the rest of the offal in the river. Ginger didn't like that.

31

At seven I began cooking. I opened a bottle of burgundy and ran the air conditioner full tilt with all the windows closed. I tried to create fall inside. A deceitful October came across my mind and I could smell apples and burning leaves in the air and on my clothes. The sound of high school football from a block away. I could feel the weight of a jacket on my shoulders as I walked through the woods. I wished for perpetual fall. I wished for baseball in October but I knew Detroit and Cleveland would be retired for the season.

I browned the rabbit in my large number ten skillet. That skillet belonged to my mother's mother, a kind Norwegian immigrant scarred by the depression in North Dakota. After removing the meat I made a sauce with the remains. I cooked down the vegetables and the hearts and the kidneys and the livers and then strained out the vegetables and sent the rest through the food processor and returned everything to the skillet to simmer. A little wine went in at this point for good luck. Never were my meals the same because I didn't exactly know how to cook. I had picked up a couple of tricks through my years and incorporated new ones when they happened along but just as often I would forget something else. The trick with the guts was something new I had read about in a magazine and tried twice with no ill effects. You've got to try even if you're just one man in one little house next to a wide brown river. Unfortunately life isn't the sole property of our cultural centers.

32

The food ready and my house clean I waited for Emily. I didn't wait with a lonely man's anxiety. An unusual calm descended over me. Possibly it was the cool air. Heat had always affected my mind in negative ways. Paranoia and irritability often coincide with humidity above ninety percent. In my head I rehearsed how I would greet my guest. An impossible kiss seemed best.

With the windows closed and air conditioner creating a low, pleasant white noise I did not hear Emily's car pull in the drive way. Her white knuckles tapped lightly on my back door and I was shocked out of my dreams.

As Emily came in and I was speechless. She wore her hair loose and it hung to the small of her back with a luxurious weight. It slid across her sheer white silk blouse. I had never seen hair like hers. Most red hair had a copper wire texture but Emily's did not. It was smooth and graceful. Unable to stop myself, I looked her up and down. Underneath her knee length skirt she wore nylons. I hadn't seen nylons on a calf in a very long time and I was enamored. It was almost too much for a man to bear.

"You look great," I said with all my Ohio subtlety.

Emily laughed at my stupidity. "I brought some wine," she said holding up a bottle. I thanked her and shut the door behind her, once again looking her up and down, repeating my obviousness.

"You look good, too," Emily said. "I like your slippers."

I wore a red pair of wool Norwegian slippers under a light brown pair of moleskin pants. My mother had brought me the slippers as a gift from a trip to the homeland six years ago. I told this little story which Emily called, "sweet".

We had some wine out of the open bottle and sat on the couch, talking about little things, about work, the library, my eye, the dog. Ginger had settled down and seemed content to lie on the rug in front of the couch and stare at Emily. For once the dog showed some intelligence.

"It sure is different in here than outside," Emily said.

"How's that?"

"It's cool."

"I tried to create a false fall," I explained. "The stew is more of a cold weather dish so the air conditioner is atmosphere, I guess."

"It's nice."

"Fall is my favorite season," I said.

"Why?"

"The air. The light. The birds. The smells. Just everything about it."

"I don't mind the heat," Emily said.

"I'm sorry. Are you cold? I could shut off the air conditioner. I wasn't thinking."

"No, no. I like it."

"Are you sure?"

"Yes… Although, could I borrow a sweater just until I get warmed up?"

I went into my bedroom to fetch a sweater and Emily followed me and Ginger followed her. I pulled a green V-neck from my shelf.

"My mother knitted this for my dad when he was stationed in Korea. The winters are nasty there."

"Your mother sounds sweet."

"She's a mother alright."

"Not everyone is so lucky."

"No, I suppose not."

She held the sweater in front of her, appraising it, and I noticed her nipples showing through the blouse hard from the chill. My ears burned and I blushed. I have never been bashful and this astounded me. Emily noticed and she returned the blush. We both laughed and then her breasts were swathed in the war sweater. I loved her right then. I wanted to tell her so. I wanted to ask her to marry me. I wanted to hold her close to me through all the winters to come.

"More wine?" I asked.

She nodded and smiled and I was lost for good, or so I thought.

We went over to the stove and peered in at the stew. It was the color of wet earth, rich and subdued. I cut the bread and Emily sat down at my little table. I had thought of putting a couple of candles between us but the cliché scared me away.

"So, I'm to pretend that it is November?" Emily asked.

"That would work."

"Is it raining or snowing outside?"

I looked through the window above the sink at the fading summer night. Nothing was in the air except heat. The highway radiated like an oven cooling with the door open.

"I wish it was dark outside. Let's say it's not raining. The real rain hasn't started yet. Only the leaves fall like snow." I ladled the stew into two bowls. "Mornings are cold and the midday sun feels empty, defeated."

"And you like that weather?" Emily asked.

"I love it. It's the only weather that makes any sense."

"I like the color."

We both sat with the bowls in front of us and the bread between. Emily smiled and pointed at her bowl. I nodded and she used her fork to pick out a piece of meat. She chewed and didn't say anything too soon.

"It's good. Rich."

"Cold weather food."

"It tastes like it looks, and I mean that as a compliment."

I was a little defeated. Why had I chosen this meal? She had asked. My doubts chased away my own appetite. "Try dipping your bread in the sauce. You should still taste the wine in your mouth with the meat." She did and continued eating and drinking. But Emily was not suited for this meal. It was a stew for men eating in the presence of wood smoke and gun oil. She deserved something better, something more refined and delicate. I would have to check out some new cookbooks. I had never cared what kind of food Rochelle warranted. A selfishness sat like a roof on top of my house. Never had I read that different people called for different dishes. People had favorites and tastes but was there more to it than that? Did Emily's luxurious body call for lemon chicken and a salad? Or seafood? I was confused.

"That was good," she said. She had finished her bowl and was wiping it clean with a piece of bread. My own stew had hardly been touched.

"Didn't you like it?" Emily asked.

"Yeah, I was just thinking."

"I noticed that. You're not much of a dinner conversationalist. Your eyes kind of glossed over and you drifted away."

"I'm sorry. I think I was nervous that you wouldn't like it."

Emily smiled and wiped her lips with the paper towel I had given her as a napkin. "That's sweet, but don't worry. I wouldn't storm out of here if you served me mac and cheese. Plus I liked the stew. I really did. And that was the first rabbit that I have ever tasted. That's quite an accomplishment. Now you eat yours while I go put some more lipstick on." She stood and walked to the bathroom. I followed her with my eyes. She was amazing. I didn't know what to think. She said the words that soothed my soul and her presence was beauty and grace.

33

Like she told me to, I ate. The stew tasted fine. I drained off my glass of wine with the hope of settling my nerves. I cleaned the table and put the dishes in the sink for later. Emily reappeared from the bathroom. Her face was perfect and a small smile curled to the right side of her mouth. It was like a smirk but it was more. It was more honest and open. I felt ill.

"Should I open your bottle of wine?" I asked.

"Yes, please. I shouldn't drink too much more though… because of the drive." Emily was once again looking at the spines on my bookshelf. When she bent over her hair draped down one side of her neck and ran parallel to her thighs. A lust that had been missing finally showed itself in my body and I was reassured. Before I had been a boy in awe of some sexless teacher, boss, officer, upper classman. But now I again felt my feet and my body. I was comfortable in this wave of warm blood. It was as if I had just been awarded home field advantage. My fans, my people cheered me on and I was comfortable now as I was on factory or forest floor. Standing straight, I rolled my shoulders back erasing the slouch that came with thought or indecision. I filled both glasses out of the new bottle and brought this beautiful woman, this full-bodied, red haired, red-lipped woman a glass of the dark wine. For possibly the first time in her presence I offered a confident smile. She stood up, taking the wine from me. I looked slightly down toward her green eyes.

"Thank you for coming," I said.

She smiled up at me and saluted me with her glass before taking a sip. Emily returned to her bent position and continued her survey of my books. A suspicion grew in my mind. Was she that good, that confident in her mental and physical perfection that she could will my soul into reacting? She reached past my thigh to the shelf and pulled a box out.

"You have Scrabble. Do you want to play?"

Her smile gave me no more clues. We set up the board on the coffee table, filled our racks, and the game began slowly.

I started with "rat" and wished I had at least used "tar". She consistently used six letter words and only by foxing her out of double and triple word scores did I manage to keep the game close. What did I expect playing against a librarian?

Emily took the victory. Had the game been close I would have tanked a few shots. That lack of originality embarrasses me but some tactics are just classics. No one argues against surprise or a flanking move. But Emily simply out played me. She emptied her rack over and over again and used difficult letters with ease. Only once did I turn her head, "fescue". It was a word I learned from my dad.

We gathered up the letters and twice her hand brushed mine as I held open the bag. The wine made my hair feel alive but maybe it was Emily who did this.

"That was fun," Emily said and sat back on the couch. "I haven't played Scrabble or any board game for years."

"Why not?"

"I don't know." She smiled again and then patted my knee in a slightly patronizing way. "But I do know that I shouldn't have any more wine."

"Alright." I sat my glass down too. It neared ten and Emily thanked me again for the evening. A silence soon crept in between every other sentence. I began to agree with her unspoken thought that the time had come for her to leave. Doubt ran too rampant to make the air smooth. Only Ginger, curled on the carpet by the door, seemed relaxed. What next? It was obvious that the worldwide tradition of drunken bodies colliding in the dark would not work for us. It was true that these half steps and positioning created more and more anticipation but that anticipation felt awfully similar to anxiety I took both wine glasses to the sink. Emily stood and now smoothed her skirt where it traversed her hips. She picked up her purse from the bookshelf and drew out her keys. Words rushed past my eyes and ears but they lacked order and the combinations that I could understand were not possible. I couldn't fall to her feet and beg her for mercy. It just wasn't possible.

Emily bent over and stroked Ginger. The dog enjoyed her touch and stretched legs in appreciation. I was jealous of the dog. Then Emily turned to me.

"Your sweater," she said. She reached down to pull the sweater over her head. "I don't want to walk away with your mom's sweater."

"You can keep it," I said.

"No. I couldn't, and it's still hot outside." She pulled the sweater off and as she struggled to free her hair I was caught by the image of her body working. It was as if Emily had slapped her figure across my cheek like a hand and said snap out of it or wake up. She handed me the sweater with a smirk, that same smirk. I could have hugged and kissed her right there, I should have, but I didn't.

"I'll walk you out," I said and opened the door. The air hit like a wet cloth. I groaned and said, "disgusting."

Emily followed me and said, "It's not that bad. It's summer. I like being able to feel the air. It's sensual, don't you think?" She was behind me on the stairs.

"If you say so," I said.

We walked to her car. The stars were out and the moon reflected on the river. It was a nice night, my prejudice notwithstanding. Bats looped overhead and the willow stood silent and still. Emily opened her car door but the bell and interior light were intrusive so she pushed it closed again without latching it. She stood close to me, looking up into my face. Her breasts were almost touching me. I was half blind with a witless smile.

"Thank you," she said again.

I thought of not kissing her. I thought of a control of time and place that I could possess if I didn't kiss that beautiful upturned face. But control of the fates is overrated. I kissed Emily. She kissed me back. It was a nice kiss, soft and tender. My bones lost tensile strength and I almost swooned. But it was only that one kiss and then she pulled away.

"I'll talk to you tomorrow," she said. Then she drove away.

I didn't wave or shout anything after her but just stood there under the moon and the stars, in the midst of all that Ohio flatness and smiled like a complete dullard. I then picked up a rock from the driveway and sent it into the river. "Hmph," was all I could manage.

34

Upstairs I cleaned the dishes and then sat in the silence on the couch. The house felt empty. I noticed the sweater laying were it was dropped next to the door. I went and picked it up and true to my wish it was fragrant with her. I inhaled it deeply, too deeply, some of the mothball undersmell came through. But if I just held it to my face and breathed, her scent came to me. It lingered and was potent. I reached over, turned off the reading light and laid my head down on the sweater. I went to sleep that way, with her smell.

My mind was steady like the river. I went to sleep content in the arms of possibility that a woman's scent and smile posed. But during the night, clouds of doubt and defeat drifted over my sun. I was visited in my dreams by a woman with whom I had a relationship of thought rather than action during school. She came back to offer me fresh refusals, new and original forms of an old tune. I don't know if tears came to my eyes on the couch but in the ether of my head they poured and when I woke I had to clear my vision with the back of my hand. It's the injury, I told myself. My eye patch had escaped during the night. It lay on the couch pillow next to the balled up sweater. I was tired of the pirate costume and wanted my normal life back. Was life ever normal? Yes, actually, it was. Most of the time it was. Whatever took up the majority of your time was your normality. Spaceships are normal for astronauts as mines are for miners. I stood and stretched, tired of my mind.

BOOK FOUR

1

Driving into town with Ginger, I tried not to think too much of last night's kiss. What did I really expect of Emily? Perhaps love. More like sex and some conversation. Passionate loves are doomed from the start. That is a law.

The factory's parking lot was full and as I approached the door I could feel and hear the thump of production. The smell of oil and metal is a beautiful perfume. The perfume of purpose. I walked past the timeclock, through the pressroom floor, to the back corner where my little war machine was being assembled.

Sean saw me coming. "Showing up when the work's almost over. Just like you."

The tooling guys were installing dies. Three stamping presses were anchored to the floor in a line, next to them was a new parts washer, a giant red basket machine that would be filled with solvent. A three-button control panel told the machine to dip up, down, or agitate. I liked that, "agitate". That's what I was there to do.

"We decided that, instead of a shear press, you would get to wash your own parts. The aluminum will be cut just like everything else." Sean pointed through the wall toward the materials building where incoming metal was stored and then cut down into blanks for the presses.

I decided not to argue with Sean. It was a valid idea and I'm sure not his. "Makes sense." I turned from him and headed for the new setup. But two steps in I couldn't resist turning and asking, "Don't you have some old ladies to be babysitting?"

He gave me the finger, "don't you have some whore to be fucking?"

Now I thought this odd on two levels. I was referring to the elderly under his command on the pressroom floor but what had he thought? And the whore-fucking jab. That made no sense. It was like air and breathing, water and river, cats and dogs. Even if he was still upset, three years later, about Rochelle then it just proved his idiocy. And I felt no need to defend her honor. I waved Sean off and continued on.

"You guys are really making time," I shouted over the factory din.

John McGraw turned and flashed me a smile of accomplishment. Not too many things had gone wrong yet. It was unusual for processes that involved several different minds to fit together first try. McGraw pointed to the next press in the line and shouted, "one more, then we'll run some tests. If everything works we could go into production tomorrow." I raised my eyebrows to show amazement.

"How's the eye?" John asked.

"It's fine. Just wearing the eye patch to humor the doctors. I'm ready to come back to work if Turnbull lets me."

He pointed to the presses, "this could change his mind."

I smiled.

John went back to fitting. A forklift came in carrying the last form block and I helped wrestle it into place on the bolts of the press frame. It was satisfying, being a part of the work. I would come back after lunch for the first tests.

2

I went to the library to kill an hour. Though I wish I had been thinking only of Emily, I was enraptured with the machine. Women could soothe my soul, but body and mind belonged to the floor.

As I opened the door I realized how wrong my thinking had been. Emily was at the front desk, red hair piled high. A smile tore across her face. She reached her hand out on the table and I covered it with mine.

"Hi there," she said.

I couldn't say the words in the back of my throat. She put her other hand on mine, looked over both shoulders, and whispered, "go up to poetry, I'll meet you there in a few minutes."

I stood in the tiny aisle waiting for her with an awkward erection. Can you have a hard on for love instead of lust? I kicked the little stool into the corner and sat down. Emily's footfalls were soft on the carpeted stairs. I watched her waist approach through the gap between rows of books. She rounded the corner and pulled her skirt above her knees before kneeling in front of me. She took my hand.

"I thought of you last night. Everything you said. I couldn't sleep." She kissed my knuckles.

"I slept well," I said.

We walked over to the balcony railing. "I want to keep us

a secret… from Mrs. White."

"Why?" I asked.

"I don't want to look like a, I don't know, a hussy. Mrs. White's evaluation matters to my grade."

I was taken aback by her concern of grades over me.

"Please," she said.

I couldn't refuse her. I needed whatever she was prepared to give. I thought it was more simple than it really was. It wasn't an original mistake.

"Alright," I said.

She straightened up, kissed me and then left. I sat on the little stool with tingling lips and a pained penis. I pulled a collection of Robert Service and read until both sensations were gone.

3

As I walked down the library steps I pulled the eye patch from my head and stuck it in my back pocket. The light hurt but I was tired of playing pirate. Ginger was asleep on the bench of the truck. She looked at me for a moment when I slid in next to her. I talked to her of love, about the powers that control your body as well as your mind. It was a familiar conversation and she wasn't impressed.

"You're fixed. You don't understand. I don't even know why I talk to you," I said and she cocked an eyebrow. I reached over and mussed the hair on her head and then drove to work.

I didn't like leaving Ginger in the cab all day. I rarely brought her to work but I wanted to see the first tests so I pulled the yellow rope from the toolbox and tied her to the hitch with the gate down so she could sleep in the shade. I poured some water in her margarine dish and set it behind the rear tire.

Quality Control, Turnbull and the tooling men formed a circle around the new presses and John McGraw who held a piece of folded aluminum. I joined the crowd, peering underneath armpits at McGraw pointing to an edge and explaining the stress. Jeff Krager ran his hand over the part, feeling the measurement. He led the party back to the granite table inside his office where design plans were spread on the table. Krager painted some patches blue before scratching reference points on them. He then measured and remeasured announcing the numbers out loud.

"That's one," Justin Bullough said. "You got two more for us?" he asked the tooling men who were standing together off to the side like expectant fathers. McGraw nodded and they moved toward the door.

I reached for the part left on the table. "What's the concern Krager?" He pointed at an edge I thought looked kind of thin. "It's an aggressive bend. We were worried about losing too much thickness, but we're within the limits."

The jaws of the press were being slowly closed to make sure the form blocks lined up. Confident that the halves wouldn't crash into each other and destroy a week's worth of work, McGraw picked up a blank from the pallet lying on the floor to the side and oiled it with a small paintbrush. He placed it against the stops then stepped on the foot trigger. The cams in the works spun round and the upper jaw came down with a smooth bite. I had goose bumps. McGraw pulled the piece out and handed it to Krager. He asked for two more. McGraw looked at me and asked if I would care for the honor. "Hell yeah," I said, making Bullough laugh.

I pushed the flat aluminum against the stops, stood back, then stepped on the trigger. My future sat there folded in the open jaws, ready to be pried out.

The third press wasn't ready and everyone went back to their jobs. I stood with my hands in my pockets watching McGraw work. I wasn't clocked in so I felt safe with this obviously lazy posture but quickly I felt less safe. I was the only one who knew I wasn't punched in. I wished for a broom to push or a dish to wash. I didn't notice Turnbull approach from behind.

"Where's the eye patch?" he asked.

To my credit, I didn't jump. "My eye's better, and I'm not on the clock." I wished for those words back as soon as I said them.

"I didn't ask if you were," he paused. "Then why are you here?"

"I wanted to see the tests. The patch is in my pocket. I want to come back to work."

Turnbull didn't answer. He watched McGraw slowly open and close the third press. His thick glasses magnified his eyes so they looked proportionate to his giant body. Ten years, almost ten years I had worked for and occasionally with this man. I did the jobs he assigned me without too much back talk, only enough to say I was alive and thinking. Ten years I had trusted him with my future, trusting he considered my work more of an asset than a tool. Finally, the step up appeared in front of me and I wasn't even sure he approved.

"See how they keep oil on the dies?" Turnbull pointed at the press. "If you put on too much it will pool and the top and bottom won't fit together. The oil can have a greater thickness than the material and the stops won't set right. Not this though. The aluminum is thick. But you've got to oil. You don't want the dies to gall. You know what that is?"

"Yeah, like when you assemble an engine." It was basic stuff, factory 101.

"Exactly, metal sticks. Once, years ago, when you were still in grade school, we had dies stick so hard I had to use a sledgehammer to separate them. They were ruined. Ten thousand dollars for a penny's worth of oil. You got to think. Think about the cost. That includes man-hours, materials. Too many people here think they're just another machine. Fuck, we could design trigger pushers. People are paid to think and to watch. Be cognizant dammit." Turnbull removed his glasses and rubbed the bridge of his nose. I wondered how much the lenses weighed. He put them back on. "You're not fucking with me. Your eye, it's good?"

"I'm ready."

"Alright then."

The third press was finished, the test pieces passed.

I drove home and waited. I waited for the next morning

and I waited for Emily to call. The sky turned gray and clouds stacked upon themselves. I took a shower leaving the bathroom door open in case the phone rang. It didn't.

4

Clean-shaven in my underwear I sat on the couch and opened a can of beer. The light over the river was now ominous. I was trying to read a book about the Fins in World War Two. They were tough people. But I kept thinking of work and of Emily. I struggled to concentrate. I grew tired and a little angry. She didn't call and when I heard a car on the gravel drive I had to hurry to the bedroom and pull on a pair of wrinkled khaki pants. She knocked on the screen door, unused to walking right in.

Emily wore a tee shirt with a cartoon mouse's face on it and a pair of jeans. The shirt seemed tailored for a seventh grade boy but it fit her curves nicely. She held up a bottle of Gin.

"I thought we could have some cocktails," she said.

She crossed the floor and hugged me tight, pressing her breasts against me. I kissed her cheek and then her neck. She let go and walked into the kitchen. "I'm sorry about today," she said, "but try to see it from my position. I've only been at the library two weeks and if I start dating the first patron I know by name it won't look good. We'll work it out, don't worry." She was pawing through my refrigerator. "Do you have any tonic?" When I said no, she came over, opened her arms and brought me tight against her body. "Play my game and I'll make it worthwhile." She squeezed me tighter than before and I wondered if she hadn't been drinking already. "I think I have some tonic water in my car. I'll be right back." She pushed open the screen door and disappeared down the stairs.

I hadn't thought of the library until she mentioned it. Maybe I should have been more concerned but I remained concentrated on the facts. She was beautiful and let me kiss her. The line at work was starting to come together. Everything pointed to a newness in my life.

When Emily opened the door I was still standing in the same spot she had left me.

"Geez, don't take it so hard Warrell. I said I'll make it worth your while." She rubbed my arm as she passed.

Emily made us drinks and we retired to the couch. We talked, mostly I listened conscious of our age difference. Emily put down three at a fast pace and would refill the glasses before they were even empty. She became excited at her own stories and then mispronounced words.

Finally, she set her drink on the coffee table and then turned to me.

"I like you. I really do."

This is getting ugly, I thought. She pulled her knees up on the couch and knelt over me. When I set my drink down she kissed me hard. She was more forceful than I would have thought and I could feel teeth through her upper lip. Oh well, I thought, maybe this is just how they kiss in Cleveland. But her intentions were clear and I just tried to keep up. Emily pushed me back and laid her full weight upon me. Her tee shirt rode up and I felt the pleasant valley of her lower back. I released the clip that held up her long red hair and it fell over me. It was thick. It made more than a tent. It made a cave. We fought like that for a while, confined by clothes on the couch. She ground her hips on me and it became painful. We had to quit or move on. It was up to me and I hesitated. In my ROTC program this was also my short coming- failure to use initiative. I heard the old sergeants voices in my head urging me on to be technically and tactically proficient. Her kisses led me to doubt the technique side. But pain is a good motivator and I asked, "Do you want to go to the bedroom?" Emily smiled and pulled herself off me. In a distant classroom Staff Sergeant Eric Hanel leaned back in his chair satisfied that I had finally learned something.

As I turned off the light over the couch, a white flash lit up the river quickly followed by thunder. We both stopped and looked toward the window. "Was it raining when you drove up?" I asked. Emily said it wasn't. The lightning hit again. It came with a deep wallop like someone had kicked an empty barrel. Ginger whimpered and she slunk with her head and tail down to the bedroom.

"It's odd," I said. "She doesn't like thunder but she will hunt."

"Maybe she can tell the difference," Emily said.

A double strike and then the wind started in every direction. Several large drops hit the glass and I realized the windows on my truck were down. I scurried for some shoes but I had waited too long. By the time I descended the stairs and rolled up both windows I was soaked.

5

I turned off the kitchen light and made my way to the

bedroom, my eyes slowly adjusting to the dark. Lightning lit the room and I could see Emily in bed, covers pulled up to her neck, hair spilling in every direction. The image stayed in my eyes after the darkness again filled the room. I reached my way to the bed, to her outstretched hand. She pulled me toward her kiss. Flashless thunder rattled the old panes.

"Is there room for me?"

"Yes, but not for your clothes."

I could hear a smile in the dark. I took off my shirt and was fumbling with my pants when I realized I was standing on the pile of her clothes. I stripped and climbed in beside her. I feared that first touch. Feet and lips only, please. We cannot control the core, only the periphery. And then Emily reached over and pulled me against her. Her body was warm and soft along the length of mine. But we were too new for a routine and our awkwardness was like a third person. Elbows and knees hit then backed away. I was too polite. I didn't even know if she liked her ass held.

Emily's body was a land to be explored and I was becoming the man to map it. I pulled the sheets down to memorize the hills and valleys in the white flashes. But Emily protested that she was cold. She didn't feel cold I told her and she giggled. It was nice.

We went slow. We betrayed nothing. I worried about coming too fast and stayed away from situations that didn't have an easy way out. Her body fired and leapt with every touch. She made noises that were little more than the sound of her breath. But these winds, these stops and starts of her lungs had a terrible effect on me. At one moment I wanted to cry. Never had I been so close to beauty, to natural unaffected beauty, to the philosophical concept of Truth.

Emily's hair swirled around us. It was a scarf around both our necks. I inhaled it and coughed. Emily laughed. It got caught beneath my elbows and pulled on her painfully. I apologized and we began again after gathering it in a safe place.

Eventually her breaths became louder and quicker. She reached for me but only brushed past and then clawed into my kidney. Emily pulled me closer and atop her. "I want to come with you inside me," she said. It was almost too much. I had heard language that made sailors blush but this was almost more than I could take. Meaning and power are always dependent on context.

That earthly heaven, that ecstasy wrapped in thunder and lightning was momentarily broken by the ungraceful rummaging of my nightstand for a rubber. Emily laughed and pronounced my depot convenient. There might have been a suspicion in her voice or possibly it was doubt in my heart. I felt lost for a moment, even though I was locked between this woman's legs. Slowly, the music and intoxication returned, then her breathing shortened and again I was skewered by her fingernails. I fought myself and tried to stay in the race but when we ultimately joined amongst the booming and light I failed. Emily took the reins, whipped the horse and was able to save the day. By the time she came I was already crippled by a cramp running from my hamstring to my foot. Afterward I kissed her cheek and neck but she was elsewhere. I felt her body hum in prolonged delight and was jealous. She was alone.

We fell asleep and I woke later to dark silence. Emily's back was to me and I rubbed her flank. The storm had stopped. I should have seen the quick summer thunderstorm as an omen instead of the pleasant soundtrack to our sex. I listened to Emily breathing and the refrigerator's hum in the kitchen until I fell back asleep.

I woke for good at six. I had slept in. I tried to wake Emily with some gentle petting but she wasn't responsive. It would have been pleasant and appropriate to lie around in bed throughout the morning but I couldn't. Work was already on my mind. This would be my first day back since injuring my eye and I felt the excitement of Ginger before a hunt. In the clear light I looked for the dog. She was sleeping in my closet on boots and dirty laundry. Everyone was breathing and whole. We had made it through the night. I managed to get out of bed without waking Emily and moved off to the kitchen. I didn't know that I could sing and drop glasses without waking her but then everything was new.

A shower and coffee, a clean uniform and a beautiful woman asleep in the slanting yellow light. Every few minutes I would hold the door trim and look on her again. Emily had rolled over and faced away from the window but that was her only stirring.

At 6:40 I started to worry. She slept on and it was almost time for work. I worried. I wanted to wake her. I wanted to poke her with a stick. Should I let her sleep while I go off to work? Should I politely hurry her off at the same time? Under doctor's orders I wasn't yet supposed to be going to work but I had already asked and was locked in. What could I do? I couldn't call and say that my eye was acting up. The first production pieces were going to be run today. Was I to let someone else work this first day? What if something went wrong? What if something went right? No, I had to go to work.

I kissed Emily on the cheek. She smiled but made no waking movements. "I have to go to work," I whispered. She didn't stir so I repeated myself a little louder but still no response. I rocked her shoulder back and forth. But still she didn't respond. It was time to go to work. I couldn't delay any longer. I shook her again and called her from her sleep. Emily's eyes opened wide, brows raised like I had just burst through her front door. I explained that I had to go to work and to lock the door when she left. Emily smiled and reached towards me for an embrace. I held her and then let her go. She was back asleep before I left the room. As I drove to work I worried about things she might have found if she nosed through my house. I couldn't think of anything too damning. There were some photos but what could one expect? We all live lives full of different people and different chapters.

7

It was wonderful to hear the thump and arc of the machines, to watch the men go back and forth getting in each other's way and hear the shouting and greetings and curses. The bite of the time clock was pleasant although the one punch on my blank time card seemed lonely. I found Turnbull but he merely said, "See what you can do."

There were no blanks cut so I walked down to the shear presses. Number Eight, filling in for a vacationer, fed the far press sheets of steel. I could feel its regular bite though the soles of my boots. The near machine was silent. Its operator, Charlie Novak, was missing. Chuck was a drunk. It wasn't a rumor but a confirmed fact. Neither doctors nor jail could wean him from the bottle. His station standing empty in the morning wasn't a call for alarm or even worry. Often Chuck would stumble in after ten and work straight through without dinner or break until his orders were completed. Because the shear presses supplied the stamping presses with their raw materials for the following day Chuck needed only to show up and get his work done. I had never heard management explain why they tolerated Chuck whereas a few tardys anywhere else on the floor would bring swift reproachment. But then management doesn't explain, it issues, it decrees. And who was I to demand equality under the rule? The rules more often than not bent in my favor.

It was commonly supposed that Chuck would be dead within a month if he didn't have the obligation of the time clock. Who knows, the county may have been paying Chuck's salary to save on jail and hospital costs. Maybe he was the illegitimate son of Zachary Bullough or of God. Most likely it was a combination of pity and seniority. Show up anywhere five days a week for thirty years and you're going to build up some favors. Beside all this, be it material thickness or blank size, Chuck never made a mistake in his work and mistakes were costly in this first step. It was even something of a spectator event to watch the old man sweat and talk to himself while pounding out basket after basket of blanks. As riddled as his alcoholic mind was he knew his material and that counted as competence. A sober Christian was hardly ever the peer of this stooped old man.

I stood on the press table and looked for Chuck. From on high I could see from the plasma presses on one end of the building all the way into the stacks of material on the other. "Eight," I yelled. Octavio looked up at me and tipped an imaginary bottle with his thumb and pinkie out. I nodded and then jumped down. I slid into Chuck's workstation and dialed my blank size and then locked the controls. I had to pick the aluminum with the overhead crane but it was still on top of its pile because of yesterday's tests. I enjoyed controlling the crane, enjoyed its astounding strength, but always worried about its claw opening and spilling 4x8' knives. I envisioned the sheets coming down one by one instead of the heavy crash that was more likely. In my nightmare the sheets rained down on the men trying to escape cutting off a foot then a crawling hand, then a leg or a head. I would surely be cut in half along the belt line and would have to watch my legs, still in the green work pants, lay twisted as the blood drained from my abdomen. But this didn't happen. I survived again.

I checked my measurements against the work order three times before I pushed the trigger and then I measured the first piece to be positive. I cut the rest of the bundle and neatly stacked the blanks on a pallet. The aluminum was delicate. It could easily scratch.

I found a lift truck driver and convinced him to pull my box to the new presses. I went to work. I pressed the aluminum and then stacked the newly formed pieces in another box. After I had filled that box I used a hand truck to pull the box over to the washer. Piece by piece went into the washer, was agitated, and then was dried off with a rag before being stacked in yet another box. This final box was plastic and special for the trip to Indianapolis. Cut, stack, move, stamp, stack, wash, dry, stack, ship. I wondered how all this movement could ever be worth the cost. But everyone knew that the government had a checkbook with no ledger.

8

I worked. I checked my watch and set the timer to record how long it took to complete fifty door jams, a hundred. Extra time had to be allowed for switching presses and either fetching more blanks or getting a box carted away to shipping. I cut total time by ten minutes between the first and second runs. It became a challenge (I am well aware that painting the fence wasn't really fun) and I sought to bring my times down. A foolish pride of ownership came to me. I imagined great compliments and rewards. Finally my life was moving in the right direction. I should have seen all the signs but I saw none.

Turnbull came up behind me. He was measuring the thickness of the aluminum with the micrometer he carried in his pocket when I turned around. I was scared but acted nonchalant. His measuring didn't make sense. He should have been worried about the actual dimensions of the parts not the metal. I could find the right material. It was marked with bright red tape proclaiming, "DOD Approved".

"How many of these do they need per day?" I asked.

"Thousand."

"They make a thousand trucks a day?"

"UTT needs a thousand total, every day."

Turnbull looked into my empty shipping box and then kicked me in the balls. Actually he said, "I'm giving you another man starting Monday. Adam Smith." And then he walked away.

But that is what it felt like, a kick in the balls. Adam Smith was a horrible worker. He complained, gossiped like a teenage girl and dragged his feet. He wasn't just a slow worker he actually dragged his feet. I wondered what part of his shoes wore out first the toe or the heel. Adam Smith was a troublemaker that each division head kept trying to pass off on his counterpart. Someone was screwing me and I had an idea who that was.

9

My concentration was broken so I took my dinner break. I clocked out and drove home. Emily's car was still in the driveway. Truthfully, I hadn't thought of last night. I had been completely focused on work. I wondered if that was a bad sign. I decided it wasn't. Rather it was just selfishness. Emily was sitting at the kitchen table when I opened the door.

"I was hoping you'd still be here," I said. She smiled and I hurried over and kissed her upturned face.

"Are you on lunch?" she asked. I was, I said. I asked how she had slept and she said fine but she couldn't remember what I had said to her that morning.

"I told you to lock the door."

"Oh, I thought you said something else." She went back to flipping the pages of a nudie mag I kept in the bathroom. The air was uncomfortable. I doubted the wisdom of coming home for lunch. Her wrists moved with a snap that warned of things to come. If we were going to fight I needed to get it going, my break was only an hour. I looked at my watch. Dammit, I thought, only forty minutes left.

"Is something wrong?" It was pulling the pin on a grenade and I knew it. I admired my bravery.

Emily was quiet for a moment and then it came. She started with a sigh that I suspected would turn into a sob, but it didn't.

"I've never done that before," she said. "Not sex, I've done that enough, but sleeping with someone right away. I mean, damn, it was like our first date. I'm not a slut and I don't want you to think that. I like you, but we shouldn't have…"

I apologized, though I wasn't sure for what. I went to her and kissed her face again. She smiled a weepy smile and I worried that the situation could still get worse.

"Maybe it was just waking up to no one. You were gone and Ginger was in your place. She's nice and all, but it's not the same." Emily smiled. Her eyes were wet.

"We could try again," I said. Why was I only a foreman qualified as a universal question because I was obviously brilliant. She whispered "ok" and then stood up and placed her face against my chest. We went to the bedroom and when I asked her, "clothes or no clothes?" she said no clothes. We lay under the covers although it was too hot. She rested her neck in my armpit and her nose against my jaw. We lay there for twenty minutes, in silence. It was nice.

"When do you have to go to work?" she asked.

"I'm not sure, now that I'm my own boss. Old style would be pretty close to now. Should I be pretending that it's morning?"

"No that's all right. This is good." She kissed my ear. "Do we have time?" She pressed her body against mine. It was a just universe that had brought me into a position of decision-making. We "made love"- her term and it "worked"- mine.

10

My dinner break stretched into the next hour. What the hell, I thought, why not take two? It wasn't as if today was a real production run. The line wouldn't be under the gun for a couple more weeks. Turnbull couldn't even give me an answer when I asked about shipping dates, which was odd.

So we took Ginger for a walk along the river. Emily didn't have to work. I wished I didn't. We held hands. I considered asking her to marry me. She was beautiful, smart, and seemed to like me. Despite this, I decided to wait. We took turns telling more stories of our lives, little things that we thought were important and worth sharing. Eventually my stories, questions and answers grew shorter, clipped. I was thinking of work.

"Should you get going?" Emily asked.

"I can do anything I want. Right now I want to be with you." I said some more bullshit and lies but ended with, "maybe I should."

We walked to our cars and I put Ginger on her chain.

"Call me when you get home from work," Emily said.

"I don't have your number."

Emily laughed. "We really do have the order of things

all turned around." She gave me her number and we drove into town. Across the bridge I took a left and she continued on.

11

I clocked in but didn't go straight to my area. I went by the robotic welders to gain more of a perspective on the floor. My presses sat idle as I went to the shear presses next to cut some more blanks. Charlie Novak was there. His shirt was already soaked with sweat down the back and under the armpits. As I walked up I could see a drop hanging from the end of his nose. I wondered why he grew such a long beard. If he was always hot, why the beard?

"Hey Charlie," I shouted beside him. Charlie was talking to himself and feeding steel through the giant scissors as fast as his foot could push the trigger. I shouted again. This time he noticed. "Hey Chuck. Could you cut me some aluminum?"

"Already done," he said.

"I know but I need more for tomorrow."

"Tomorrow's supply is over there." He pointed to two pallets, "I already did it." He didn't smile but only looked at me. He seemed scornful of my ignorance. His eyes stripped me of any falsely assumed rank. Possibly that was the reason he had yet to be fired. He had Ahab's eyes. I mumbled my thanks and waved like the village idiot.

Instead of pulling a forklift away from the weld shop or pressroom floor I towed the pallets across the factory with the hand jack. The metal strips that served as seams on the floor impeded me but I muscled over them.

On my second trip Charlie looked up at me. "How many blanks are you going to need per day?" he asked.

"A thousand."

"They make a thousand trucks a day?"

I tried to fake some confidence. "Need a thousand per," I said.

Charlie frowned. It reminded me of the time my grandfather said I wasn't much of a man. I had no command presence. Staff Sergeant Hanel was right. I gave in to my own destiny. I became who I was. My voice squeaked like a girl. "I know. It doesn't make sense to me either."

The old man stood straight, as straight as his bones could manage and pulled at his beard. He looked at me. His eyes weren't softer but his words were. "Watch yourself Swanson. Don't get burned on this shit." He turned back to his work and went from zero to full speed. Bang, bang, bang. Cut pieces flew into the bin.

I wondered about his warning. I didn't know what he meant so I followed his example and worked as fast as I could. At a quarter to three Jeff Krager came strolling down from quality control. I was loading some parts into the washer when I spotted him.

"Can I have a couple of those," he shouted. When he got closer he said, "Taking long lunches, eh? You still fucking that little waitress on your dinner break?"

"No," I snapped.

"Hey, it's okay. I don't care what you do. I'm not the cops."

"I'm not seeing Rochelle anymore."

"Yeah right tell me that in two weeks."

"I'm serious. It's over."

"Too bad. She's built for speed. I can tell just by looking at her. But you already know that." He winked for emphasis as he reached into the box for a part.

"Take those over there. They're already washed."

"Thanks." Krager grabbed two parts and turned toward his office.

"Hey Krager, Charlie told me not to get burned on this. You know what he meant by that?"

"No… Chuck's a drunk. But maybe he's got a point. Anything new is bound to have some bumps. What I mean is, if this doesn't work out, where will that leave you? I don't think they'd let you back in as a floater. That was supposed to be temporary and it lasted, what? Three years? Once you get off the floor you walk around with a noose around your neck. Chuck was a foreman once, about a thousand years ago. He got busted back down when he really started drinking but that probably saved him from getting let go. Fuck, look how relaxed Turnbull is. He's been doing that for close to twenty years. Always the same pressure. Is it worth it? I don't think so. You should go back to school and get your quality assurance certification. Sit in air conditioning in the summer, heat in the winter. Just check the oil and make sure there's air in the tires. Let someone else drive."

"Yeah, maybe."

Krager gave me a phony British salute and headed back down the aisle to his office. I went back to wiping my parts but had no idea what anything he said really meant.

12

After work I untied Ginger from the tree. She saw me slip a couple dog bones into my hunting vest and became very motivated. We headed across the road. She seemed torn between the rewards lurking in the brush and the ones in my pocket. We walked on to my birch stand. I loved being surrounded by those white trees. Two crows came along and taunted Ginger. One stayed in the tree and screamed down at her while the other crept along the forest floor. The walker would jump into the air when Ginger got within striking range but would only stay airborne long enough to find another spot from which to taunt the dog.

As a child in Michigan I had to worry about my dog being led to her death by Mallards. They would swim dogs until they sank beneath the waves. My father had warned me about this but of course I hadn't believed him. But one day I was coming home through the woods from a friend's house when Sage, that was her name, took into a lake after some swimming ducks. I wasn't in a hurry so I sat down on a dock and watched her chase the ducks. She would gain on them but at the last moment they would beat their wings against the water and stretch the distance out. I called to her when I had gotten tired but she only glanced my way before continuing on. She'll get tired and come in, I thought. But she continued swimming and I could tell that she was losing her strength. Her pace slowed and the ducks took less of a lead. My father's story had already been in my head but now it shouted at me. More than a fear for Sage I had a fear of watching her drown. I thought about this latter and still found it cowardly. I stood on the dock and shouted and commanded but whenever the dog would make a turn toward shore the ducks would make their racket and convince Sage that she was gaining on them. I couldn't stand it any more. I ran along the beach until I came across a little fishing boat up on the beach with its oars still shipped. I pushed the boat into the water, put the oars in the locks and pulled like no fancy boy ever has. The little boat came out of the water, it planed. I shot across the surface like a water strider. As I closed in on the ducks they flew off. I yelled, "chickens", but that made no sense. Sage looked like a croc. Only her nose and eyes were above water. I reached in and grabbed her collar. I yanked, choking her and almost capsizing the boat, the rail almost to the water. Dead lifting eighty pounds. She was so tired that she didn't shake herself off. It had been that close. We went back to shore and I tried to remember what cottage I had borrowed the boat from. A man on shore helped me. It was his boat. He was angry that I had stolen his boat but I told him of the emergency and pointed at the cowering Sage as proof. He didn't care and threatened to call the cops. It was then that I noticed he was holding a rake. It was early summer and there was no raking to be done. What was he planning to do? Beat me with a rake? How absurd, I thought, a grown man defending home and property from an eleven-year-old boy and his wet half-dead dog with a rake. I ignored him and pulled his boat on the shore. I stored to oars not as he had but as they should have been. All the while he continued his tirade of private property rights and threw in some "worked hards" and mentioned the cops a couple more times. But I grew tired of him. I hadn't ever been concerned with his opinions. Concern for my dog had blocked out any fear. Finally I looked at him and said, "Fuck off". I didn't scream it as I did at passing trucks or trains but said it calmly and evenly and then I turned and walked away with my dog. The man didn't hit me with his rake. He said some more things but I didn't listen. It seemed to me that I had won something although I wasn't sure what. Something large. Something big.

My parents noticed my smugness at dinner that night but I couldn't tell them of the reason. I paid attention to my Father for some time after that waiting for some more applicable advice but it never came. Start with the battery is good troubleshooting advice but I'm not sure it came from him. That fall I shot more mallards than I needed or was allowed. With every pull of the trigger I mumbled, "dog killer". I hoped that one of those plunging ducks was the offending one but I was satisfied with general vengeance.

A few years later that dog, Sage, died of a stomach blockage. At five years she developed a taste for work gloves and athletic socks. It killed her.

I watched Ginger being led away by the crows. But I didn't worry because the stream running into the swamp was knee deep at best.

13

It was Friday so I took Emily to a fish fry. We drove down river to a little catfish joint in Florida. Florida, Ohio. Emily laughed and said she should have brought her swimsuit. I parked in the gravel lot.

We both drank beer and enjoyed the 'all you can eat'

across the red and white plastic gingham tablecloths. I dipped some fish in tartar and talked through my food. "Ohio's got a bunch of fucked up names. This was the frontier, the great northwest. There's a New Paris, a New Rome, New London, New Vienna. I bet you there are more "New's" in Ohio than any other state. People had tremendous hope when they settled here. Shit, look at towns like Independence, Liberty, Unity, Friendship, Felicity," I said counting with my fingers. "Not to mention our own, Defiance. Pretty cool name if I do say so. Although it's referring to Indian killing which is cool in its own way." Emily frowned but I continued on. "Of course this was all before industrialization. Now we should name things like Drudgery and Zombification." I dipped some more fish and then took a big swig of beer. "Just kidding," I said.

We left the third pitcher unfinished and I was painfully full as we walked out into the lot. I started the truck and told Emily I wanted to check the taillights. As she pushed on the pedal and triggered the turns, I walked to the tailgate and farted out all the gas I could. We should be safe, I said, giving her a thumbs up. We drove home through the bugs and the gloam. That night we didn't make love. We lay together like old people and were happy.

14

Following her through the grocery store I saw only her. Along the river it was the same. I held her hand compulsively. I needed the touch of her skin. At night I watched her fall asleep and in the morning I watched her wake. Actually I would get out of bed early, sliding gently out of the warmth so as not to wake her, go outside to get the paper and then read it while having my coffee. But every five minutes I would peek in at her sleeping face. There seemed to be a smile on it. Sometimes I would have to go in and kiss her cheek or forehead. And after an hour or two I would always have to return to bed and press my body against hers, to feel her warm, soft flesh against mine. And doing this I would smile and try to remain still. But soon I would be fighting with my own lust not to wake her with the demands of my body. I chastised myself. I tried to enjoy her aesthetically. I tried to embrace her with a love absent of hard-ons, a castrated love. I thought it was what she would want. That was how I thought. I tried to be inside her head and then look out at this man and read my, or her, desires. It was confusing and didn't work too well. This is how I feel, I would say to myself, I want to taste her flesh, hear her words and ultimately be inside her. So my gentle morning caresses would become more animated until she woke. Sometimes she would push me away but sometimes she would accept me. Not knowing the outcome was reason enough to try.

15

She asked to be woken early on Sunday morning so she could go to church. She needed time to go by her apartment and change. It was a conversation that we had not yet touched. She asked if I wanted to come along with her and I deftly declined. Emily drove away and I was left with the dog.

Never before had this kind of quiet been in my house. When it was Rochelle, I wanted this kind of solitude, often suggesting solo trips. Rochelle existed like a storm. She was never quiet only building. To keep Rochelle naked and occupied was not only an exercise in carnality, it was self-defense. But with Emily gone the silence was obviously a loneliness. I tried turning on music or the television. It was too early for baseball. Nothing was worth hunting. Nothing was worth doing. I just wanted

Emily back. I tried masturbating but that didn't work out. It was only nine in the morning and I was going out of my head. I wondered if I could break into the factory and get a little work done. Without a thought in my head I went to the fridge and pulled out a beer. I was sipping it on the couch before I realized what I had done. Oh great, now I've become a drinker, I thought. Too many alkies in my family already. Then I walked back into the kitchen and instead of pouring the beer down the drain I poured myself a shot of bourbon in a water glass. I took three of these before returning to the couch with my beer. My stomach burned and I felt ashamed, but gradually I felt better. I wanted Emily back, maybe more than before, but it wasn't so painful. I put on some music and started to shake my ass. My idiocy wasn't new or astounding so I just enjoyed it. I had worked up a sweat when Emily's car skidded in on to the gravel. I froze unable to decide what to do. I was still thinking when Emily opened the door.

"What are you doing?" she asked, smiling.

"Dancing," I said, although I was standing still.

"Well, let's see it."

"I don't dance in front of other people."

"I've had your dick in my mouth. I think I deserve to at least see your dancing."

I had imagined, feared actually that Emily would return from church with a saintly glow or a prudishness, but she had instantly dispelled that worry. I rocked a little, then swayed over to her. She was wearing what I had always thought of as her librarian outfit. Silk shirt, skirt and cross. Her hair was piled on top of her head and she looked studious, quiet and lovely. As I moved in on her she looked at the beer can in my hand and exclaimed, "you've been drinking!"

I scooped her waist with my arm and confessed. "I was lonely. I couldn't bear it without you. Don't ever leave me again."

She pushed me away and said, "fix me a drink. I want to catch up."

I was a little taken aback but did as she said. She drank two down like water and then we danced a little. My hands rode over her hips and back and then pulled at her blouse and skirt.

16

Mondays aren't so bad if you've just left the bed of a beautiful woman and are starting what you believe to be a new life. With motivation and belly upon belly anything is possible, even getting out of bed.

Emily tried to wake up with me that Monday. She sat at the kitchen table in her silk kimono and blinked as I scurried about gathering all I needed. I was showered and shaved in a crisp new uniform and I was excited to see what would come of the day. How many could I do? How many could Smith? I thought for a second that it might be possible for me to do all the parts. If that was so then I wouldn't have to worry about anyone else. But that was stupid. I needed help.

I sat down at the table and drank a cup of coffee. Emily slouched. Her thoughts were obvious as she was too tired to defend against my reading them.

"Why don't you have some coffee?" I asked. "It might

wake you up."

"I'm sorry Warrell. I'm trying."

I slid my chair next to her and nuzzled into her neck. When I pulled my face away her eyes were closed. I looked into the folds of her gown. Her breasts, full and heavy, pointed in different directions. I reached in and cupped one with my hand. A frown came across Emily's face but that was the extent of her protest. She really was defenseless in these morning hours. In the evening I would have to explain my wanting to hold her breasts, explain with words of praise and love. I was fascinated with her body. It was so unlike any I had ever touched. I hate to compare. It seems rude. But Rochelle hardly had breasts at all. Rochelle's body was a young boy's; narrow hips, thin arms with visible muscle. Emily's body wrapped in red silk was so different, so luxurious. When our bodies came together it was the meeting of soft and hard, only skin color could have magnified the difference. I loved the otherness. Only a narcissist wants to fuck his self-image and I could barely tolerate myself. I brushed her nipple with my forefinger and it stood up like a dandelion. A small smile came to Emily's face. I wanted to reach down between her legs but knew I would be swatted away. Instead I looked at the wall clock, 6:33. It was better that I go to work now and not risk any frustration. I needed all my strength and will. I pulled my hand away.

"I need to go."

Emily mumbled something. I kissed her cheek and stood. I filled my coffee cup and quietly shut the door behind me leaving the sleeping woman at the kitchen table. I hoped that she wouldn't fall over and hit her head.

17

My aluminum was waiting for me when I got to the presses. I was filled with a sense of power and authorship. I couldn't wait to see pallets full of finished parts. I wanted to accompany them to Indianapolis and introduce myself as their maker.

I pressed the first part, then the second, then the third. Oddly, my joy didn't fade. I smiled at the forklifts going by. I yelled hellos to passing workers. I hummed a little jazz tune that I made up on the spot although one riff was obviously lifted from the Marine Corps hymn. I felt strong and fast. I considered having an erection for effect but decided against it. Everything rolled smoothly. It flowed. Part after part reached its potential and I floated over all of it omniscient and omnipotent.

A little after eight Adam Smith showed up and I was grounded. I made a gesture of looking at my watch.

"Little late, aren't we?"

"I'm not. I can't vouch for you," he said. Smith came forward and leaned against one of the shipping boxes.

"I think we should start at seven," I said.

"You can, but I'm coming in at my normal time. I come in at eight and leave at 4:30. I've done that for five goddamn years and I'm not going to switch because you think you're little Napoleon."

How could such a little fat man be so arrogant? He pulled a cigarette from his front pocket and lit it.

"What do you want me to do?"

The tune I was humming quieted. It was obvious that I wasn't going to be able to push Adam around with threats and commands. He didn't want to work. It wasn't a secret. I was thinking on my feet, literally. While Adam smoked his cigarette I maneuvered. It was similar to the exercise in my infantry leaders handbook. I had just come across a bunker, an obstacle, and I needed to work past it. I would have to trick this lazy man into believing it was in his best interest to work hard and succeed. I would have to change twenty-seven years of wrong thinking.

"Right… whatever. The important thing is we get our numbers every day. We have to do a thousand. That's not so bad. We have a week to figure it out. I'm thinking that we should both hit the presses hard for the first three quarters, then use the last for washing and packing."

"What is that? A sports reference? I hate sports."

"Right… That's just how I divide up my day. Four quarters divided by the breaks and dinner. It's just an easy way for me to think," I explained.

"Do you call dinner half-time?"

I let Adam finish his smoke and then explained the basics of our task to him.

"It's a press. I put metal in and it puts widgets out. What's the big deal?"

"Well, this aluminum is going to be coated in Kevlar to be bullet resistant so we can't scratch it. And it's a defense contract. It's a great opportunity."

"For who?" he asked.

"Us. This could be our thing, our show." I guess I really hadn't thought of the selling points. I would have to do that later.

"Whatever. I just want my hours."

After Adam finished his cigarette we set to work. Adam's pace was slow, which didn't surprise me. I tried to ignore it but soon I was counting three parts to his one. At 10:30 his press went quiet. I looked over. Adam was smoking, but he was always smoking.

"Break time," he said. "You going to take yours?"

I went on break with this man who I wouldn't save from a burning house. Life is full of moral compromises. Even the Amish put up with shit that makes them feel less that pure. And then we worked on.

I took my dinner break at the library. Emily and I sat on a bench facing the river and ate the sandwiches she had brought. It was nice. We quit pretending not to know each other in front of Mrs. White but Emily still insisted that I didn't touch or kiss her in front of the old woman. This didn't make sense. Mrs. White had given Emily an endorsement, calling me a "nice young man."

By the end of the third quarter I had two hundred and fifty pieces and Adam only half that. It was the first day so I didn't get too upset. Washing and packing took much more time than we had allowed.

At 3:30 I told Adam I had to go check on something. I went to the time clock and punched out, setting another precedent, then I went back to work. All day I avoided any real conversation with Adam. At times I positively seethed with hate for the man. I was sure that he was planted there to sabotage my future. But as he gathered up his things and began smoking his last work cigarette I genuinely wondered what he did after work. I didn't ask and off he went. I worked on.

At six the maintenance workers began switching off machines and lights. I was still unloading a basket of parts from the washer, wiping them and filling the packing boxes. I looked at my day's work. It wasn't a good sight. It seemed impossible to ever reach a thousand pieces a day. I wiped off those last pieces in the basket and then walked for the door.

18

It was a quarter to seven when I got home. Emily was sitting in her car in the driveway. Her windows were rolled down and she pretended to be reading. I parked and shut off my truck.

"Fuck. What a day," I said.

"Hello to you, too," Emily frowned. "Now you don't get a kiss."

"Sorry, had a bad day. Come here and give me a kiss."

"No, not yet," she said. I shrugged my shoulders and climbed the stairs. Emily followed behind me. She told me that she had talked to Ginger through the closed door and that the dog was also upset I was late. I opened the door and Ginger walked past the both of us and went down the stairs. In the kitchen I opened a drawer and rummaged through until I found what I had been looking for. I tossed Emily a spare house key.

"I need to take a shower," I said. I began taking off my clothes on the way to the bathroom. Emily followed me.

"This is serious," she said.

"As serious as you want it to be," I said.

"What's that mean?" she asked.

"I don't know." I pretended that I didn't know the meaning behind the words, that it was just an offhanded comment. I was scared of their meaning and the risk. But mostly I needed a shower. I closed my eyes and let the water run down my back.

19

We had a thousand pieces done by noon the next day. That was fine except for putting us back half a day. Smith arrived at his time and, in his fashion, dove into his work. Turnbull came by after dinner to see how things were progressing. I lied and said everything was fine. We were just working out some kinks, finding our rhythm. After he left Smith turned to me and said, "Don't you see it's impossible?"

"What's impossible?"

"One thousand is impossible. Three hundred is possible for one person but that doesn't include any time for washing or packing. We would need two more people to do a thousand."

I was insulted by his defeatism. Sure Smith, Ponte-du-

Hoc is impossible and so is space flight. I really expected those words from such a man. But still… How did he figure that. Smith broke down his math for me and I had to admit, it made some sense. But he figured a man only able to punch out 200 or 250 at the most. Our presses came to a halt as we discussed our tactics. I pulled a marker from my pocket and turned over the piece of cardboard I was standing on.

"480 minutes per day. Divide that by 500 and you get around about one per minute. A minute per part. You don't think that's possible?" There, with mathematical certainty, I had proved him wrong, or at least lazy.

But Smith wasn't finished. He demanded the marker. "You're an idiot… First, you didn't subtract any time for breaks… minus thirty. And what about washing and packing? When's that get done? A quarter as you say? I'll be generous and figure only an hour. Now we're down to 390. Divide that by 500 and you get what? Two a minute. That's impossible because it doesn't figure in fetching more aluminum or moving pallets or any smaller things. With two people it's just impossible."

"What do you figure we need?"

"To win the lotto," he laughed. "But, barring that, four people, possibly three. Three would still be a challenge. Everything would have to flow without interruption. You've been here long enough to realize that's a fantasy."

I stood up straight and thought about it.

Then Smith asked me, "Haven't you worked out these numbers yet? I'd say they're testing you to see how much of an idiot you really are." Smith pushed the long strands of hair that had fallen forward back behind his ears. He looked at me sideways like a co-conspirator. "This shit is doomed. They've given you a sinking ship and now I'm on it. I wish we had a shop steward… How many minutes have we just lost talking about it? Where are we going to make that up?"

"Let's get back to work," I said.

"That's all you have to say? Jesus, you're useless."

We stepped up to our presses and continued punching our parts. I don't know what Smith was thinking about but I tried pushing the numbers through in different combinations. Something had to be wrong. It was Turnbull's job to figure out production schedules. He was an expert at the calculation of man-hours. Why hadn't he thought of this? No, there was no plot. There was never any plot. I felt ill. The back of my throat tasted like metal. I leaned on the press in-between punches. My pace slowed and eventually equaled that of Smith. I needed something in my stomach.

"I'm taking my break," I said.

Smith stopped working and took off his gloves, nodding. We both went to the break room and I pushed the buttons on the food machine that spun the carousel around inside. I looked at the selection several times and each pass convinced me again that I couldn't eat any of it. Smith opened the door and walked out to have a cigarette in the heat and sun. I followed him and we both sat on the picnic bench.

"Can I bum a smoke?"

"Since when do you smoke?" he asked.

I shrugged, then we smoked our cigarettes in near silence. I wanted to talk to him about something but couldn't figure out what. A tractor-trailer pulled its load out from the shipping building. We watched as it rocked back and forth struggling with the low gears. Black smoke burped with each clutch grab.

"I wonder if he gets laid much," Adam said.

"What?"

"The truck driver. I wonder how he meets women. I mean, I've been to truck stops and they're not filled with lookers. I've heard all those cowboys are fags. It's a macho gay thing."

"What?" I was lost. Is this what Smith talked about instead of sports?

"Yeah, they act all butch but they're really a bunch of fairies."

"I'm sure they get to meet waitresses and shipping clerks and people like that."

"Where'd you get that from? A country song?"

After we finished our cigarettes, I decided we should continue making parts and I would wash and pack later. Smith asked if my overtime had been approved. I nodded and mumbled, but in truth I had already clocked out.

20

The week continued and our little team continued to fall behind. I tried not to worry about it but regular production started on Monday and I knew that even with our built up supply of six thousand pieces a couple of weeks would erase the advantage and the trucks would be leaving with less than they needed. For ten days I had struggled with this new system. No new answers were coming. Although I hated to admit it, Smith's appraisal was looking more and more right.

At night I would go home and eat with Emily before we made love and fell asleep. But work was entering my head in the unclocked hours as never before. Was this the price of advancement? Occasionally, as Emily rocked her hips back and forth on me, I would leave the room to count parts or imagine a more efficient body movement. Twice Emily stopped and asked where I was. She quit and it was difficult to bring her back around. I tried to tell her it was the job. She complained that I didn't find her attractive. I had to beg my way back in. "I love you," I said. "I would walk a thousand miles in the rain just to see you naked." Eventually we would get back inside each other and make it to the end. I would lie about this or that, but I was thinking about work.

21

I worked till the sweat dripped off my nose like the minerals in a cave. Smith laughed and kept assuring me it wouldn't work. Even at that pace I could barely make my numbers. There was no possible way I could expect anyone else to follow my lead. That night I collapsed on the couch and slept through to the morning. It wasn't good for my love life.

22

Friday came and I was being won over to Smith's camp.

And then Chris Carlson came by. He was the king of the salesmen and I had never liked this man. He made promises to his customers and the floor paid the price. He was bald, had a big ass and small hands. I always kept my gloves on so I wouldn't have to shake his hand.

Smith looked at Carlson and then back at me. "Clue number one," Smith said. I nodded back at him. I was being won over by my enemy. You shouldn't read that literature dropped from the sky.

Carlson clawed through our shipping boxes. He put aside several pieces until he found an example of each that suited his desires. But he didn't replace the others. Smith looked at me again, this time rolling his eyes.

"Can I take these?" Carlson asked.

"No," Smith said, without turning to face the salesman.

Carlson was facing me and asked again. I suspected that he was playing into my false sense of command. He was a salesman and knew how to please the little vanities. I knew all this. "Are you bringing them back?" I asked.

"Do you need them?" he asked.

"Yes," I said.

"Sure, I'll bring them back. I just want to get them checked out, then send them over to Indianapolis to make sure everything is kosher."

I felt insulted though I wasn't sure why. Possibly it was

just this man's presence. Somehow, in my ethics his work didn't count. It was dishonest. He lied to both sides and wasn't paid for hours or parts but by percentage of money changing hands. I waved him away with both hands, palms down, like you would shoo away a child. Gloves weren't enough. I wanted my respirator to protect me against his lies. He left and I felt taken advantage of. All this worry and sweat so that another man could take another golf vacation.

23

Turnbull came by in the afternoon. Smith was just leaving. We wished each other a good weekend.

"He's really not that bad," I said to Turnbull.

"How's it working?" he asked.

"Good. We're still figuring out how it will all work but it's coming."

"How many are you getting a day?"

I looked around at the packing boxes and thought of Smith and Carlson, Emily and Rochelle, my Mom, Dad, even Ginger. I couldn't do it anymore, I couldn't continue lying.

"I don't think it's possible," I said.

"What's that?"

"A thousand. I don't think it's possible for two people to put out a thousand a day. We've tried. I've tried. Hell, Smith has tried. He really has, but we're not even treading water."

"I worried about that," he said.

That made me angry. I was too tired for too much respect. "You worried about what?" I asked. It was a question that in my right mind I would have never asked.

"When we set up this whole thing. Two people. It was cutting it too close. It's possible. I've done it. But you can't run like that day in, day out."

"Then why…?" I drifted off. I wondered what he had meant by saying that he had done it. Had Turnbull come after we had left or early in the morning and run our presses to time the work? I bet he had. On Wednesday morning, when I arrived, my rags had moved.

"Do you think you could make this work?" he asked.

I leaned against a box of unwashed parts and thought. I didn't want to retreat, but conditions were dire. "One more person," I said. "It's frustrating to say, but I need one more person. With one more we could make it work."

"You're frustrated?" Turnbull asked.

"Ah, I don't know. It's more than that. I was frustrated with everything before this new line but this is something else, something more. I've been trying everything I can to beat regret." I walked a horseshoe and shut down my machines, trying to gather my thoughts. It was time to complain or beg. Turnbull went behind our presses and leaned against the rail along the edge of the abandoned loading ramp. I hopped my ass up on the rail and wrapped a leg around a post to keep from falling back into the pit. From there I could see down past grinding, past the robots and QC. I could see all Because of the distance between us, the distance of boss and worker, I could talk to Turnbull as a stranger. I could start a conversation like two men standing in line or sitting at elbows in a truck stop.

"I'm talking of things that come to you when you are working or lying in bed. Regrets. A year from now I don't want this to haunt me as a missed opportunity. I don't want to look back and see that I could have tried harder or that it would have worked if I would have just thought about one thing. Do you understand what I saying? I'm scared this isn't going to work and that I'm going to blame myself. I'm trying to prevent that. Is there anything more I can do? I'm competent, I think I know how to do my job, even this new one. But am I missing something? It doesn't seem like this would work if anyone was put on it."

Turnbull removed his glasses and rubbed his eyes. "You shouldn't take this so personally."

"What?" I spit.

"You shouldn't take this so personally. It's a job."

"You don't take everything that happens under this roof personally, every success or failure?"

"It's my job. It's not me," Turnbull said, and for the first time, he looked at me.

"That's a lie!" I yelled. "You are what you do. Everything you do or have done, that's who you are. Thoughts and intentions don't count, only actions."

"Then you're no more than an aluminum bender."

"Sure, but I do it well. At least I hope so."

Turnbull laughed, then I laughed, too. It was a precarious judgment. I put too much thought into my work. It interfered.

"Is this what you want to do with your life?" Turnbull asked.

I didn't say anything. It was a question so unrelated that I couldn't even consider it. Turnbull put his glasses back on and stood. "Well, see what you can do." He walked off toward the pressroom. I sat on the rail and didn't know what to think.

24

Emily and I had a nice domestic weekend. She went to the library on Saturday and I mowed the dirt before taking Ginger for a long walk through the woods.

Sunday, after Emily got home from church, we sat around and drank a second pot of coffee. Emily moved from couch to chair to bed reading about ten books. Professional journals, history, fiction, poetry. I used to be impressed with my own reading but I was an amateur. I didn't even like reading in front of her. After a while she got up and went to the fridge. She sliced some mozzarella with the tomatoes that we had bought at a roadside stand. I was pretending to listen to the Tigers.

"Do you want some?" she asked.

"No, I think I'm going to drive out to the dam and throw the ball for Ginger. Want to come along?"

"Go ahead. I'm going to stay here and read."

I drove down river so I could watch the water fold over the spillway. At one end of the park there were kids smoking pot and looking at engines. At the other end a family was having a reunion. Ginger chased the tennis ball without much enthusiasm.

We sat down and watched the water. The almost perfect arc of moving brown water was only disturbed in two places by debris caught against the wall. And that's when I understood. Emily didn't need me, and it was a good thing. She was complete. She wasn't looking for anything outside of herself. She was the most complete person I had ever met. A woman without ache. Even religion was a way of discovering something that already existed inside her. Emily was a Lutheran Buddhist. There was no void that I satisfied and it was good. It was refreshing. Rochelle always needed. Rochelle needed me to fill something in her soul. Rochelle was desperate for that thing and sometimes that thing was me.

Me? I was not complete. I was never complete. Crimes through generations past haunted my nights and I needed work to give purpose to my day. And between those shifts I needed a woman.

25

That night as I got ready for my softball game Emily was still reading. As a courtesy I asked her if she wanted to come and surprisingly she agreed. The game went well and I watched Emily talk to Jill on the bleachers. It was still close in the seventh and Mario came over to me before I led off. "Don't swing at the first pitch," he whispered in my ear. A perfect strike. The second pitch was over my head but I went for it anyway and tomahawked a double straight up the center. We pulled away after that.

26

I clocked in at five to six and found a note from Turnbull taped to my press.

DON'T MAKE ANY MORE PARTS.

I was confused. Samples had been sent and QC had thumbed up. I wanted to talk to Turnbull but I knew he was in the Monday morning staff meeting. That sometimes lasted until nine. I walked across the breezeway to tooling. John McGraw was there turning on his machines.

"At least you could have brought coffee," he said.

"Do you know about this?" I asked, closing the space between us.

"Seriously, coffee would help." I turned and went out back through the breezeway past the robotic welders and grinding and past QC. I went to the break room and paid for two coffees out of the machine. Then I made the trek back to tooling.

"Thanks," John said. On a large drafting desk he sorted plans. "I got these last week." He pulled a plan and put it on top of the pile. "They're different parts. The same with different holes. Little differences but completely new blocks. Like a model change. I bet…" he opened a file cabinet and pulled out another plan. "Yeah, look at the production numbers. That's next year. See?" He pointed to a long sequence on the first plans. "See? Last year," he pointed to the plans out of the file. "I'd say you guys have been making back stock. These new blocks will make the current run."

"How long?" I asked.

"Shit," John looked again at the plans. "It's not "rush" tagged. Two weeks?"

27

Waiting for Turnbull to get out of his meeting, I drifted over to welding where Mario put me to work. I found Adam at break. He was at the table under the oak tree reading a book I had never heard of. I shook a cigarette from his pack.

"We were making last year's parts. They weren't wrong, just the wrong year."

"Whose fuck up is that?"

"I don't know. Not mine," I said.

"You gonna ask Turnbull?"

"Maybe."

We finished our cigarettes. Adam went back to the press-room and I went back to welding. I felt alright. It was just a delay and more importantly, it wasn't my fault. I took my lunches with Emily and at night we cooked dinner together and made love.

28

It was the last weekend before school. Emily read more and more. I asked about the books. They were all for the upcoming semester. She had read almost the whole load, beforehand. It was stunning. No one told her to do anything. She just thought of plans and executed. Emily never lost good intentions at the bottom of her purse.

29

We got ready for a welcome back picnic. Emily asked me to come with her and at first I was a little nervous. We had existed only with each other. All our time was apart or together but not mixed with others, except for the dog. There was a morning wind and the heat was not bad. Not long after coffee we had our first gin and tonics. I put on records that matched the light. Emily came out of the bedroom wearing a sundress. It was tight across her breast and loose everywhere else. Her hair was pulled back into two long braids. Her sunglasses were already on top of her head and her feet were still bare. When she moved her dress swung side-to-side, transforming her walk into a dance. I stood and went for her. She let me kiss her neck down the long lines of her shoulder.

"You look great. What should I wear?" I asked.

She laid out clothes on the bed, talking to herself as she designed an outfit. A pair of green work pants cut off at the knee. A yellow plaid short sleeve cowboy shirt. A close brimmed straw hat. Canvas tennis shoes and black socks. I dressed as I was told. I promenaded. I catwalked as only a factory man from Ohio can. Emily laughed and clapped. She was happy and therefore I was happy. Love, love, love.

She stood and caught me in mid stride. "Don't button your shirt so high. You can show a little skin." I kissed her forehead and pulled her against me. She pushed away. "I like these snaps," she said, then pulled them all open in one quick movement. "Ready access." I was so full of love. Emily kissed me in the hollow of my chest. My heart fell down again and again like a drunk man stumbling down a hall. I put my hands on her shoulders.

"Don't, you'll drive me crazy. I'll have to have you." She pulled out of my reach and I worried that I had said something wrong, that I had offended her somehow. Emily pulled her panties down from under her dress and left them lying on the floor. I watched her face. Emily went to the bed and gathered her dress up around her waist. She leaned over, her bare feet planted on the wooden floor. Like a land-sick sailor, I weaved the couple steps toward her bare ass. I reached for the spot between her legs. She was more than wet. She was soaked. I was quickly inside her. "I can't last," I told her, panting. "Don't," she said, and I didn't. Afterward, I took a step back and she dropped her dress before kissing me on the lips. "You're a good man. I want you to be happy," she said, giving my dick a little tug. Emily walked out of the room and I could hear her in the kitchen fixing another drink. Her panties were still on the floor.

30

The world looked quite rosy through my green foundry glasses. All my fear had gone and Emily was the banner under which I would march. The party was in the backyard of a house over by the college. We drank beer out of red plastic cups and I followed Emily through the small crowd. Things I supposed, ideas I had mulled were confirmed. Emily was asked advice about classes, about jobs and internships, about graduate schools. Everyone said hello and most solicited something from her. Emily was cool. She took each question and answered as though it was for herself.

Most of the students were girls. A few men drifted around—boyfriends, husbands. I got to talking with one of the guys while pumping the keg. His name was Pete and he was also an almost teacher. He was thin and already had grey streaked through his black hair. He would teach history and coach baseball. I asked his opinion on the proper age to teach a curve and we were fast friends. He worried about the harm done to young boys' arms in the pursuits of selfish coaches. Emily waved to me occasionally as she made her way through the party. I was happy dispensing beer and talking baseball. I knew it was her party. Once she passed by on her way inside to use the bathroom. After saying hello to Pete she leaned in close to my ear. "You're dripping down my leg," she whispered. She disappeared in the house and my brain fogged over. Pete continued on about the neglected right field but I couldn't hear him. Later he asked what I did and I told him about the factory. We were filling cups for two girls and I could see by the way they tucked in their chins that my stories didn't satisfy or reaffirm their opinions. They wanted to hear it was dead end drudgery, monkey work. But with Pete it was different.

"It's alright," I said. "It's the same most every day, but I don't mean that in a totally negative way. You know what to expect and more importantly what is expected on you." I didn't tell him that I made as much as most teachers.

I got a little too drunk and was berating the Tigers yet again for their lack of a closer when Emily finally came to me and said she was ready to go. Pete and I shook hands genuinely and said it was nice meeting each other.

31

That week I filled in for a vacationing shipper. I had done it before and knew how to fill out Bills of Lading and all the paperwork. It was odd to be separated from production by that little distance of the breezeway. Isolated in baby-blue collar land.

Emily began school. At night before and after dinner she worked at the kitchen table. I tried to live quietly. I would do the dishes and then retreat to the couch or to my little office to work on the Bismarck and listen to the Tigers on AM. I wanted Emily to have a comfortable place to study. I didn't want her to go to her apartment or the library out of frustration. I ceded territory. I would have moved to the garage if needed. I would move.

My aching hands were soaking in the dishwater. Emily had spread her things: texts, professional magazines, notebooks and loose papers. I looked over my shoulder as she made notes. The words flowed from the pen she held in her long fingers. I watched her hands. Her right found passages, walked from resource to resource. Her left all the while kept writing. It was agony for me to write even a letter yet her words flowed and flowed. I couldn't even copy that fast.

Every word, every word that she put on paper neared the end. In a few months she would finish school and leave. Emily had mentioned working in the Defiance school system but she said the market was always full because of the college and career-wise it wasn't anything special.

"Do you want some tea?" I asked. Emily looked up, confused. I repeated the question. Emily smiled nodded and returned to her books. I lit the stove and put the water on. Ginger got up off her rug and came into the kitchen. Pavlovian response to the sound of gas. Ginger leaned against the pantry cupboard and then slid to the floor. I watched the water until finally it was ready. I made two cups and then brought one over to Emily. She looked up and I passed her the tea. Emily talked about "special needs" children but she was talking to herself, working something out. I stared at my tea.

"I love you," I said.

"I love you, too."

I went back to the sink and put my cup on the sill. "If you get a job somewhere else, I'll move," I said, looking out at the world. A couple crows circled high above the field. Silence, for too long. "I mean, if you want me to. I would." Emily's chair scraped on the wood floor and I looked back. She was coming towards me. Her eyes were large and shined. Emily kissed me on the neck, pressing her nose against my collarbone. She returned to her seat and rummaged through her bag. She pulled an envelope from it. "I was worried about showing this to you," she said. Emily held out the envelope for me. I took it and leaned against the sink as I read. It was from Ohio University. It was a scholarship offer with a teaching assistant job thrown in. "That's a good program. It's not too far away and it's not forever. Have you ever been to Athens?"

"No," I said, trying to understand.

"It's pretty. It's hill country. I went down there to visit in high school. I was also accepted by Syracuse in New York, but not with a full scholarship and it's awfully far away."

I went to the bookshelf and pulled a plat map. "We

should go down there," I said.

"When?"

"This weekend. We could leave Friday night or Saturday morning. It's not too far. Looks like around four or five hours. If we left in the morning we could be there before lunch and then camp in the woods on Saturday night."

"Camp?"

"Yeah, I have a tent and all that stuff. It will be fun."

32

Friday afternoon I was finishing my week in shipping when Adam came across the gap. I was sitting at the desk on the loading dock overlooking the river. Adam shambled out to the dock. He pulled a chair and leaned it against one of the posts. He pulled the book from his back pocket and sat down.

"Can I help you?" I asked.

"Naw, I'm alright." Adam went back to his reading.

"Shouldn't you be working?"

"Suppose." His legs swung in the air.

"What if Turnbull comes by?"

"He won't." Adam flipped a page. "They're all gone-Turnbull, Bullough, everyone."

"What about Sean?"

"What about him?"

I laughed. Yeah, what about Sean. Fuck him. I pulled out a car magazine from the desk drawer and read. I asked Adam if he wanted a pop and then walked down to the machine outside Tooling and bought two. I brought them back, handed Adam his and then sat down.

Adam put his book down on the plank floor. "I heard we're starting back up Monday," he said.

"From who?"

"Just around, but it's true. Dale cut blanks today."

33

We left Saturday morning at five. Emily thought we were going to take her car and I assumed we would take my truck. Emily argued for air-conditioning and cruise control. I argued for the dog. We both didn't want to insult each other. She didn't trust my truck outside of the county and I viewed her car as a mark. No one fucks with a man in an old truck as long as he looks like he could hold his own. And as long as we broke down by the side of the road and not in the middle of the engine I could fix it. I won and tied Ginger in the back. We pulled out and headed south. Emily fell asleep.

We made good time and Emily woke up outside of Columbus. She smiled and I rolled down my window and she rolled down hers. The sun was bright in the morning and the air was heavy with humidity. We pulled over for gas. As I pumped Emily went into the store and bought us two ginger ales and two small bags of chips. I let Ginger out of the truck and she peed in a planting strip before I helped her back into the bed. Emily got back in the truck and I looked around.

This part of Ohio seemed to be all outskirts. Not country, not city. The same depressing chain stores every quarter mile. We got on the bypass and swung around to the south. We drank our ginger ales and Emily's red hair blew all around the cab. Some went out the window and some tickled my ear. We laughed and smelled the change in the land. The smell of towns, the smell of cut grass and industry. Countryside, livestock and fields. Sometimes neither pleasant but most of the time both were. It was something we would have missed had we ridden in her air-conditioning. I wanted to remind her of this but feared she would take it as an insult which it was. We broke the grips of the city.

A fire at a tire dump slowed us south of Lancaster. Black smoke charcoaled the gray sky. Fire trucks had one lane of the road blocked but the fire fighters didn't seem in much of a rush to do anything. A good number of them stood around talking in half their turnouts as we inched past. Ginger stood on the toolbox and occasionally barked. Some men laughed, most took no notice. Emily placated the dog by feeding her chips through the slider. Past the fire the road opened up again. I shifted into high gear and Ginger climbed down in the bed.

34

Outside of Athens we stopped at a cafe. Over our sandwiches I told Emily the plan. I would drop her off at the college while I went and made our camp in the National Forest.

"You're not coming with me?" she asked.

"No, you should do this by yourself. You don't want me standing around with the dog when you're trying to get the feel of things. We will meet up later and you can show me the highlights."

We drove into the city center with its brick buildings and old trees. The streets went off in different directions and changed grade at whim. So unlike our own little piece of Ohio flatness. I pulled over to the sidewalk. Emily opened the door but didn't get out. We would meet back at five and then get some supper. Emily had an appointment at one. It really didn't leave much time. We kissed and then I pulled away from the curb and went looking for the state park.

35

I tried not to look too lost as I drove through town. The Defiance tag on my plate would mark me but then I noticed a New York plate and a couple blue Michigans. It was a real university that drew students from all over. I knew I wouldn't be mistaken for a student. I looked at the young men walking the sidewalks and a fleeting jealousy flashed through me.

36

The state park wasn't spectacular but it was close. Ginger was happy to be freed and she looped the perimeter sniffing and scenting all she could in this foreign land. As I assembled the tent poles I wondered if there were any working coalmines in the area. I had never even been underground. As a kid I was told about the salt mines underneath Detroit. "Off to the salt mines," and "Another day at the salt mines." It's the dread that makes us human. I looked down at my feet and wondered if there was anything below them.

But then I already had a job and I had been avoiding thinking about the factory and what Adam had said. Would we really start up on Monday? Would the new line really begin? I wouldn't allow myself to hope. As an antidote I went back to thinking of life down in the mines. Maybe we would go on strike and shoot at each other- the scabs and the union men. Once I had the tent set up and our spot properly claimed I loaded Ginger back in the truck and we went driving around. We took random rights and lefts on whatever felt best and got good and lost in the green hills. Little houses, not much more than shacks with porches, rested back up off the roads. Chickens ran free and old cars rusted into the grass. For some reason it made me happy. I imagined living in one of those houses with Emily and Ginger and some chickens. I began to feel good and wanted a side of beer to go with my driving and dreaming. At the next gas station I bought a six-pack but drank slowly. I didn't want to get stopped and find myself in a pile of trouble that I couldn't explain to anyone except the dog. I didn't even know what county I was in. Ginger and I spent the rest of the day like that just driving around. We even glimpsed the Ohio River for the first time in our lives. When it got close to time I turned and headed back for town. It was easy because every road sign had an arrow pointing the way. Lost must be a common experience. Outside of town I stopped at a gas station and topped the tank off and got rid of the empties.

37

We turned the corner and sure enough Emily was sitting on a low wall waiting for us. Ginger stood and wagged and barked like she ran into Jesus at the corner store. Emily smiled and waved. There was a parking space so I pulled over and we got out. I went over and sat next to Emily. Ginger was sniffing the people passing by on the sidewalk and I had to snap my fingers to get her back over by us.

"What do you think?" I asked.

"It's nice. A girl from my program gave me a tour and said some really positive things about the faculty. Do you want to take a walk?"

"Sure," I said and went back to the truck to pull the keys from the ignition.

"Do you think Ginger should be on a leash?"

"Naw, I'll keep her by." We started walking. I did think the dog should be on a leash but the only thing I had was the yellow nylon rope. We walked. Emily pointed out buildings as we went. Later, we went to a bar that Emily's guide recommended. We locked the dog in the truck and went inside. It was full of college students. We ate some sandwiches in the restaurant then moved into the drinking half. There was one stool open at the far end of the bar and Emily sat on it while I stood. We both looked around as we talked. Emily went to the bathroom. I stood with my foot on the bottom rung of the stool. A group of boys wearing baseball caps were drinking next to us and one of them slid onto Emily's stool without looking at me. I was a little stunned because it was so obvious and intentional. Shit, I thought, now I have to say something. I put my hand on the boy's back.

"Hey," he turned toward me. "Hey, my wife was sitting there," I said.

"So," he said and turned to face the lined up bottles behind the bar.

Great, I thought. He was a little bigger than me and looked fairly athletic and he was with a whole pack of shitheads. Great, I'm going to get my ass kicked over a bar stool in some town where I don't know a soul except for the ones I brought with me.

"Hey, just move. She was sitting there." I could see Emily coming back. The kid rolled his eyes but got off the stool and went back to his herd. Emily came back and sat on her stool. I drained off my beer and gave the bartender the two more sign. Emily seemed to be enjoying herself when the kid in the hat turned toward us. He spoke to Emily.

"Your husband wanted to kick my ass over a bar stool. He's a real gentleman," he said pointing at me with one finger of a hand holding a drink before he left.

Emily looked at me with a strange look. "That guy's a jackass," I said. What could I say? Nothing had happened. The bartender delivered our drinks and I paid for them. We drank but didn't talk. Emily continued to look around. I looked at my bottle.

38

Outside the bar a cool wind was blowing. We loaded up and headed out of town to our camp. Before we reached it rain began to fall in large drops against the windshield. Emily had hardly said anything. When we nosed into our parking spot it was raining steady. I shut off the engine and we sat there. The rain beat on the roof above our heads.

“I’ll pay for a hotel,” she said.

“I’ve got money,” I said. I had more than five-hundred dollars in my wallet and I wasn’t camping to be cheap.

“Congratulations.”

I got out of the truck without saying anything and went through the rain to the tent. I pulled the four stakes and then released the poles. The little house collapsed on itself and I gathered it into a ball. The bags, mats and my little candle lantern were all still inside. I carried it back to the truck and then stuffed it underneath the toolbox. I had to make another trip for the stakes and poles. Back in the truck my wet clothes fogged all the windows. Three bodies on the bench. Emily’s car would have been more comfortable. I lit my watch and it was nearly midnight. “Well, let’s go,” I said. Emily hadn’t said anything. She was just sitting there looking out her window. She may have been sad or seething. It had gotten too dark for me to tell.

39

Every hotel was closed for the night. I pointed the truck north out of town. Ginger slept with her head against my leg and Emily crashed out against her door using my sweatshirt as a pillow. There would be some all night hotels and restaurants outside Columbus, I thought. It was the state capital. Eventually I got on the bypass and the lit signs kept streaking through the night sky. My plans alternated between driving through and stopping for the night. It seemed whenever I had the opportunity to stop I wanted to keep pushing. We left Columbus and a tiredness attacked me. My eyes burned and a hot knife stabbed me between the shoulder blades. I knew I had reached the end and needed to pull over before I flipped through the median and became a small blurb in the local papers. Emily stirred when we took an exit a little fast then fell asleep again. I looked for a place that was dark and out of the way to hide and sleep. Behind a closed restaurant had all the atmosphere I could have hoped for. In fact it had so much atmosphere I thought we might just get robbed or killed. I started the engine again and looked for someplace less dark. We ended up spending two hours parked in front of a volunteer fire station under their mercury vapor light.

I woke before dawn. The rain had stopped and it was hot and muggy in the truck. I rolled down my window. The frogs were singing in the ditches. I started the engine and got the wheels rolling again. Emily stirred. After a while she woke. Her eyes were puffy and she had marks from the sweatshirt on her face. "I feel like shit," she said. Then Ginger woke and I knew we would have to stop and let her out. We pulled off at a cafe. Emily pulled her toothbrush out of our bag and she wandered off before the coffee came. I seriously wondered if she would come back. Life didn't scare her as it should. She could just walk out the back door and beg, borrow or steal a ride and disappear. But she didn't. She came back and we ate in near silence. I think we both wanted to fight but were too tired. Everything about Emily at that moment bothered me. Her superiority. Her left-handedness. Most of all the fact that she didn't need me. That was the problem with a complete woman.

We were back in Defiance by the early morning. Emily put her things in her car and gave me a cold-lipped kiss and then drove away. I took a shower then slept.

41

Of course the line didn't start up Monday but Adam was right about Dale cutting blanks. I asked Turnbull about them and he confirmed that the following Monday we would begin again. My troubles with Emily made me put more hope into work but that hope was temporary because Emily came over after work Monday and we made love on the couch with most of our clothes still on. That week I filled in for Dale Novak on the shear press. I think he was on vacation. I hoped so. Another Friday came so I left the plant. At the corner store I bought a can of beer for the drive home. I considered stopping off at one of the bars to have a few but decided against it. I was hoping that Emily could give me something that I needed.

42

Inside she was stirring a pot on the stove. She smiled amongst the mess she had made in the kitchen. Ginger sat at Emily's feet sweeping her tail back and forth across the floor.

"I think I've finally surpassed you in her heart." Emily pulled a piece of sausage from the pot and fed it to the dog's snapping jaws. "See!" Emily smiled in her little victory.

I set my lunch pail down and approached the two of then in a low crouch. Emily stood, spoon in her hand, confused. But Ginger knew to fear. She scooted her but around away from me but couldn't pull her attention fully away from the enameled pot that held the sausage. Ginger looked at me now fast approaching and back up at the woman who gave her sausage and then back at me but it was too late. I sprung and tackled the dog. She went down under me on the linoleum floor, legs splayed. I kissed the dog loudly on her floppy jowls and her eyes bulged in fear. After I had pinned the dog to the point of panic I finally relented and let her up. Ginger stumbled away from me but quickly circled back around towards the sausage pot, this time on the other side of Emily, the woman separating us. I stayed seated on the floor and leaned against the cupboards

"Don't you wonder what I'm making?"

"Sure."

"Spaghetti with homemade noodles."

"Sounds good." I lied. I turned over on hands and knees and started again toward the dog. Ginger whimpered and her glances quickened back and forth from food to attacker.

"Leave the dog alone. You still haven't kissed me. I swear if you could fuck the dog you wouldn't want me around."

I stood. I wanted to tell her not to talk that way but didn't want to sound prudish. "Do you want a kiss?" I asked.

"Yes," she said and tilted her cheek up toward me. "Have you been drinking?" she asked.

"I had a beer on the way home. I thought of stopping at a bar and getting drunk. I don't know why. Work sucked this week." I rattled off a description of difficulties as she stirred and seasoned.

"Please don't become like that… one of those men that drink every night after work and avoid their wives… play softball and bowl."

"What's wrong with bowling and softball?"

"Everything. Don't you like me?"

"I love you," I said opening the fridge and grabbing a beer. "Do you want to go for a walk?"

She protested that she had to continue minding the pot and asked if I really appreciated all that she did for me. I wanted to say some things that I didn't. Finally I grew tired of her reasons and got up for my walk. She wanted to come along but then complained when I reached for my gun.

"Is that all you do in the woods?"

"No, I've done other things," I said with a smirk, thinking of all the stumps Rochelle and I had fucked on. Emily understood.

"Kill or fuck, how original. You live such a full life."

43

I didn't want her to come but I didn't say anything. I walked down the stairs and she followed. As we crossed the road I wondered why I didn't like to hear her say 'fuck'. I liked the word. I liked the meaning and the action. But somehow she made it sound dirty, tarnished. She turned fuck into a cuss word. It made me ashamed and embarrassed. There were words that I used with her and then there were words that I had used with the other and they were languages. I spoke one to Emily and one to Rochelle but they didn't translate to the other. They would have been incomprehensible, nonsensical. And alone, I thought, what language do I use? What language do I think? What is my native tongue? It seemed that I only used these words to express wants or desires to the other- never to myself. I knew my want without words. I felt them. But neither woman would ever know, truly know, my desire. They merely heard an inarticulate man, hobbled by a regional stinginess, mumble and spit the names, in two different languages, of body parts and motions. Or they felt a body aroused rail against obstacles cultural and personal, a man living in defeat praying for one small transitory victory. Why was I even thinking of Rochelle? We walked on and I started to talk about the dog. I explained what Ginger was doing and why. I also explained what Ginger should have been doing if she was a better dog. Then it came to me. I realized that the three of us weren't very good. We had our shortcomings that was sure. I couldn't make use of an opportunity, Emily couldn't fuck and Ginger couldn't hunt. I laughed to myself.

"What?" Emily asked.

"Nothing, I was just thinking how we're not very good."

"How so? How aren't we good?" There was defense in her voice and I regretted laughing. I regretted saying anything, anything, ever. "How so?" she continued. I waved my hand around and said "everything" as vaguely as I could. But she wasn't satisfied. I could see that she was formulating, listing, reasoning. She was prepared to defend all her actions and all her choices and it made me so tired. I sat down on one of the fallen logs that littered the woods. Emily put her hand on my shoulder and again asked, "how so?"

"Do you want to mess around?" was my answer although I knew what hers would be as sure as I knew that my grandmother's body was in the ground across the hidden river.

She pulled her hand away from my body. "No. Why did you bring your gun if you wanted to fuck?" I couldn't say anything. I put my head in my hands and for a moment wanted to cry. Emily sat down next to me. "I don't understand you," she said, "I don't think you even know me. I don't think you even see me. Do you realize what I do for you?"

The sad fact was that I did. I could see her and understand her. That was exactly why I felt so miserable. I thought of shooting her and then myself but decided against it out of love for my mother. Instead I looked up, faked a smile and said, "I'm sorry. Let's go home and eat." We did.

44

Dinner was good. Ginger had some more sausage and was happy. Emily sucked down some cocktails and I watched her out of the corner of my eye. We watched a movie on TV and I tried to fall asleep on the couch. But, noticing me fade, Emily shut off the set and pronounced it time to go to bed. We undressed and lay next to each other. Emily made kissing sounds. It was her cue for me to roll over and kiss her. I did and then lay back down. She did this several times and then said, "hey, I'm right here." But I didn't want her. I didn't want to work at it. If she wanted to fuck then she could go right ahead. I lay still. Finally she rolled over with a snort and feigned sleep with her back towards me. My eyes were open and I stared at the ceiling. I hated her. Gradually, I became tired and finally fell asleep. In the early hours of the morning desire came through my body. It woke me. I don't know what I was dreaming of but I woke with a painful erection. I slowly started petting Emily. I stroked her ass and then her cunt. I hoped to trick her body into desire. I hoped to wake her body without waking her mind. I worked slowly, very slowly. It might have taken an hour to feel some moisture. Gradually I began rubbing against her. I thought it might work. But she woke and swatted me away saying, “Don’t touch me.”

I fell back asleep cradled in an amusing hate. The absurd, the knowledge of it, can be very comforting in the absence of anything else.

45

I woke before Emily, made some coffee, pulled on some boxers and fished a quarter from the oilcan before going downstairs for the paper. As always, the gravel hurt my bare feet. A sedan pulled in the lot. An old couple laughed as they saw me struggling with my fire-walking step towards them. The man got out of the driver’s seat and put his money in the machine. “Your Sunday best?” he said to me with a laugh. His wife was giggling in the car.

“Sure,” I said.

They both waved as they drove off and I waved back.

Upstairs Emily was just beginning to stir. She talked to me from the bed. She asked what time it was. I told her even though there was a digital clock glowing on the bed stand. She must have been facing the wrong direction, I thought. The bed squeaked and I knew she was getting up. I sat at the kitchen table reading the first section.

“Why don’t you come with me to church?” she said as she passed into the bathroom.

“Because I don’t believe in it,” I said without looking up.

It was an old conversation.

"But you'd be going with me and it would make me happy," she said from the bathroom. I could hear her on the toilet. She never shut the door. It was disconcerting.

"No, anyway I'm Catholic and I don't like all that guitar music that you folks favor."

The toilet flushed and the sink ran. I thought it odd that she didn't take more showers. She said it was bad for her hair and she had a lot of it. I didn't argue. One a day seemed right to me. Emily came out of the bathroom with her robe wrapped around her.

"Can't you do something for me once in a while. I do things for you all the time." She sat down in a chair across from me. Her arms were folded. "I do things that I don't want to. You never give."

"I don't feel like going to church but I'll tell you what. How 'bout we go the cemetery instead. I'll show you where my grandmother is buried."

"Let's meet at 10:30 at the Twin Teepees. You know where that is?" As I said this I held my wrist up and looked at my watch. Emily stood watching me. She didn't wear a watch. That annoyed me in some little way that I couldn't place. I wanted her to look at her watch and respond with a "check" or a "mark". But she just looked at me with a blank expression. "Well, you better get a runnin', God's a waitin'," I said. She frowned. It wasn't my fault that other people took their existence so seriously. She gave me a polite kiss and then left. I watched from the top of the stairs as her car pulled away.

46

I called my mother but no one answered. Next I called Mario. Jill answered and I couldn't think of anything nice to say. Mario came to the phone and I asked him if he was going to watch the game. Mario was going to work around his house, mow the lawn and paint the back porch. They had a nice 1920's house in the city, wood floors and narrow halls, built-in ironing board and bad wiring. I offered an excuse for him to dodge his responsibilities but he declined. He asked if I was playing softball at five. What? I said. We had a game against the fire department. No one told me, I said. It was on the bulletin board for two weeks, Mario said. Shit, I said and then ok I'll be there. See you then, he said. OK, I said. Kiss Jill for me, I said. Mario laughed but didn't say anything. Jill hated me.

47

Emily was at church and I regretted not going with her. Was it possible to find God merely to stave off loneliness? I looked around at the kitchen, at the couch and at the bathroom and imagined her still here walking from space to space complaining about some little fact. "Why can't you just admit to..." something or another. Ginger got up from her nap and went to her bowl. She ate the last bits and pushed around her stainless steel bowl. It made the house seem even more quiet without Emily. Tears came to my eyes and I hated my own pathetic mind, so soft.

48

Ginger and I got in the truck. It was in the high 80s and even with both windows rolled down it was hot. Ginger stuck her head out and let her ears fly, unable to fight the call of genetics. I tuned in a little rock station from Toledo and tapped my fingers on the wheel. My mind drifted over escape plans. It was becoming more difficult to extract myself from my own life. Could I go back to school? For what? I didn't want to be a teacher. I knew myself well enough to know that I couldn't motivate anyone, especially young people. The military still held some call for me. If I could be given a task from dawn until dusk I might be able to fake happiness. It was the downtime that tortured me I needed to be deceived with purpose. It was the between innings that tortured me. Let me dig a foxhole and then I'll dig yours. I'll dig you a Hilton every night before I pass out. Or let me paint an aircraft carrier. Anything, but deceive me with purpose, please. But I was too old for that. What about the Foreign Legion?

I turned left over the Maumee. I drove past the turn for work and went into the center of town. Only the flowered print and blue polyester church crowd milled about. The courthouse square had plenty of parking. A beer can lay on its side in the gutter. Proof of a Saturday night. Three police cruisers were tied up in front of their building. All the cops were watching TV and talking sports. It would have been a good time to break the law. Maybe they were changing shifts. I didn't know when their changes were. That would be something to know if I had more criminal intent. My lack of immorality was depressing. In my adult life I couldn't remember wanting to steal anything. Did fear keep me from taking all that I wanted? That dream that I always dreamt, of being caught behind enemy lines without a weapon. All fire and running and hiding. It was an hour of pure panic that visited me once a week. I would wake very sweaty and very tired but equally relieved. True they never did catch me but I had to run like hell, swim rivers and hide in the root clusters of swamp trees my green-gray uniform soaked and filthy. No, to be criminal you had to be detached, to exist in some mythical rebel apartness. I couldn't pass an open gate without closing it.

The yards in front of houses became larger and larger as I broke free of the core of town. I passed the middle school and the Lutheran church. It was made of giant fieldstones and looked like a castle. I wondered if the stones were just a facade but knew they weren't. At one time it was possible to build like that, with an eye on permanence. Now it was press board and aluminum stringers but who could argue with that. Not me, I was all for progress. Put wheels on everything. Make it disposable. That old stuff only reminds us that we're not the only ones. As if the day wasn't hard enough. Here's a building to tell you that generations failed before you. You don't even possess an originality of defeat. I gave the church the bird and drove on. Emily would be in that building somewhere with completely different thoughts and good for her.

49

Passing Emily's apartment I saw her car in the lot and pulled a hard u-turn without looking. Ginger slammed into the door and rolled into the foot well. "Sorry," I said. I had never before been to Emily's apartment although I knew where it was. Ironically, Rochelle only lived a few hundred feet away, off the main road in a four-plex buried by a row of houses. Emily's apartment was on that road.

I had to read the mailboxes to figure out what unit she lived in. The brick building had six on three levels, fairly big for Defiance. "DODDS, EMILY" lived in the basement. I walked down the short stairs and pounded on the door.

Emily answered with a surprised hello. I asked what she was doing there with an investigative tone and was not immediately invited in. I mentioned breakfast and church and even the dog. It was my idiot play. Emily stood aside and waved me in. She told me that her mother had called and they had talked past the church hour. They both decided to talk instead of going to church. Her father was out of town on business and the mother-daughter truancy was going to be their little secret.

"Well, it's all the same," I said.

"What is?" she cocked her head.

"Church and talking to your mother. It's all under the same goodness umbrella. I just find it odd that your starting times are the same."

Emily smiled with a look of pity.

"Let me change and we'll go to breakfast," she said.

"No, don't. You look beautiful and I like looking at you when you're all decked out."

"Alright, I'll just freshen up." I was looking around the apartment and Emily noticed.

"You can sniff anything you want," she said.

I protested that I had never been to her apartment and it was all new. I had a right to be curious. I had tasted her most private flavors. She smiled and waved a game show wave. This showcase could be yours if...

Emily went in the bathroom and shut the door. I went to her bookshelf first. It was filled with mostly textbooks. She had a heavy dose of women authors and an uncomfortable amount of psychology. Willa Cather saved her though. She had a small picture collection of her family and friends. Two gold frames held pictures of Emily and a boy who I chose to believe was a relative. I went over to the bedroom and switched on the light. A double bed with a flowered comforter was centered on the wall. Everything in that cinder block cell was sparse but that is always the way with students. Neat, but nothing too personal.

"Find anything incriminating?" Emily asked from behind.

"Just looking. Does the bed work?" She smiled but didn't answer. Her phone rang and she went to the kitchen to answer it. I decided to lie on her bed half hoping that she would be inspired to prove its functionality. Her voice came around the corner; she was talking to a friend. I rolled on to my side and examined her bed stand. No pictures. Just an alarm clock and a collection of e.e. cummings. In the drawer I fingered a letter from a C. Davis of Barcelona, Spain. It wasn't a very Spanish name, I thought. Better to not think about, I put the letter back. There were some travel packs of tissue and to my surprise a vibrator. I wondered how well used it was. For some reason I doubted Emily's conviction for this little machine. I didn't exactly know why. It seemed more of a symbol than a tool, an accoutrement of the modern girl. It was chrome and not too offensive. I tested the batteries. They worked. I put it back and closed the drawer.

She came back to me. "Find anything?" she asked.

"No, no. It's nice in here. The cinder blocks make it cool.

You almost don't need an air conditioner."

Emily was leaning against the doorjamb. She looked out toward the small living room and the ground level windows and asked what I wanted to do. She knew what I wanted to do but it wasn't going to happen.

"Do you want to go see my dead granny?" I said in a chipper voice.

"Let's go get some breakfast first," she said.

50

The three of us, man, woman and dog, piled into my truck and we drove to the Twin Teepees out on Highway 24. It was a 50s era roadside diner in the shape of two giant Indian teepees. One teepee was a cocktail lounge and the other was the restaurant. A gas fire burned in a center fireplace of the dining room year round even when the air conditioning ran at full blast. It was odd to sit by the fire while your ass froze two feet away. The Indian Room was favored by the retirement crowd. Rochelle and I used to come there when we needed bloody marys on a Sunday morning.

We entered and were temporarily blinded by the shift in light. Emily clutched my hand in the darkness. I couldn't imagine what this did to the old people but maybe it wasn't so harsh filtered through cataracts.

A waitress as old as the clientele made her way toward us. She wore the traditional polyester zippered dress with a cardigan. Rochelle owned one of these dresses and sometimes wore it to Mags for fun. On those days she would put her hair up and stick a hundred pens and pencils in it. I remembered fondly unzipping that dress. The correlation disturbed me. Maybe kitsch is the tie that binds.

"We haven't seen you two in here for a while. Where you been hiding?" the older lady said much to my displeasure. I mumbled something very ambiguous and looked sideways at Emily. She had a slight smile on her face. Instead of being angered at the mistaken identity she was enjoying the discomfort that it brought me.

I had my usual corned beef, over-easy, wheat. Emily had a terrible habit of special ordering but I refrained from correcting her. Anyone who special orders has never touched a shovel. They have no understanding of work. Eventually I recommended the bloody marys to Emily saying that they were very good. "Oh? Do you come here often?" she replied. But by that time I was tired of dwelling in the doghouse so I said, "I used to," and let the silence come. Emily waited through it for a couple of minutes and then started another polite, non-confrontational conversation. We talked about the weather.

51

I turned into the cemetery and then onto one of the side paths. Pinecones cracked under the tires. A few hundred yards in I stopped the truck on an oil stain and killed the engine. It was quiet.

"I don't like pulling off the trail here. The ground is soft and I have the feeling that over the years people get misplaced. I don't want to drive over anyone. Come on," I said as I got out. I didn't put Ginger on a leash. Luckily she wasn't a male and I didn't have to worry about her pissing on any head stones. With Emily trailing behind and Ginger out front we walked down the trail. The pines drooped their boughs, calm in the absence of any breeze. It was nearing noon and the temperature had climbed well into the nineties. I sweated as I walked through the garden of the dead. I veered off the path to the left and walked straight for a marble tree stump. It stood over six feet tall and looked like a young black oak poleaxed by lightning. "Now look at this," I said as I reached up and held one of the truncated limbs. Emily held her left hand over her mouth. She looked terrified. I let go of the stump and walked back to her.

"It's horrible, ghastly. How could you bury her under something like that?" she asked.

I let out a belly laugh. "This isn't my grandmother's grave. She's buried over there," I said, pointing to a newer deforested section of the neighborhood. I quickly walked back to the stump. "This is where old. . ." I had to look at the name carved on the side. "This is where old Adolf Oetzel lives. 1892 to 1936. He's the devil. This is where Satan lives. Yep right here in little old Defiance, Ohio." I patted the stump for effect. Emily hadn't taken a step closer. "If we came back here at night and stopped where the truck is now you will see the devil's face. No shit."

"I'm not coming back here at night," Emily said with conviction.

"It's something to see, really." I told her how the local kids had taken me here when I first moved to town. I told her how it was just a phenomenon caused by the headlights, that it wasn't anything evil. She just couldn't see the mystery.

Further down the trail we inspected my grandmother's grave. It was very plain compared to Adolf Oetzel's. She was buried next to her husband, Fred. His first wife was on his other side. I liked Fred. I liked his straightforwardness. I hoped he liked me when he was still walking the earth.

"You should have brought flowers or something," Emily said.

"No, if I brought flowers every time I came out here I'd be broke. Anyway she doesn't know the difference. I come out here for me, not her. She should give me flowers and you see the problem with that. Just the logistics!" I said with a laugh.

But Emily hadn't found me clever or amusing for a couple of weeks. I thought it might be her school or my job but most likely it was us. "Just drop me off. I have to study," she said on the way home. I kissed her before she slid out of the truck and her lips felt like earthworms, cold. When I left she smiled at me but as her mouth went up her eyes went down and the pain was obvious. I smiled and waved and pretended not to notice anything.

52

I cruised through town in second gear. I drove toward work but pulled into Mario's alley. Mario spent almost every Sunday afternoon in his little workshop attached to his garage. Jill worked Sunday afternoons and this left Mario free to work on little projects, watch TV and smoke weed. He had built this little clubhouse for that purpose. It was his retreat and Jill pretended not to notice. Jill wasn't a prude. She just wanted a lot from life and from Mario. Mario's good nature was his downfall. Good humor and too much soul. Mario could pull the wagon but Jill had to drive. He just belonged somewhere else. He should have been a landscaper in Hawaii, a surfer, a holy man subsisting on fish tacos. But his family was here.

I killed the engine and knocked on the shop door before opening it. Inside Mario stood next to a storm door with a screening wheel in his right hand. I wondered why he pretended. I hadn't surprised him. My truck's pipes were a theme song always announcing my arrival. Mario's guitar lay on the workbench, a new package of strings on the body.

"Brother. How goes it?" I asked.

Mario shrugged and went back to his seat next to the guitar. I went to the corner and sat in my usual seat next to a little fridge. A TV looked down from the corner, high on the shelf. The Indians played on without sound. I pulled two cans of beer out and set Mario's on the bench without opening it, preserving his choice. "Thanks," he said with his back to me.

"New strings, huh?"

"Yeah. It's about time." He inserted the pins and wound the knobs. I crossed my knee and relaxed. I knew he wouldn't restring and tune without playing some. I loved hearing Mario play, following him on the little tours he led. He hit notes on different strings and adjusted by ear. Satisfied, Mario opened the beer and took a sip. He held the guitar on his thigh.

"What's up?" he asked.

"Nothing," I said. I wanted to talk about Emily but I didn't know what I wanted to say.

Mario's right hand started and then his left guided the tune. I looked up at the TV and sipped my beer. I couldn't look at Mario when he played. It seemed too personal. His image, his watery eyes and Buddha belly blocked the music. So I watched the silent baseball and toured the landscape that Mario painted. We went through the Smokey Mountains, through the south and across the border. We saw work and women and everything that man had seen for hundreds of years. Eventually Mario quit playing but the music continued on in my head. Only when he lit his pipe did I notice the difference.

I stood and stretched. "I should get going," I said. "See you tonight."

"Five o'clock," Mario said.

53

At home I mowed the dirt and brown weeds that passed for grass and continued drinking beer. It wasn't that Mario's music had made me feel better but I felt better about feeling bad. I even washed my truck before softball game.

The fire department had never been much of a challenge for our team. They were too loose. They had two paid full timers but the rest of the crew were volunteers. A dentist, a schoolteacher, a mechanic, a factory worker. They lacked familiarity. These hobbyists didn't know whose wife was sleeping around, who hated who, or who was on a lucky streak. We had that for years. Even Sean and I knew where the other would be at all times. Our animosity wasn't disruptive. It was dependable.

The fire department had a new third baseman. He was a plumber and a drunken idiot spouting this and that over his gut and pigeon toes. And unluckily for him it was a night where I utterly controlled my swing. Inexplicably for a right-hander he played towards the gap. I seized on this and sent fouls curving belt high over the bag, my fairs would kick chalk ten feet past it. I am not a large man, neither in size nor spirit, and I made this oaf throw his body to the ground again and again, eating the talcy dust. Mario and Sean gave us power and rest of the guys caught the ball when needed.

54

That night Emily slept in her apartment and it was the first night we spent apart. She claimed that she had some studying to do and I didn't protest. It was nice to have the quiet although I couldn't read. I kept hoping for a phone call.

As I lay in bed I thought about how I really did love her. I wanted to call her but I wanted to respect her privacy. I tried to masturbate to the thought of her but I kept being distracted by passing trucks and the shifting evening light. Looking around the house, I realized I didn't own any pictures of Emily. I would have to change that. I wasn't prepared for her absence. In the end, I fiendishly sought out some hidden pictures of Rochelle and came looking at the other woman's curved back and small breasts. Afterwards, I again thought of Emily.

BOOK FIVE

1

Monday morning came with the smell of coffee and after-shave. All the buildup was over. One thousand doorjambs would have to leave shipping every afternoon for Indianapolis. It was difficult for me to sleep much past four. I wished for Emily to be there to tempt me back to bed. But she was sleeping in her little cinder block cell over the river across town. I had fallen asleep confident in my solitary strength but now I wished to kiss her hand, her sleeping face.

Ginger and I went for a walk. We crossed the road and hugged the edge of the wood. The early gray light lived only in the open spaces. Unable to concentrate on anything save my nervous stomach we walked very fast. We broke free of our home wood and streaked across the soy field. The ditches were empty, dry. Dew was the only moisture. I walked as fast as my short legs would throw me. Despite my best efforts my watch became a strobe light. 5:12, 5:14, 5:15.

I walked so far that I had to jog back to the house. The early morning foot falls of work boots on dried dirt banks sounded across the empty fields. My breath and Ginger's bell were the only other sounds. Nearer the woods the morning birds came and nearer the road the sound of traffic. Trucks and cars went up and down from Toledo to Fort Wayne. The day was starting.

I had worked up a sweat but I didn't change. At 5:42 I headed for the shop. It was much too early but I couldn't delay any longer. Ginger was tied to her tree with water and food. The back door was locked and I was off to work.

2

Monday. Monday can be everything. It can be another spear through your soul or it can be one of the last lifelines thrown from a passing boat. For me, everything started on that Monday. Finally I was confronted with what looked like a real opportunity. True, the day's order was already filled with all our past work. We couldn't even consider losing ground. I didn't need to check the board for assignments. I knew what needed to be done. Little time was wasted before I was punching out the first pieces. I figured that if I could do 500 pieces then the other two men could each do 250 then move on to washing and packing.

The other man? At that point I still had hope. I didn't yet know who my third man was going to be. I thought Adam Smith had been a challenge. But after working with him I thought Smith would be fine if he could be kept motivated. He needed to be inspired to believe in the value and purpose of work. True, he was too focused on the results, but he had shown promise. I considered it my duty to save his soul. I was an evangelist of work, of toil and the redeeming value of unending defeat. Everyone would rather lie around doing nothing other than drinking, eating and fucking but that didn't get roads paved. The world was not static. The world was a wheel. Progress was the call and production its foundation.

One hundred pieces stood ready for washing by 7:30 when I turned to see Turnbull's approach. I wiped my hands on a rag and stepped from my station.

"This is going to work," I said with a smile that presumed victory.

"Do you still want a third man?" Turnbull asked without acknowledging my optimism.

"Yeah, sure. Why?" I asked.

"We don't have any extras right now." Turnbull looked at the southern wall behind which the pressroom thumped and banged its presence. "The weld shop has orders to keep everyone busy throughout the rest of the month and giving you Smith took all the slack out of the press room. As it stands Sean has twenty-seven people for thirty presses. Luckily, right now he doesn't need to run all thirty. I wanted to hire someone new but the front office hasn't ok'd that yet. They want to see that this line warrants the expenditure on someone new, benefits and all."

"They want to see the line work but they won't give me the man power to make it work," I said.

"Right," Turnbull said.

"If I did get the numbers with only two people then they would say that I didn't need the third man."

"Now you're beginning to understand how things work," Turnbull said.

"I swear no one besides me wants this to work." I threw the rag I had been clutching at the trash barrel. It spread its wings mid-flight and fluttered to the ground well short of the target.

"You might be right." Turnbull looked down at me with a seriousness on his face. I didn't know what to say or ask. "But I've figured out how to give you some more muscle at least for the time being. I'm going to pull Jack Sumney off maintenance.

He'll be your third man whenever we don't have a pressing need for him."

I let out an uncomfortable laugh. "Have you told him of that plan?" I asked.

Turnbull smiled. "Not yet," he said.

Jack Sumney was more than a man. He was an icon, an example, a cartoon. He was disinterestedness incarnate. He was a man without friend or comrade. He worked in complete isolation and this was by his own choosing. The other two maintenance workers operated as a team but Jack remained solo. Whether doing electrical, plumbing or machine repair he made no small talk, just did the job. He punched in and punched out for ten years with a minimum of words. And like the distance the rich create that becomes an insult, a person who doesn't want to know you becomes your enemy. People need to know that the pain is the same, that the next man in line isn't winning.

On top of it all was the issue of "Tom." Jack Sumney called everyone: man, woman or beast, "Tom." He didn't walk around saying, "Hello Tom." Mostly, he didn't call anyone anything. Workers could be called by their job titles. Go ask maintenance, QC or welding. But when the universal didn't fit, it was Tom. "Tom did this wrong," or "When this was Tom's machine."

I turned back to my press. Either it would work or it wouldn't. You couldn't worry too much about these things. Some things were guided by fate or the front office but the results were often the same and definitely not in your favor. I laughed to myself and thought of Emily. I loved her even more at that moment. I wished she could walk across the factory floor and kiss me.

3

Smith showed at his usual 8 a.m. He walked towards me down the aisle from the break room gently carrying a paper cup of vending machine coffee. I waved at him with a genuine smile. He wasn't so bad. You just had to know him. Maybe you had to work with him to understand that he wasn't such a bad worker. He just looked bad doing it and what he said, the almost constant complaining, made you think he wasn't getting anything done.

I walked over to the trash barrel and searched through it until I found a discarded coffee cup. I looked at the two cards printed on the side and then the one on the bottom.

"What do you have?" I asked Smith as he walked up to our station.

"I don't know but you have a two of clubs hidden. That's my cup from Friday."

I threw the cup back in the barrel. "Guess who we got?" I asked. Smith just shrugged his shoulders. "Jack Sumney!"

"Oh shit," Smith said. "You know I've never really talked to that guy. He's called me Tom a few times though. I thought he was in maintenance."

"He was and still might be on occasion. Turnbull's going to break the news to him."

Smith finished his coffee and threw the cup towards the barrel. He missed. I would pick up the cup later. "Oh shit. This is doomed. Brush off your resume Tom, we're going to be on the streets soon," Smith said.

"It's not that bad," I said as I went back to my press.

Smith turned his press on and looked over at me. "Yes it is," he said.

4

We worked. Jack Sumney showed up just before the dinner break. I'm not sure how long he stood behind our back watching. I finished my supply of blanks and turned to get more when I saw him standing with his hands in his pockets. He was a tall, thin man in his mid-forties with black greasy hair that fell just below his ears. He wore a wispy mustache and a pointy goatee. He was a good mechanic and a good machinist. He had been comfortable with his job and by the look on his face I knew that he blamed me for the change. He didn't scowl but had somehow kept the insolent look of a teenager all these years.

"Hey Jack!" I said with a false happiness. His expression didn't change. Smith noticed the commotion and turned around. It was up to me to force any conversation. "Turnbull said you were going to help us out?" Still no response. I gave up the politeness. "You have the third press." I pointed. Jack moved that way.

"If we were union this shit wouldn't happen," Adam said to Jack.

"Shut the fuck up!" I yelled at Smith. Adam had twice tried to bring the union into the shop. It was a long and difficult argument. I wasn't anti-union. I was anti-rock the boat, especially if it seemed to be headed in the right direction.

Sumney didn't say anything to Smith. "Are all the blanks the same size?" he asked no one in particular. Smith and I answered yes in unison. Jack picked up a blank, oiled it with the small paintbrush from the coffee can then pushed the aluminum against the stops. He pressed the triggers. The top jaw came down and opened. Adam and I watched like we had never seen this happen before. Jack pried the piece from the form block and held it up to us. Smith smiled and I gave Jack the thumbs up. We all went back to work.

5

At eleven Adam and I broke for dinner. We looked at Jack and I said "dinner" but he continued working and never looked at us. As we walked to the time clock Adam asked what I was doing for dinner. I had thought about going to the library or at least trying to track down Emily. I was curious to see if she had missed me the night before. Smith asked if I wanted to go to Mae's and I said sure.

Mario was at the time clock, in line. He gave me an odd look as I walked up laughing at a Smith joke. The man was funny in his own way. I asked Mario if he was going to Mae's but he was on his way home to take dinner with Jill. I had the feeling that he didn't approve of my new association.

Smith and I drove to Mae's in my truck. Adam was back on the union subject.

"You see, don't you, that since we're at the top of the floor pay scale that they can let us go if this thing doesn't work out. Then they hire in some new people at five dollars less. That saves the company ten thousand dollars per employee. If they axe three of us they could hire four new guys at the price of three. Don't you get it? That's where we need the union. That shit just isn't fair," Adam protested.

"Life isn't fair. And your idea is that we're doomed. How do you know that this isn't going to work out? We're doing fine today and I don't see why we should fail. Especially if we get a permanent third person."

"You think Jack is that guy?"

"I don't know. He had a good spot in maintenance. I don't think they want to lose him. I don't know though. You've got to admit we have a motley bunch," I said.

"See? You're starting to see it my way. They put all the pains in the asses on one boat and send them over the falls."

"Now you're back to being a defeatist. I'm not ready to concede on the first day. I still think this is a great opportunity. Once we really get our shit wired this is going to be a good assignment."

"Mark my words Warrell, if we ever get so it's comfortable, our third guy, whoever that ends up being, will get yanked." Adam was pointing his finger at me. I guessed that he was trying to be earnest and serious.

We sat down at a little table against the wall. I stirred the spoon in the hot mustard jar nervously as I looked around for Rochelle. I couldn't see her but I knew it wasn't her day off.

"You still date her?" Smith asked.

"What?"

"The waitress. Do you still see her?"

"No. It's over," I said hopefully being truthful.

Smith pushed his chair back. "Order me a beer will you."

"You a drinker?" I asked.

"You my boss?" he asked and then walked off towards the bathroom.

Rochelle came up behind me. I was still stirring the mustard. She asked me if Smith was my new girlfriend. I told her that he was. I ordered two beers and two barbeque pork sandwiches with chips. Rochelle looked good but I didn't tell her that. Her hair was a little greasy and a little disheveled but in a way that told you that she would never keep you waiting. She seemed angry but I was getting used to that. I treated her with indifference which probably stoked the anger. What else was there to do? Rochelle walked away and I didn't watch her go.

Smith came back from the bathroom. He was all soft edges. He wasn't obese but would need to keep that in mind as he went through his thirties. He sat down.

"Did you order?" Smith asked.

I said I did. Then Smith ungracefully asked me how Rochelle was, "in the sack." I told him that I would rather not talk about it but he said if you're not seeing her anymore then what's the big deal?

"Do you want her back?" he asked.

"No," I said, looking around to make sure she wasn't sneaking up on us. "But I still have feeling for Rochelle," I said in a quieter voice. "I don't know exactly what that means but it feels… ungentlemanly to talk about her."

Smith laughed. "Fuck all that. You're either with her or not. And you owe no loyalty to exes. That's a worldwide rule. Anyone who thinks otherwise still wants to fuck their ex. Is that you?"

"Sure, but that's not the point. It's over between Rochelle and me and now we have to move on. And that being so, I have to keep a polite distance… in thought and touch." It was my turn to laugh a little. "And I like the food here so this is how it has to be."

As if on cue, Rochelle turned from the order window and worked her way through the tables toward ours. I nodded her way to Smith and our conversation paused.

Rochelle set the baskets that held our sandwiches and chips down in front of us. "Oh, I'm sorry I forgot your beers. That's bad service isn't it," she said with false abashment. She went off towards the bar.

"Sounds like she doesn't hold any politeness for you," Smith said.

"Yeah, but she controls the food and drink."

Rochelle set our beers down. They spilled over the side and formed little puddles around the glasses. "Mr. Warrell here doesn't like to drink or drinkers for that matter so I forgot your drinks. It's so strange," she said to Smith. He just sat there and smiled at my expense. Rochelle walked away without looking at me.

Smith turned to me, still smiling. "She really doesn't like you," he said.

I was putting hot mustard on my sandwich. I shrugged my shoulders. "I have too much going on to worry about what Rochelle thinks of me." I bit into the sandwich. It was worth putting up with a little hate.

"But she was a good fuck, right?"

I smiled with my mouth full and said, "the best," through my food. This delighted Smith and he turned his attention back to the woman. I knew that I had opened the door for a million questions but if he kept putting up the numbers then I would sacrifice a little of my past.

Luckily he didn't ask any more questions that day. We finished our beer and then had two more while we finished our sandwiches. We tipped well and left. No punches thrown. No dishes broken. A successful operation.

6

Back on the floor all three presses stood silent. Jack was gone. We assumed he had taken his dinner break and hoped he would return. He didn't. In the third quarter we shut off the presses and began washing and packing. Smith and I took turns loading the washing basket and running the controls. At first both of us thought that running the machine would be better than loading and unloading the baskets. But after fifteen minutes of inhaling the solvent fumes we thought otherwise. It was a sensation that would entertain a high schooler but frightened middle aged men. A light-headedness let you know that you were doing damage to your brain. Thank God you have five billion brain cells, Smith said. I wondered where he got that number but he didn't know. Between the beer, the fumes and the work I began to feel ill. But I knew I would get accustomed to it, like everything.

A little before three Turnbull came in to see how things were going. I tried not to smile. I was a little high when I told him we were doing fine. Smith laughed feeling the same way. Then Turnbull asked how Jack had worked out and I didn't know how to answer. We hadn't seen him since before lunch. I didn't say anything about it. I merely said, "fine." Turnbull told me with a frown that Jack was working on a robotic welder that had broken. I felt that I had failed in some way.

"Well, they're loading your first shipment right now," Turnbull said. "Keep it up."

He walked away and I looked at Adam. We had the same idea. We wanted to see that first truck off. He turned off the parts washer and we walked through the sunshine and the heat between the two buildings to shipping.

The shipping building was the oldest of the three in our little village. It was home to the original factory and constructed of giant foot and a half square beams. The wood plank floor upstairs was made of 14-inch wood planks set on end, thousands of them, and sturdy enough to support loaded forklifts. The freight elevator sagged a bit when you drove on to it and I thought that it would be the first to fail. The building already had near a hundred years of rough use.

The truck was still backed up to the dock. Phil Peterson was loading the last crate. We were disappointed that the truck was a regular short haul line truck. We had expected something more. I wanted to see a truck with US Army painted on the side but that didn't make any sense. The world was what it was and that meant things got done according to rules of efficiency instead of aesthetics. It was how it should be. No frills, no brass bands, just heads down and straight-ahead.

We watched as the driver signed the bills. Phil pointed to lines on the papers and the driver made a motion too informal to be significant. The driver climbed down the ladder off the dock and we wished him good luck. The truck pulled away and we hustled back through the shipping building so we could catch it as it passed through the open breezeway between the two buildings.

"Does this make us part of the American war machine?" Adam asked.

"I think it does," I said with a comfortable grin.

Things got better with Emily and they got worse. I focused my attention on work. With three people we could make our numbers although I was still working a couple hours a day off the clock. Jack's animosity mellowed into an understandable loathing for press monkey work. I noticed he occasionally laughed at Adam's antics. He did these polka-style dances that always turned into riding a horse. But these smiles were rare and

I could see they pained him. He didn't want to be us. It's hard to be indifferent with three in the bathtub.

At break we stood around smoking cigarettes. I bummed one from Adam just to fit in. The rain hadn't started yet and we were still smoking under the oak tree behind the weld shop. Jack even followed us out there. He didn't join in on the conversation but he was there and that was something.

Adam was eyeing Jack. It became his mission. To figure out who Jack was. When Jack wasn't present Adam would speculate on Jack's nature. Adam's favorite theory was that Jack was actually the fourth Bullough son but through some evil deed or by an illegitimacy he had lost his claim to the throne. So he had a job with decent pay and was always passed over in the layoffs. I liked that theory, too. It was the same one I used on Dale Novak. But it was good for explaining the unexplainable. Like God. The couple of days following Adam's invention of that history we watched Jack out of the corner of our eyes as we went through the work day waiting for him to betray some sign of royalty. Of course he didn't. But it was fun and the time passed.

Adam had a habit of asking Jack questions point blank. "Where'd you go to high school?" or "What year did you graduate?" Mostly Jack would stare back at Adam and then return to his press. Adam thought it funny but it made me uncomfortable. In some way I could understand Jack's desire to be separate. It seemed plausible that Jack merely wanted to work, to exchange a few hours of his life for the money which bought him food and put a roof over his head. Why was there this social need around work? We didn't congregate because of friendship. The friendship always came later. We were brothers born of the need for money, which isn't as bad as it sounds. People who demand too much out of their short lives prove that they have not really touched the marrow of it. The principals and laws elude them. They have little knowledge of themselves or history. Life is a losing struggle fought with sickness, war, age and ultimately death. Soothe it with the balms of love, friendship, or religious thought, but never forget that these are only coverings across the open sore that it is.

Walking back from the oak tree one day Adam turned to Jack and said, "You look like a Civil War soldier." I looked at Jack and saw Adam's point. With his droopy mustache and longish hair Jack could be wearing the Union blue instead of the factory green. Then to our surprise, Jack spoke.

"On weekends I'm a Sergeant in the 53rd Ohio."

Adam and I looked at each other with raised eyebrows. To our greater surprise, he continued. "It's what I do. History. The Civil War. In August I took a week off to go down to Virginia for a reenactment. There were 30,000 people there. The fighting was only a day. Most of the time we sat around our camps cooking, singing, playing music. It's a good time. I play the fiddle with another couple of boys from my regiment. That's the best part, the music and the stories. The guns are fun but that's more for the spectators. A lot of them come out though most are rooting for the Rebs as if that would make a difference. Southerners are odd. They really take everything seriously. They all claim to be related to someone, mostly Forrest and Lee. It doesn't make sense, numbers wise. But let them think what they want. It doesn't hurt anyone. People think all sorts of funny things and even set their lives by them. My Great-Great Granddad fought with the 53rd Ohio but I don't make a big fuss about it. If someone asks I'll tell them but that doesn't make me anything too special. Just a guy whose relative didn't get shot or die of the flu. People are odd."

We walked back to our building and despite ourselves Adam nor I asked another question. We couldn't. We were overcome by the amount of information we had just received. It was as if we had witnessed something great or terrible in the old sense. We had to think about each of the words, about the meanings of the phrases. We made it to our stations and turned on our presses and started working.

Turnbull came by after lunch and pulled Jack out for some repair work in the weld shop. As they walked away Adam and I finally found our voices.

"Do you believe that shit?" he asked me over the din of work.

"Maybe you just need to ask the right questions," I said.

We both shook our heads and went back to our machines. It would take until the afternoon break before we could once again talk sensibly. But then we didn't talk about Jack. It seemed that we had said all that could be said on the subject.

8

Monday night was wash night and we were at the laundry mat. I ungracefully watched Emily's ass. She was studying, leaning on a table next to the bank of dryers. I was in the corner playing solitaire and sipping beers from a six-pack I had hidden in my basket. Emily shifted her weight back and forth from foot to foot and her ass hypnotized me. A triangled yellow polka dot kerchief held her hair back, peasant style. Emily's lips formed words as she read but I couldn't make out what she was saying.

One dryer thumped and another whined developing a bad bearing. I didn't get up and grab her. I didn't tell her how wonderful I found her backside. I played solitaire and sipped beer and let her be.

As we folded the last load and Emily made her two piles, the one that went to the river house and the other to a small student apartment, I reached over and grabbed her wrists.

"Don't," I said.

"What?"

"Don't separate. Quit pretending. Just bring all your stuff out. I can't stand the thought of you being somewhere else."

And then, in the yellow light of the laundry mat, in front of the big window for everyone to see, we kissed. We kissed long and slow with our hearts and our blood. And when we had enough we said that we loved each other and then put the folded clothes in any basket.

Later, after Emily had finished studying, she woke me with a delicate hand and light kisses. She came easily and quickly. As I worked towards mine she reached back and held my balls, gently squeezing until she had it all.

I faded towards the darkness with thousand pound limbs. Emily laid her head on my chest and I could feel the warm tears.

"I can't," she said.

I didn't argue because I was tired and what was there to say that I hadn't said?

9

Adam took the afternoon off to take his mother to the doctor. Jack was off elsewhere and I was alone. I went looking for Mario. I found him in welding on his knees doing custom work, flipping his shield back and forth checking his beads. On his desk were the plans and I sat on the corner and tried to decipher them. It was something for the dairy plant but that was all I could figure.

I tapped the bottom of his foot with my boot. "What?" he said beneath his helmet.

"Want to go to dinner?"

"When I'm done," he said, then struck his arc.

I kneeled down and tried not to look at the blue light. I could feel my face getting tan. "When? I'm on break now."

"Are you off the clock?" Mario asked.

Of course I wasn't. Mario knew that. Punching the clock was the last thing you did before exiting the building. He knew that. I wouldn't waste minutes. "But I'm hungry now," I whined. That made Mario laugh. His shoulders shook and the arc stopped. It started again but then he laughed and quit. Mario crawled backwards out from beneath the dairy thing.

"You're such a little girl," he said.

"Yeah, but I'm cute."

We drove to Mae's in Mario's truck and he took a couple

of hits off a half-smoked joint in the ashtray. I looked out the window.

"You set such an example," I teased him. "Leadership, responsibility, integrity."

"How many people are in your section?" he asked, seemingly unrelated.

"Three," I said.

"You don't count yourself jackass!" We let it lie at that.

10

Rochelle was back in fine form. We sat at a wall table and turned our attention towards her. Every man was looking at her. She had her sleeves pulled up and was flexing her muscles for the table of cops, who nodded in approval. She did have nice arms. Rochelle smiled and then pulled up her shirt and punched herself in the stomach a few times.

Mario turned from the cops. "Did Ian ever find out about you and Lisa?" he asked.

"Nothing happened. What could he find out about?"

"His wife gave you head in the bowling alley parking lot," Mario said in a low voice.

"It was practically nothing. We were both drunk."

Rochelle came and took our order. I was thinking of Ian's gun. His gun was made to kill people. That was a fundamental difference. But he seemed like a good guy, a little dumb but basically good. On the softball field I tried not to talk to him any more than I talked to the other cops. We had nothing in common, I told myself. Yet I worried.

"How are things with the librarian?" Mario asked.

I told Mario that Emily wouldn't make the move out to the river house and that it disappointed me. I told him of her parents. They wouldn't like the way it looked. And Emily could study away from me and the dog.

"You love her?"

I nodded.

"She loves you?"

I nodded again.

"Then I don't get it." Mario pushed his chair back. "I don't mean this to sound bad. I don't mean anything bad. But could she be using you?"

"No," I said without thinking. "For what? What could I be used for?"

"I don't know. Experience? Maybe she's slumming it. You know, getting dirty, getting fucked by a man before she goes off and marries an accountant."

I stole one of Mario's cigarettes from the pack on the table and leaned back in my chair. On the wall above me was a black and white photo of the Defiance High School championship football team. Krager was on that team. Turnbull was on that team. I inhaled and heard voices from across the room, the laughter and Rochelle's ordering. But I was too insulted to hear Mario. He knew I had been to college, that I had almost been an officer of Marines. He knew that. I was truth with a big "T". He should know that.

"Christ, she doesn't even have a job." Mario took a bite of his sandwich that had arrived unnoticed by me. "Where is she going to work after she graduates?" he continued.

"I don't know. A school," I said, still looking at the football players.

"Which school?"

I hadn't told Mario of my trip to Athens. Emily's future was unknown even to Emily.

My gaze had shifted across the room to the order window. Rochelle was looking back at me and she nodded. She was too far away to be nodding at anything in Mario's conversation. She was acknowledging my stare. It didn't work with you either, I thought.

"Shit man, why you got to be so anti-love."

"Easy, brother," Mario said. "You know I'm not anti-love. I'm just looking out for you. I want things to work out. I do. I just want you to be careful, to look at everything."

11

Mario's concerns came back to me later as I pressed parts alone. His few words made me doubt all of Emily's. His words came back to me at night as I sat on the couch, as we sat on the couch. Maybe I should have led with words but when you doubt words are the first to fail. I led with my hands. I reached for one big beautiful tit. Emily swatted me away.

"I don't feel like being kissed."

What? What is that? You struggle. You fight. You dodge bullets, punches, drunk drivers. You survive life to come back to this, to know that blood is for something other than bleeding. The small things become big things. Everything took on too much meaning. If she accepted me, I was suspicious. If she denied me, I was righteous.

Each night before bed, more and more I stole away to the bathroom or my office and fucked myself. It was self-defense. I was trying to avoid confrontation like crossing a street to bypass a group of drunks. I wanted to fall asleep happy with the woman I loved. And if that wasn't possible, then sated. So I came quietly into toilet paper behind the bathroom door. I thought of Emily and sometimes I would steal a passing kiss or glancing grope to get started. Mostly it was her memory I fucked. That is important. I didn't want any other woman. Emily was the one I loved, the one I wanted to be with and I was trying to find a fix.

12

Monday morning I woke in a panic. I couldn't remember my dream but it was probably one of the running kind, dreams where you dodge and make good moves but never lose your pursuers. Those dreams were different from the kind where you are in a fight and your body is slowed by some internal freeze, as if gravity was centered in your stomach. I was sweaty. My hair was wet as were my legs and back. Emily slept facing away from me. The clock glowed 4:27. A little early but what can you do when your mind won't play along? I got out of bed, took a shower then headed for work.

13

At six I walked through the front door then the locker room without punching in. I knew it was stupid to throw my time away but I considered it an investment. Our corner of the factory was dark and I turned on the overhead lights. I turned on all three presses and thought of doing twenty-five pieces on each. I'll give everyone a head start, I thought. I was worried because our buffer had been brought down to only a few parts. The o-three stock was completely empty so I started them first. Our little radio was tuned in and I worked away, happy to be doing something.

Adam came in an hour early and I didn't notice him standing behind me.

"Are you punched in?" he asked wise to my schemes. When I said I wasn't, Adam said that was stupid and that he wouldn't ever be caught doing anything like that. Adam had brought a dozen donuts and a Thermos of coffee and we had a little break right there in front of our presses. We talked over the weekend's events in very vague terms, and despite the machine oil on my fingers the glazed donuts were wonderful.

Loaded with sugar and caffeine, we set back to work. Even though we couldn't have real conversations over the production din it was nice to have Adam next to me. At seven-thirty Jack showed up, showered, hair slicked back.

"Kill any Rebs this weekend?" Adam asked.

Jack smiled and shook his head, "No. None this weekend."

I snuck off and clocked in. Our presses slammed open and shut all morning. By the time for our first break we were ahead of schedule. It was a false standard because I had shown up early but numbers were numbers and we were reaching ours. I wanted to call my father or someone. See? Things might work out after all.

Of course it couldn't last.

14

We were all walking back from break smoking cigarettes and laughing at the crude stories Adam was telling of his weekend conquest. I doubt anything he told us was true but his stories were funny nonetheless.

"She was big as a cow. No shit…"

The laughing stopped when we saw Chris Carlson standing in our zone. Jack said, "what the fuck," under his breath. When Carlson saw us he came forward.

"You guys need to stop production," Carlson said.

"Why?" was all I could manage in the voice of a teenage girl. It felt like someone had jumped on my chest. I looked at Adam and Jack. Adam had no expression at all. Jack looked like he wanted to hit the salesman.

"United Tracked Truck went on strike this morning," Carlson said. "We don't know how long it's going to last but they're not going to take in any parts. As of this morning we are losing money. Don't touch any more aluminum. I have to find Turnbull." We watched his bald head speed away.

"He doesn't control shit," I said trying to rally the troops. Adam shrugged his shoulders. Jack said he could always go back to maintenance. We waited for five more minutes. I kept looking at my watch. I grew more and more worried about losing time. We were ahead but any glitch could erase that quickly. Finally I looked at my two work mates who were smoking cigarettes and leaning against the boxed parts and said, "Fuck him! We don't stop until Turnbull tells us to." Jack nodded and Adam shrugged his shoulders. We went back to work.

15

It was almost dinnertime when Turnbull came over. The three of us turned off our presses and gave our boss all our attention.

"Did Carlson tell you guys not to make any more parts?" Turnbull asked, although the question was aimed at me.

"He's a salesman not a production manager," I protested. A forklift went by and the driver looked at us a little too intently. I wondered how many people knew about the strike. In a factory rumors are more contagious than smallpox.

"No. You did right. It's his fault if the margins are that small. You guys continue on and make your numbers. We'll just have to wait and see about the strike. As I understand it the sticking point is about retirement benefits and the two sides aren't that far apart. If things got too out of hand the government would step in because of national security. So you have the Pentagon covering your ass. Don't worry about Carlson."

"Yeah and we can make up our buffer," I said. Turnbull frowned. I regretted saying anything. Why couldn't I keep my mouth shut? He had said all that needed to be said. All my life I had jumped in with the wrong comment at the wrong time. I made a resolution with myself to only talk when I had something to say, but that wouldn't last through the day.

Turnbull pointed a finger at us and said, "No slacking! This isn't a vacation. I'll still be watching." He swept his finger so that it covered each of us and we nodded in recognition of its power. And then he walked away. We waited until he was out of hearing distance to speak.

Adam spoke first. I was still holding my promise to myself and Jack rarely spoke no matter the situation. "Hot damn! Who wants to go out to lunch?" he said.

I looked towards the open bay door and could see rain coming down. It was a gentle soaking rain, like a spring rain, good for beast and crop. I wondered what it would be like to strike.

16

As we walked to the time clock Adam asked again if I wanted to go out to lunch. I turned him down. I wasn't feeling too well, mentally. Not that I told him that. I was thinking of Emily and worrying about us. It seemed odd that everything could have happened in three months but there it was. I could look it up on the calendar in my kitchen at home. I had colored in a corner on the day that we first kissed to secretly mark our anniversary. I knew it was a girlie thing to do but that's what Emily inspired me to do. I was so hopeful.

But now? I was worried. As I walked outside and through the parking lot towards my truck I was overcome and on the verge of tears. I held them back but in the rain I could have played them off. I worried not that she no longer cared for me. I worried that our relationship had reached a plateau where it would stay for the next fifty years. Every three minutes my mind would oscillate between gratitude and dread. Yes, this was really wonderful to have a beautiful woman to share your life with, to hold your hand while we watched movies and to erase your library fines. I thought, if she could just kiss me right then I would be saved, a nice kiss on my neck that raised the hairs along my spine.

My heart raced. I feared I was having a nervous breakdown. I thought it might be related to work but kept thinking of Emily. She was at school and therefore impossible to track down. I thought of driving through the campus to look for her but knew that would only hasten my collapse. The sight of students utterly defeated me. I would be filled with regret over my own failed attempt at higher learning. Instead I drove to the grocery store.

As I pulled into the parking lot I had almost talked myself into a normal heart rate. I went over the "facts" as I knew them over and over again. I had work. I loved Emily. She loved me. Ginger was dumb but loyal. I had the best house in town. My truck was rusty but mechanically sound. Those kinds of things, over and over again. Money in the bank, good health, hair on my head. It almost worked.

17

I got some fried chicken from the hot case at the deli. On the way to the checker I passed the beer cooler. For some reason it called my name and without too much thought I grabbed a 16-ounce can of beer. I read the tabloids as I waited in line.

"Drinking your lunch?" a voice asked from behind.

I turned and saw Rochelle. My heart leapt and then hit the floor, trampled by a marching army. Something else inside me, lower, was like an excited dog thumping its tail against a linoleum floor, riding its butt like a sleigh. She stood just under my chin and I put away the paper without folding it correctly. She looked good. She was wearing an old work shirt with the name "Earle" sown on the breast, an old pair of jeans and tennis shoes. Her hair was up in pigtails and she looked sassy for a middle-aged woman, not pitiful or trying.

"You're up," she said pushing my elbow forward towards the checker. I still hadn't said anything. In my confusion I could barely pay for my lunch.

"I'm glad I didn't go to Mae's," I finally said.

"Why?" she asked and paid for her bleach and fabric softener. I asked if she was doing laundry. She called me Sherlock Holmes. We cleared the check-out aisle and stopped before the doors. It was raining outside. I held my little bag and didn't know of anything to say.

"Are you still dating that girl?" Rochelle asked.

"Yeah… and you?"

"None of your business," she said. And it wasn't. A silence drifted between us and I looked out to the parking lot.

"I'm going to go see my grandma and eat some fried chicken." When too stumped I often stated facts. I could have said it's raining or my truck is rusty, but I didn't. I looked back down at the woman. She was looking out toward the parking lot.

She turned her face up towards mine and asked if I wanted company. My insides turned over on themselves and I knew that killed dogs. I had lost one that way. Was it fear? What had I to fear? Really. I said, "sure".

We climbed into my truck and I put my lunch on the bench. Rochelle put her goods in the middle also. I pulled out and we listened to the wipers flap, flap.

"What's her name?" Rochelle asked.

"Emily," I said.

"That's nice," she said looking forward out the windshield.

"It is. It sounds older, classic. Not one of those new names, like Amber, Chelsea, Tiffany. I hate those names." I was rambling.

"How old is she?" Rochelle interrupted.

"Twenty one," I said.

Rochelle laughed. "Cradle robber." I said that she acted a lot older than that. Then I said she kissed me first, not the other way around. I regretted saying that. Rochelle was quiet. We drove past Emily's apartment and her car was in the lot. My breath disappeared and I felt faint. But what was I really guilty of? I asked myself. Plenty in the Catholic tradition, was the reply. I opened the beer and took a long drink. It helped but the fact that it helped almost made me feel worse. Almost.

"You seem nervous," Rochelle said with a smirk. She was enjoying my discomfort.

"Some days work is tough, this is one of them." I hadn't lied. I thought about it. I hadn't lied yet and promised myself not to. I turned into the graveyard, drove back to the Devil's stump then killed the engine.

I pulled a breast from the bag and bit into it. The skin flakes exploded and flew over my shirt. I laughed a little to myself and was again glad for our uniforms. What did I expect? Rochelle pulled her left leg up and tucked it under the other so that she faced me. She reached over and picked up my beer. Without asking she took a sip. It made me angry, like the old days. Rochelle must have noticed the cloud come over my eyes because she laughed. And I laughed a little, too.

"How are things going? Seriously," I asked.

Rochelle shrugged then looked away. The windows were fogged over and for a moment it reminded me of better days. Rochelle drew a heart in the moisture of the passenger window. It was such a girlish thing to do yet it didn't seem pitiful. How could this woman manage to exist like that? Maybe it had to do with her eyes that stuck out from her skull like she was pressurized with sadness. The rest of her body belonged to an oil field worker, a roughneck, but her eyes were pure kitsch. They were constantly sad in the grotesque.

She talked toward the window. "I might move away. My cousin, Sara, the one who lives in Columbus said I could move in with her. I don't know though. Some days I'm ready to move to Chicago or St. Louis on my own. Just start over on my own terms. A whole new life. Do you think that's possible? Thanks to you I'm debt free and have money in the bank. So anything's possible, huh?" Rochelle was crying softly, but just in the eyes turned toward the opaque window, not in the chest or the stomach. "I don't know. I thought of moving away three years ago. Before we started. Then there's Mae's and as stupid as it sounds I feel tied to that place and not in a bad way." Her voice steadied. "I feel like I belong but I don't know what that's really worth. When I open the door in the morning I like it. I like turning everything on and putting on my apron. I like talking to all the men at lunch. I would miss all you assholes if I left. But working there and living in my little apartment alone gets depressing. I want more." Rochelle looked at me with her eyes clear.

Finally I thought it safe to bite into my second piece of chicken. It would have been rude in the middle of her story. Rochelle smiled at me but I didn't know why.

The emotion was completely gone from her voice. "There's someone in town that's been trying to woo me. But I'm playing hard to get."

"Really," I said.

"Yeah, you won't be happy when you find out." Rochelle reached over and took my beer again.

I tried not to play the guessing game. I looked at my watch and it was time to head back to work.

"Do you want me back?" she asked in a voice that was suitably frivolous. Do you like the color red? Do you want more soup?

"What?" was all I could manage. I took my beer back from her and she said that I had heard her. I started the engine and put the defroster on full. "Do I want you? That's a horrible question…"

"That wasn't the question. I asked, do you want me back? There's a big difference. I have never questioned if you wanted me." She reached over and patted my lap in a vague way. I put the truck in gear and we slowly weaved out of the graveyard. I concentrated on the road and wished for something spectacular, zombies, anything. But she wasn't distracted. "Just answer the question. Yes or no."

"No," I said. I had to say something and I couldn't say the other.

The windows were beginning to clear. A big truck passed and its wave of wind and water rocked us back and forth. I turned on the main road and steered back to the grocery store where we had left Rochelle's car.

"Wow," Rochelle said, then sat quiet. "I didn't think you had it in you. She must be really good." Rochelle was looking out the window and I was looking out the other as we passed Emily's apartment. Her words filled me with dread. I felt very alone.

"Do you love her?" Rochelle asked.

"Yes," I said.

"Well then… You deserve to be happy. And I'm happy for the both of you." Rochelle grabbed my beer and held it up in a toast and then finished it. I felt the worst I had in a very long time. We pulled in the parking lot and Rochelle got out.

"Don't be a stranger," I said.

"What are you talking about? I'll see you tomorrow at lunch." She slammed the door and I pulled out without watching her get into her car. The bleach and softener were still on the bench next to me but I couldn't force myself to turn around.

18

At the presses Adam asked me where I had gone and I said the grocery store but left out all the fireworks. Although I did want to talk about it Adam would ask all the wrong questions and therefore it was better not to talk. When I got into my truck after work the laundry supplies were gone and I was happy for that.

I drove through the rain. I loved the sight of my house coming into view around the corner. Beautiful, beautiful home, I thought. Emily's car was in the driveway. I bounded up the stairs in three leaps. She was at the kitchen table studying. I went over and kissed her and then pulled her to her feet. I kissed her neck and ear and was holding her ass in my hands when she pushed me away and said, "Don't manhandle me." I thought, but that's what I am, right? She complained that she was studying and I didn't want to hear any excuses so I went to the closet and pulled out the Bismarck. I set it on the coffee table. The foremast was ready for gluing. I didn't feel well but it wasn't the Eastern front,

I reminded myself.

Emily's voice came in to me. She was calling my name. I asked her what but she wanted me to come to her so I did. Emily was in bed with the covers pulled up to her neck. I inferred that she was naked so I pulled off my clothes and got in beside her. She said some more things about studying but I didn't want to hear her voice. It ended up working and after I was a little depressed because I really felt better. I was ashamed it was so easy. But it was.

19

We tried to keep abreast of the strike situation but our local newspaper, The Crescent-News, didn't cover the news in far off Indiana. It might as well have been Paraguay. Where was Paraguay? Occasionally on the public radio station out of Bowling Green I would hear of the strike but never anything of great importance or relevance. "United Tracked Truck is on strike for the fourth... fifth... sixth day." And if the commentator focused in more depth it was about the people and not the process. Joe Lunchbox has been out of work two weeks and his twelve dirty-faced kids are running out of Twinkies. I hated the human-interest angle. Tell the truth. Let's hear about the causes, not the effects.

We continued working and the shipping warehouse began to fill with our parts. The odd thing was, now that the blade was removed from over our necks, the job became easier. By the end of the week we were reaching our quotas without worry. I still worked an hour extra but that was half of my previous off clock time.

The strike moved into its second week and there was no let up in the rain. Puddles began forming in the parking lots and low places. The corn was not yet picked and the field down river from my house was swamped under the gathering water. Only the tassels could be seen above the new lake. Pheasant season was set to start in the first week of October but the mud made walking impossible. I had scouted the woods on the off chance that the birds might have taken refuge there. It was the only walkable stretch of land for miles. The small drainage stream had turned low laying swales into full swamps. My beloved stand of birch now remade itself as a cypress swamp. I wished for a johnboat so I could visit those trees. Ginger couldn't maneuver in the deep mud and stuck unusually close.

One day we happened upon a pheasant. Ginger never saw the bird and I didn't point it out to her. I was stopped on the narrow deer trail that ran the western edge of the wood when I turned to see a rooster pheasant sitting on a pine branch at head level. He stared at me. I was carrying my gun, although taking him wouldn't have been legal. I looked at him for a couple minutes and was overcome by pity. The water had chased this bird into the trees as if he was a robin or a jay. I wondered where his nest was. Floated away probably. It was the first time I had ever seen a pheasant in a tree.

20

United Tracked Truck struck for three weeks. Jack, Adam and I filled shipping with parts. Management grew nervous about the money we had tied up in shelved parts. The line was to be our first experiment in "just in time" production, yet because of the strike we were pilling up stock like we had just emerged from the Industrial Revolution. After the second week

Jack was pulled from our ranks and sent back to maintenance. He genuinely seemed reluctant to go and visited us whenever his assignment carried him past our zone. Adam and I forged on. Our personal numbers continued to climb and we laughed at the fact. We now had time to smoke cigarettes. Adam began wandering off more and more so I reminded him of Turnbull's warning and he promised me not to wreck our good thing.

Water filled our parking lots and began invading the shop floor. The pressroom had sunk in the clay over the sixty odd years that the machines thumped down on the floor. The water invaded through the open bay doors and I would see Sean push the waves back outside with a giant squeegee. Adam took to calling him Ohio Moses.

The first talk of flooding came from nowhere. One day we were talking about puddles and messy fields and the next we were talking of flood stages and cresting heights. It was days later when newspapers and TV talked of the possibility. I felt confident because although my house was on the riverbank it was possibly the highest point in the county. The world could cover over and the River House would still stand there like a little Gibraltar. True it was only a matter of tens of feet but in this billiard tableland the littlest differences were made great. What is the saying? "An Everest in Kansas."

After the amusing anecdotes of flooded basements and holy shoes were digested we began to worry about real issues. Peterson Metal, built at the confluence of the Auglaize and Maumee, was squatting on prime wash-over land. At breaks, and during dinner, small processions of workers sloshed toward the rivers and observe the change in height. The angry brown water that now carried trees and debris was only six feet down a gentle slope. Men would bend low putting their heads nearer the muddy ground in efforts to guess the remaining buffer. The Bulloughs made regular visits to the bank.

I saw Turnbull out there. He didn't look at the ground or the river but up the river. I thought he was manifesting more genius but after he had left I trudged out there to see what he had seen and was disappointed. Up river was the bridge that led to my house, a railroad bridge and then a bend. Nothing was suggested. He had only been thinking. But he could have thought in his office. Why did he have to drag me out in the rain?

21

When I first looked at the clock it was exactly 4 a.m. I closed my eyes and pretended for another twenty-seven minutes. Somehow Emily had tucked the sheets in around her body between us. I tried working my hands toward her flesh but her weight was firmly on the fold. Hopeless, I thought. It was then that I noticed the rain had stopped. I left the bed with a smile. After searching in vain for any news about the strike on the radio I left for work.

The solvent in the parts washer needed to be changed. I had been avoiding it but a sheen of old oil now washed across the surface like a miniature Prince William Sound. Changing the solvent wasn't a tough task. Old solvent out. Clean the insides. New solvent in. Simple. The fumes inhaled throughout this operation take at least two grades off your education. But I had some to spare.

We decided to work half a day then change the solvent after the dinner break. First we walked down to maintenance and checked out the needed equipment: funnel, non-sparking electric pump, two pairs of heavy rubber gloves, two respirators, and hazardous waste placards to affix to the barrels when we were done.

I borrowed a forklift from QC and fetched four empty barrels from the pile then three full barrels from the solvent stock. The solvent barrels were kept in a large cement tub to prevent ground leakage. All our gases and oils had similar containment cells.

Our section was up against an old loading dock that was sunk into the floor. It was no longer used and was now wasted space. Lucky for us the overhead door was on the uphill side of the factory and the water hadn't yet worked its way in. Adam came up with the idea of placing the barrels in the pit. That way we wouldn't have to use the pump. Gravity would do our work for us. We could merely turn the valve on and off. I complemented him and he played it off unconvincingly.

We filled two barrels without a glitch. Adam and I had switched positions. He was now in the pit with the hose and I was stationed at the valve. I wanted to make sure all the old solvent got drained. And then it happened.

"Oh shit!" Adam shouted. "Oh fuck! Stop it! Shut it off!"

My head had been stuck deep in the washer but I leaped for the valve. I closed it and looked over the rail at Adam. He was looking at me. He pointed to the bottom of the barrel where a steady stream of solvent was shooting through a hole. It was a fork hole. Someone had punched a hole in the barrel with a forklift. I didn't do that, I thought. But that really didn't matter. The barrel was in the good pile and I hadn't checked all its surfaces for holes. Why should I have?

Adam tried to cover the hole with one rubber glove but the flow was too great. It sprayed over him.

"Be careful!" I shouted down to him. "Don't do that." I jumped down in the pit to watch the barrel empty. The solvent was forming a little pond at the bottom of the slope but was steadily disappearing down a drain.

"Where do you think that leads?" Adam asked pointing at the forming whirlpool.

"The river," I said.

"Should we tell someone?" he asked.

I looked around. No one was near. No one had seen our fiasco.

"How full was the barrel?" I asked.

"About half," he said.

We watched the rest of the solvent drain out without saying anything else. What could we do, really? When the flow stopped I went over and tipped the barrel on its side and shook out what was trapped below the hole. I found a barrel dolly and then switched out the punctured one for another from the "good" pile, this time checking all sides.

Adam and I went on to thoroughly clean the washer. We did it in silence although the respirators helped with that. We had to use the pump to refill the machine. And while it went about its work we finally took off our masks.

"It's a good thing it happened down there," Adam said pointing at the pit. "If the barrel had been up here… shit." He looked around imagining the spill. I looked over the lip of the machine and watched the rising liquid. Adam continued, "So this should stay between us, huh?"

"I think so," I said reaching over to switch off the sputtering pump. The barrel was empty. I put the pump in the next one. "It shouldn't have happened but there was nothing to be done once it did. Right?" I wanted to say something about the river, to minimize our mistake, but I couldn't think of an excuse that wouldn't sound like one. I wanted to repeat the maxim that "dilution is the solution to pollution" but in practice it wasn't so catchy. Adam helped me push the barrel dolly up the ramp. We were both outside when the first heavy drops hit. They were big. The sky was throwing water balloons. Adam got hit in the back and stumbled forward three steps. He looked up, "this seems real," he said.

We didn't talk that much for the rest of the day and clocked out at three. I wanted the day to end. I wanted to go to sleep and awake to something new. It's one of the blessings of having a bad memory. Every day is new and full of possibilities. I drove home through the rain listening only to the flap, flap of the wipers. I had a headache and felt nauseous. I didn't like the solvent. I didn't like dealing with it.

22

That night the land went through a visible change from

wet to saturated. The runoff ran both ways. It bumped into itself and sought something that no longer existed.

The next morning the water began to fill the empty loading bay behind our presses. I thought the drain might be clogged. Rags lay around in almost every corner. One could have migrated over the drain. I went down to maintenance and borrowed a pair of tall rubber boots from Jack. He asked what I was doing and when I told him Jack followed me back to the presses and he and Adam watched me enter the ugly water from the safety above.

The boots were only knee-high but I thought that would be enough. The most difficult thing was walking down the wet ramp without falling. The boots wanted to keep your ankles straight but I needed them to bend. The soles were lugged and built for soil not concrete. Twice my feet tried to escape me but I caught myself before going down. Those two laughed each time, rooting for my fall.

When I made it to the drain I dragged my boot across the grating. I couldn't feel anything blocking the water.

"Do you want a plunger?" Adam asked.

"Maybe that's all she can take," Jack said.

"Who?" I asked.

"The drain, the river, the whole water table," Jack said. "Maybe the water is coming up the drain, not going down."

"Yeah, like a basement." Adam was obviously proud of his thought.

I was uncomfortable standing in the oily water. "So what? Just live with it?" Jack shrugged his shoulders and Adam didn't say anything. I began the slow walk back up the ramp.

Of course I didn't make it. My right foot slipped out from beneath me and I had to put my left hand down to stop my fall. Both boots filled with the slimy water and I swore for two minutes straight. And, of course, Jack and Adam laughed. I wasn't angry at them. I wasn't angry at anyone. I had tried to fix something and it didn't work. It was better than not trying.

But I was uncomfortable. My pants were wet from above the knee down and the cuff of my shirtsleeve was wet. I took off my socks and threw them away. I wore my work boots over bare feet. I suffered through the rest of the day that way.

23

After work I drove straight home and took a long hot shower. I was hoping that Emily might come home and be compelled to join me. The water ran on the back of my neck until I was almost asleep. Steam coated all the windows, but only Ginger's eyes were on me when I stepped from the shower. I pulled on my wool sailor pants and a sweater before going to the kitchen for a cup of tea. It was six and Emily still hadn't shown up. I phoned her apartment and she answered.

"What are you doing?" I asked.

"Studying," she replied. Her voice was distant.

I told her of my day, of falling in the dirty water and of the rising tide. She didn't seem concerned. The college was far enough inland that they probably hadn't even noticed the coming flood. I couldn't criticize her though. Only people in the flood path were concerned. Others had a detached interest but that was all. I told Emily how I had turned on the heat and made tea. I told her that I had put flannel sheets on my bed, which I hadn't, and that I might turn in early. But she only grunted an acknowledgement. I was uncomfortable. It felt like begging and that was the opposite of what I wanted.

"Okay well, I'll talk to you later," I said in an effort to end the torturous call.

Then Emily found her voice. "What do you want, Warrell?" she asked, a sudden volume to her words. "Do you want me to race out there so you can…" She couldn't find a word.

I leapt in like a bomb squad. "I just wondered what you were doing. You weren't here so I called. I wondered how your day was."

"Then how come you never asked?"

It was true. I hadn't, so I lied. "I did. I told you how my day was. It wasn't good and that's all. You act as if I had some other motive?"

"You do!" she shouted. "You want to fuck me so you can go to sleep with a smile on your face. You don't care how my day was. You only think of yourself. You and your penis. Is that all that exists?"

I was confused. Where did she get this? I did want to fuck her. More than that I wanted her to fuck me. But where did she get the idea that such a thing was wrong or bad? I felt guilty of something. Selfishness, maybe.

A long silence sat between us.

"Hello?" came from her side. And then she went on, "I want more Warrell. I want to share my soul. I want to share my ideas, not just my body."

The pleasant hard on I had been enduring faded away. I wanted to tell her to get a job but I knew that wasn't fair. I wanted her to know that sex is sometimes a medicine and not always a dessert. I tried honesty. "You're right, I do want to fuck you. I don't think you can doubt that I love you but I also lust for you. I don't want to make love to you. I don't want to share anything special. I want to fuck you. I wish you wanted to fuck me."

"There's more to it than desire," she said. Then the silence returned.

I was confused and had a headache. I didn't want to talk to this woman anymore but I couldn't hang up on her.

"Maybe we want different things," she said. "Maybe I want more."

Was she trying to end this? Was she trying to end us? My brain pounded. Why was she so difficult? Where did she exist? In some future? I couldn't take it anymore.

"I'm going to go now," I said, and she hung up.

24

My eyes burned and I knew I wouldn't be able to fall asleep. But I wanted the day to end. I wanted the next morning to come. I wanted the next chance that sunrise would bring.

Possibly by getting good and drunk I could find sleep but that would mean passing through the stages of melancholy and anger. I wasn't ready for the possibility of tears. I opened the back porch door and looked out. The rain was coming down in big drops, straight down. Maybe it would flood. I looked out through the darkness but couldn't see the river.

Ginger walked up behind me and then slid to the floor with a thud. Her air rushed out of her lungs. It was such a defeated sound that I had to laugh. I bent over and stroked her head. She raised one eyebrow seeming to demand an answer. Possibly she only wanted reassurance. But I had neither to give. They were things in short supply.

"If it weren't so wet we could go for a walk," I said to her. The word walk hadn't even twitched her. Possibly she had her own regrets, her own demons.

I went to the closet and pulled out my rubber-bottomed boots. Sitting on the couch I laced them and looked and the prone dog. She still hadn't moved. Maybe she needed more sunlight. I'd heard of people becoming depressed at the lack of sun. Something to do with vitamins, I thought. But I'm not sure that was applicable to dogs. Do you need a sense of self to become depressed? Is it the fruit of consciousness? Some days I wished I had studied some of that quackery, psychology.

Boots on, I grabbed an old Army coat, my dad's jacket. I put a wool crusher on my head and went down the stairs. I drove back towards town through the rain. The stoplights were not yet flashing. I looked at my watch and to my surprise it was only 10:45.

The factory was obviously dark. Only the mercury-vapor lights were awake, creating small circles of blue-white light at the corners of the buildings. That was where the rain was really visible, in the light. The parking lots were almost completely covered by the storm water. The islands and archipelagos we tried to navigate by were one by one swallowed by this new sea.

Driving past the office building I noticed some lights that were still on but as I got closer I noticed the cleaning service van. For a moment I hoped for a scotch with the boss. Justin Bullough would invite me into his office and ask my opinion of everything factory. But not tonight. Only two middle aged Guatemalan women roamed the offices pushing vacuums.

I didn't make it to the cemetery. Instead, I pulled into the parking lot in front of Emily's apartment. Her kitchen light shown through the pulled curtains. In the past I would have sat in the truck for one or two hours staring at the door and those curtains. But I got out of the truck and marched right up to the door and knocked. My heart raced like mad and I thought I might black out. I prayed she wasn't at home just to spare myself, but she was.

The door opened without a chain or a "who's there?". There was no peephole. She opened the door and stared into my face without expression. I don't know if she expected me or possibly someone else. Her void swallowed any hope I had of saying something. We stood there looking at each other. I couldn't talk. I knew I should say something but I had no idea what.

"Yes?" she asked.

"I feel terrible, Emily. I love you and want you to be happy." I wanted to be happy too, but I didn't say that. "I'm sorry for anything I might have done… Can I come in?"

She moved to the side and I walked in. Emily shut the door behind me.

"You look like an idiot," she said. I looked down at my high-water bell bottomed Navy pants and my rubber boots. I went over and sat down on her love seat.

"Can I stay here tonight?" I asked. She said I could. I grew a little more excited and said it would be fun, new. Her face clamped down and I held back any more words. She said that she was just about to go to bed and just had to wash her face. I moved off towards her bed, leaving my jacket on the small couch. Before she entered the bathroom I asked her again why she didn't like my pants.

"They're dorky," she said and closed the door.

I made my way to her bed thinking what a horrible word, so ungraceful. I didn't mind her not liking the pants as much as I minded her summation of them. But I was cautious of being critical. She was entitled to her own opinions, I reminded myself. I undressed, got into her bed and waited for the woman I loved to join me. In a short time she did, wearing a pale blue nightgown. It was enough to show off her delicious curves yet tell me not to touch. Normally we did not wear clothes to bed. I wasn't. But I knew she must have a purpose in her dress. I told myself resolutely that I wouldn't do anything that might come across as sexual. My erection refused to be a team player, but what could I expect?

Emily climbed in next to me and shut off the light. She

lay on her back and kept her hands to herself. I rolled over and kissed her goodnight. Surely she felt my penis against her thigh but I couldn't help that. I really couldn't. Her breathing slowed and she actually fell asleep. I thought of her vibrator in the bed stand next to my head and wondered what she looked like when using it. What did she think of? How often did she? These were torturous thoughts. Eventually I also fell asleep.

25

As I slept the valve holding my guts down malfunctioned and stomach fluid spilled into my throat. Filled with bile, and panic, I woke trying to swallow the corrosives back down. I went to the kitchen and drank a glass of water and then a glass of milk but none of it helped. The fluid no longer threatened to drown me, but the acrid taste was in my throat, nose and mouth. I fixed a piece of toast and ate it in big chunks, trying not to chew. I wanted the jagged edges of the toast to scrape away the residue. But that didn't work, either.

Eventually, I went back into Emily's bedroom and lay next to her. She was sleeping with a feminine snore and had not woke. I didn't find sleep again. I watched the clock tick over and over until four.

I got up and left. I scooped my clothes off the floor and dressed by the streetlight shining through her kitchen window. The world was still dark. Rain blew in sheets. At least something was constant. I tied the laces on my boots and locked the door handle behind me. I wondered if the grumble of my truck would wake her.

With the defrost and wipers going at full I turned left out

of Emily's parking lot and continued toward the cemetery. The gates were open and I drove in. I wound around to the back and said, "Hey Devil," as I passed his stump. The rain hid his face. I stopped by my Grandmother's grave. I turned off my lights but didn't get out.

"This seems serious, Gram. I think it might actually flood. What do you think I should do?" I sat there for a little while and then looked at my watch. It's blue light lit up the cab. "Yeah, you're right. I should get to work."

Driving out of the cemetery I had to creep across a large pond that had formed in a low spot. Head stones stuck out of the water like shipwrecks. I thought of the dead floating against the top of their cells as if they wanted out. The water was almost to my doorjamb. I could hear my pipes go temporarily under water. Wup, wup, wup. Blurp, blurp. Wup, wup.

Pulling on the road I pushed the accelerator down and drove a long alternating fish tail through three gears. I'm sure people living along that stretch weren't as soothed as I was by the small block roar but sometimes you have to take care of yourself first. As I passed Emily's apartment I loaded the carburetor and then pulled off the accelerator sharply causing the truck to backfire. I smiled and barely slowed through the sleeping town not bothering a glance as I went through the flashing yellow lights.

In my driveway, I slid through a U-turn and sprayed gravel against the closed down service station. I killed the engine but she ran on and on finally stopping with a hiss. That concerned me. "What the fuck?" I asked aloud.

But to tell the truth I felt good as I climbed the old

wooden stairs. I felt like dancing, although I didn't know why. I realized that I felt better than I would have if Emily had fucked me the night before. If she would have seized me and made me a prisoner of her desires it would have only produced confusion. But as I opened the back door and was passed on the landing by a full bladder dog I was confident in my knowledge. It had taken me thirty-five years to learn a couple of things in life, but these few I knew well and could count on and navigate by.

I didn't bother making coffee. I changed into a fresh pair of greens and laced up my boots. Ginger clawed back up the back stairs and I let her in. She passed me and collapsed on the rug. I went over and stroked her wet fur. Her eyes looked droopy and she breathed heavier than usual. "Are you sick?" I asked. I checked her food and water and then petted her some more. She seemed tired. Maybe she's depressed, I thought. I would come home after work and spend some quality time with her. A dog needs more than a rug to lie on. I turned on the radio for her and put a new rawhide bone in her food dish for her to find later, a surprise gift. Then I locked the door behind me and descended the stairs.

26

A different world greeted me at work. Two large dump trucks were spilling dirt along the far edge of the parking lot. They were beautiful machines, shiny paint, chrome and running lights. A portable generator attached to a light pole sprayed its artificial sun into the rain towards the river. Turnbull walked through the scene dressed in rubber boots and a yellow rain suit. I got one of the last remaining parking spots against the shop wall. The rest of the workers would have to park in the neighborhoods to the south, as half our lot was now a construction site. I walked through the water towards Turnbull.

"What's going on?" I asked, right hand shielding my eyes from the light and rain.

"We're going to build a dike. Another storm is moving down from Lake Michigan and that will put the river over all the banks," he said, and as if to emphasize his point, a front end loader rumbled around the corner of the shipping building. It put its bucket down and acted like a bulldozer pushing the gravel from our parking lot into the new dirt dumped by the trucks toward the advancing river.

The rain soaked my shoulders and hair. I liked seeing the construction equipment work. I wanted to drive something, anything. "What do you want me to do?" I asked.

"I want you to make 02s, 03s and 04s. We have these guys until noon." He pointed at the loader that was reversing for another pass. "But after that we might need people off the floor to work out here."

"I'll do it," I said, eager for a change.

Turnbull gave me the nod then I walked towards the time clock and the coming workday.

I hadn't thought about Emily. The lights were on and the presses were running. As I put my first piece of aluminum in her image came to me. What would I do? What was even possible? Did we exist in her concept of love? Most definitely not, I thought.

Maybe it's not possible. Maybe nothing is possible between two people. Even the best marriages, those without the mutual bitterness, seem more like co-conspiracies than loves. Where could I go to get applicable advice on such matters? What book could I read? You couldn't go to a professional unless you believed in their beliefs. One had to know the building blocks. What is your concept of the soul? What is your take on happiness and what worth do you ascribe to it? Do you believe in the subconscious? What school did you go to? What school are you of?

If you didn't ask these questions then the advice given was surely to be more evangelism than technical reason. Surround yourself with people that believe how you wish to believe! Otherwise talk to some foreigner. Talk to a German if you don't speak the language because the conversation will be just as valid.

27

During the breaks crowds of workers walked into the changing landscape. Berms were growing along the river's edge. I couldn't understand why they pushed all the dirt and gravel out of the parking lot. It was a hole now deeper than the lowest edge of the berm. Maybe it was motivation. If we didn't stop the flood at the gates all would be lost. Or possibly it was a secondary line, a pond to catch the blow by, to contain the rain and runoff. It was still raining, harder than before.

We went back to work. We worked on with a sense of purpose. This is good, I thought to myself. Hot damn, this is really living. Can't you taste it boys? This is the marrow. The only thing missing was a good fuck and a steak sandwich. I knew where to get the sandwich. And unfortunately I also knew where to get the fuck.

To my discredit I had never noticed the tilt of the land before. Now such things gained great importance. I don't know if I had thought everything was level, but now I could clearly see that the long shipping building was a couple feet below the main factory and the weld shop a good five feet above that on the slope that led straight into the neighborhoods.

A lot of people were walking around and not a lot of work was getting done. On three occasions other than my breaks I walked away from the presses and went to look at the water or the trucks or the other people looking at the water or the trucks. By lunch the loader had disappeared and then shortly after that the rumble of the dumps left us as well. They were promised elsewhere, a middle school I later found out.

The bank they had built looked formidable. I was impressed. A dirt berm formed a large "J" with the curve facing up river and the tail tying into the slope east of the factory. It was a sound defense. It gave protection for up to five feet more of flood height. Any more than that and the river would flood us through the neighborhoods and rush in through our rear. But there is only so much you can do. The river was already up ten feet and another five was a good insurance. One more storm was known of and after that… Well, we would have to see.

The odd thing about a crisis is that nothing changes. The world could be on fire and you still want a beer and a short skirt still made the blood flow.

28

Back at the presses Adam was gone. I couldn't be mad at him for something I had just done, walking away from the job.

We weren't going to get our numbers, but with the back stock sitting over in shipping no one was worried. I worked at a leisurely pace thinking of everything. I thought of Emily and would get so cramped up that I had to shout out loud. Then I thought of the river and of work.

Adam came back with his eyebrows raised and the corners of his lips turned up. No one loved being the first to know something like Adam. He really could have been something if he would have put any effort into it. He was a natural detective or spy. Anonymous and ubiquitous, he could walk by, start a conversation and record all that was said before the talkers even knew they were talking. He was such a nobody that you didn't realize that you were answering someone else's questions. But I didn't like to stoke his fire, so I didn't ask him anything when he returned. I didn't ask him where he had been—my gentlest reprimand.

He turned to his press and put in an aluminum blank but couldn't even make it through a push of the triggers.

"Guess what I heard," he said.

"It's raining," I said.

"No, man. I'm serious."

"It's going to flood," I said.

"Oh, shut up. I'll just tell you. They're going to make us fill sand bags. A sandbag machine was just brought in and starting tomorrow morning everyone is going to be out there in the rain." He nodded his head at me as if by agreeing with himself he would convince me of something. Look, two people know it's true.

"I'm not doing it," he said, finally. It wasn't what I was expecting.

"Why?" I asked.

"I'm not paid to fill sand bags. I'm not paid to get wet. This is my job and it's all I've signed up for. Let some other fool stand out there and drown."

"You're afraid of drowning?"

"I just don't want to work outside in the rain." Adam crossed his arms. He was set in his opinion, sure as a teenage girl.

"I'm going to work out there if they let me. Fuck! You're getting paid either way and we do this every day. Outside is a different world. Granted the weather isn't too nice but it's healthy and exciting. Look at the river. This doesn't happen everyday. Shit Adam enjoy life for once."

"I don't know. It sure is wet... and cold." But his mind was changing.

"Just think, in a couple of years when we're all sitting around remembering the flood what are you going to say? What did you do during it? Watch? Work you same job or man the barricade with the rest of us?" I didn't exactly know who "us" was but the one thing Adam hated worse than not knowing was being left out. He played softball, very badly, just so he could be part of the conversations Monday at lunch.

"What about the line?" Adam asked softly, almost confused.

"Shipping is full of parts. There's no better time for a flood. Shit, we might be able to do both. Think of the overtime!" I mentioned that just to rattle him. Adam didn't like working a minute over forty hours. He thought it a crime that any man should have to work more than the sacred forty. Eight hours work, eight hours play and eight hours sleep was his mantra. I think he slept by stopwatch.

Adam's head began bobbing again. A conclusion was reached. At least that was how it appeared from the outside.

"Maybe... Turnbull is having a meeting with everyone first thing tomorrow. I'll listen to what he has to say," he said.

29

After work, I went upstairs and opened the door. Ginger was lying on the rug where I had left her. She looked up but didn't shove me out of the way like usual. I dropped to my knees and stroked her head. I asked her what was wrong but she just moved her eyes. Her breathing was short and fast. Ginger had been sick before, dog flus and colds, but never had I seen her so docile. I looked around but there wasn't any vomit or shit, nothing. She had worked her new bone over some. As I was playing detective the dog got slowly to her feet and made her way down the stairs to do her business. Another day of without improvement and I would take her to the vet.

Emily's car pulled into the lot. My two loves slowly climbed the stairs. Immediately I asked Emily for her medical opinion. She thought Ginger looked tired, but the dog's tail still thumped at the sight of the full-breasted woman and that was enough for Emily. I wished she was as gracious with me. Look at my erection like a wagging tail. Instead, I offered her some tea.

We sat across the table from each other. The tea steeped and so did we. Emily wanted words and I wanted… I'm not sure what I wanted. The only thing I could have wanted I gave up wanting a long time ago.

"It's really going to flood," I said.

It was all Emily needed, an opening. You could almost hear the rush of air escape her as all that was pent up came forward.

"It's been flooding. For a week now people have been losing homes, cars. Where have you been?" She gripped her mug with both hands.

"What I mean is, it's going to get serious. All that stuff lost is just stuff. They can get more. But now the river looks like it's going to push through the south side of town. You should see the wall we have around the plant. It's impressive. Tomorrow we're going to start sand bagging, then we'll see what the river can do."

"You're only concerned now because it might touch your life. You have no idea of anyone else."

She was becoming annoying. I wasn't guilty of solipsism. I only meant that possessions were one thing whereas a job was something different, and more. The ranking, as far as I could rank things, went: life, work, stuff. But I didn't want to talk about any of this. I didn't want to hear about heirlooms and wedding pictures. That was sad enough, but seeing a man without a paycheck was much worse.

Instead, I said, "I don't see you out there handing out blankets with the Red Cross."

Emily pushed her mug away from her. "How would you know what I do when I'm out of your sight?" She pulled the mug back and watched the steam boil out of it. She talked in a low voice. "You have no empathy, let alone sympathy for anyone. You don't even know how bad things have got between us." She looked up. Her eyes were shining. I didn't know what to say so I didn't say anything. She continued, "I don't know how much more of this I can take. Shit Warrell, you haven't even asked what's going to happen when I graduate. I graduate in December, by the way." Her last sentence was firm and hard.

I knew when she was to graduate. I knew her options, or at least thought I did. She would tell me when she knew, when she had made a decision. I had thought of it but I said, "you do?" Before she could reply I got up from the table and went over to the dog. I petted her head and asked Emily if she thought Ginger was sick. It must have been some final straw in that woman's head because she pushed her chair back, grabbed her purse and stormed out, making sure to slam the screen door. I was still looking Ginger in the eyes and it angered me that Emily's noise upset the dog. "If she had a job she'd know what they're worth," I said to the dog.

30

That night I watched two cowboy movies on the couch with the dog. I drank scotch and gave Ginger some turkey from the fridge. Looking back now I think that was the best spent night of my life. I mean as regards quality. Gradually, I got drunk and tired. Then I carried the dog to bed and we slept together on that old bed like we had done a thousand times before. When I woke she was dead.

As I made my way to the kitchen in the half-light of the morning I saw her on her spot on the rug. I didn't need to see the pool of blood next to her muzzle to know she had gone. There was something in the air, a feeling. I walked past her and began to make coffee. As I poured the grounds in the filter my eyes fogged over and by the time I flipped the switch my hands were shaking.

I went over and knelt next to her dead body. I touched her and the tears came full. I wept long and hard. I wept like a woman you see on TV weeping over some third world tragedy. When I could breathe again day had lit the world. I poured some coffee and cried over Ginger a few more times.

What do you do with a dead dog? If I were still at my parent's house up in Michigan I would drag her behind the barn and bury her with all my other dogs. But I wasn't in Michigan and I didn't own this land. I thought of the woods across the road but it was too wet to dig anything. Ginger wouldn't want to be buried in Ohio ground anyway, I thought. She had come down here with me and would surely want to return. I knew the vet cremated dead animals. I decided to take her there so I could take the ashes back north.

In the toolbox of my truck I kept a blue tarp for covering loads. Pulling Ginger's body to that tarp, I alternated between laughs and moans. It was ridiculous and sad. A dog that was so good shouldn't be treated so matter-of-factly. I apologized again and again, then closed the bundle with two bungee cords.

My day was just beginning, yet I felt very tired. I changed for work then carried the dog down the rain slick steps for the last time. If I fell and broke my neck we would be together again, I said to the heavy tarp. But I couldn't handle the shame of being found with my best friend wrapped up that way. I had to get things done. I made it to the wet earth and momentarily debated putting her in the cab with me but she liked the bed and I put her there. Ginger was a dumb dog. Let us not forget that because she is dead.

We drove into town to the vet's. I pulled in the driveway and looked at my watch. It was 6:43. I was late for work. A sign above a button next to the door said, "ring for emergency". I didn't ring. I was sure I was too late. I just wanted this man to burn up my dog and make her transportable.

A light shone from the kitchen window and I crossed the lawn toward it. The vet was at his breakfast table eating cereal with his wife. I knocked on the window and he motioned that he would meet me at the clinic door. He did and we talked about Ginger's last week and he guessed it was congestive heart failure.

"Nothing really to be done," he said, although that may have just been to make me feel better. Truthful or not it was nice to have a name put on it.

I carried the dog in and he said I could keep the tarp if I wanted. Looking at the bundle I knew what it was and almost broke down again. I asked if I could come back for it and he said I could. I never did.

31

I got in my truck alone and headed for work. What was done was done and now I had something else to concentrate on. I expected to see the dirt bank crowded with people passing sandbags when I pulled into the lot but the wall was empty. Our parking had disappeared under the TVA project and only ten cars lined the factory wall. It was strictly a bosses bunch. I had to park three blocks away in the neighborhood and walk back down through the rain. I didn't have a raincoat with me, just a blue mechanics jacket. But I didn't have rubber boots either and somehow this made it better. You don't want jealousy between body parts.

Inside the plant all presses were empty and silent. No one milled around the floor. I guessed that the meeting was still on and made my way at a trot towards the break room. The break room was big enough to fit everyone in for a meeting but not large enough for anything else. You couldn't move an elbow without jabbing a coworker. A few that feared crowds spilled out the door toward maintenance. Of course Adam was there. I slid in next to him leaning against the wall. We could hear people asking questions inside the break room and Turnbull answering. Someone asked about overtime. Always, the questions about overtime.

"Where you been?" Adam asked me in a low tone just above a whisper. It reminded me of being in school.

"My dog died last night. I had to take her to the vet."

"Aw, no. I'm sorry." Adam looked me in the eye and I thought he was genuinely sorry. Emotion fed emotion and I thought I might cry.

"Don't say that! You'll make me ball like a little bitch," I said and elbowed him. Adam seemed to understand and mouthed the word "sorry" again before turning his head to listen to the meeting. The sound of chairs sliding came from the open door and then the voices became full. The meeting was over. People began filing out of the room. Adam and I strayed over toward maintenance.

Jack came out of the room, saw us and walked over. "Looks like we're together again," he said. We followed the crowd toward the locker room. People pulled coats and boots from lockers and from bags stored above. Then we went out into the rain. It didn't take long for my feet to get wet. I looked around. Most people had dressed for the job. Adam came through the crowd. Even he had gardening boots and a cheap plastic poncho.

"If your dog died why'd you take her to the vet?" he asked.

"Cremation," I said.

Adam nodded his head and we walked together toward the yellow sand bag machine. It was a simple idea. Dirt was fed into a hopper that was connected to three chutes. A bag was placed around the neck of the chute and then a door to the hopper was opened with a foot pedal. A crowd was gathering around the machine. A stack of shovels lay on a pallet next to three pallets of empty sand bags. Some of the shovels were new and Adam grabbed three. Jack and I thanked him.

Some of the knuckleheads from shipping began pitching shovel loads of dirt from the berm into the hopper. It was twice the work of filling a bag at ground level but they wanted to see the machine in action. When enough dirt was in they filled a couple of bags. It was a slick operation. Obviously the hopper was intended to be filled by a front-end loader or something with a bucket but none was around. The bags had ties attached to them and were finished off with nice bows. There was a little discussion about the proper knot but the conclusion was that it didn't matter.

Jack, Adam and I were standing in the rain with one foot each on our shovels the handles grasped with both hand at the top. Jack's was mid chest. Adam's was in front of his mouth whereas mine was at my adam's apple. We turned to see the commotion coming, a storm within a storm. Turnbull led the Bulloughs, the engineering department and to my disgust Sean.

"Knock that off!" Turnbull shouted and everyone moved away from the machine in obedience. "That's not for you. The county is on the way to pick that up. We're going to do this the old fashioned way," he said with a smile that elicited groans and laughs depending on back health. One thing was certain, Turnbull had the system already worked out and we were going to follow it. It was useless to volunteer ideas when he had his mind set. Only the fact that he was usually right made the situation tolerable.

Turnbull began dividing the labor. The strongest were at either ends of the line and would rotate. The filling and placing were the most strenuous. The middle of the line was stocked with the elderly, the female and the infirmed. Adam and I were sent to fill but Jack was sent to place.

About twenty minutes later a county dump truck with a

small equipment trailer rumbled into the mud of our parking lot. The driver neatly swung the trailer around and backed it square against the sand bag machine. He got out and after he was finished giving us disapproving looks he tilted the bed of the trailer and hauled the machine aboard using a hand come-along. He secured it with a couple of straps and then splashed his way out.

We set to work. There was about fifty of us and although we hadn't started till nearly 9:30 by dinner break we had done a pitiful amount. We were working on the back slope of the western edge and all our slipping and sloshing had amounted to was about ten feet of bagged line. It was discouraging. Adam and I started grumbling. That is what we did inside and it came naturally to fall on our usual habits out in the rain.

At five to eleven, Turnbull came out and told us all to take an hour lunch but didn't tell us why. Although no on talked about it everyone knew that only a hot lunch would get us through another half of rain, river and work.

32

We crowded the little restaurant and the coat rack quickly became a coat pile. By the time I got there all the edge tables were taken and the middle tables had been pushed together to form one long table. I was waved to the far end by Mario and ended up sitting next to Sean. It was the price of bad parking. Some men had ordered beers but I was too soaked to think of anything but coffee. Rochelle was pouring behind the bar and I whistled a short peel that made her turn. I motioned the one more and she smiled back and nodded.

It was only after I had the warm mug in my hands that

I could hear the conversation around me. Sean and Mario were talking about their basements. They both lived in the same neighborhood. Instead of taking orders Rochelle just started bringing sandwiches. She would come from the kitchen with a tray and say, "Who wants pork?" Hands would go up and shouts would go out. It was more efficient than treating us like individuals. No one seemed to mind. And even though I was one of the last to arrive I was one of the first to eat.

Sean turned to me with a full mouth and said, "It was nice of you to show up."

I looked around the table and I saw Adam's ears perk up. He was sitting four chairs away on the other side of the table. But Sean failed at his attempt. I was too tired to be baited. I was too tired even to tell him to fuck off.

Mario tried to diffuse what he misinterpreted by saying, "I'm sorry to hear about Ginger." I furrowed my brows questioning how he knew and Mario pointed towards Adam. I looked at Adam but he turned away from my glance and took a bite of his sandwich. I didn't need him running around telling people to be nice to me.

Later, as we grabbed our coats, Sean came over to me.

"Need a pair of boots?" he asked.

"No. I've got a pair," I said.

"I meant a rubber pair. I've got extra. I bought all they had at the store yesterday."

"How much?" I asked.

"Ten bucks."

"How much did you pay for them?"

"Ten bucks," Sean said.

I doubted him. He probably paid seven. Sean was a real go-getter, and an ass to boot. Nothing would have pleased me more that to tell him to go piss up a rope. But I was tired and my feet were so wet they hurt. I reached in my wallet and gave him a ten-dollar bill. We walked to his car. Sean drove a pitiful little sedan, newish, no character at all. The man lacked any style. I figured he must have been squirreling away all his money in stocks and real estate. I bet he owned a fleet of rental houses. He would be a perfect slumlord. He was a perfect short stop.

Sean opened his trunk and a row of boot stood heels up so you could read the size. He did buy the whole stock. I pulled out a pair of elevens and thanked him. He said he was sorry about my dog and I said so was I.

33

I parked in the same neighborhood spot and walked. Again, I got back to the lot a little later than everyone else. There was a surprise waiting for us. The engineers and toolmakers along with the welding department had made us our own sandbagging machine. They had even painted it in the company blue and stenciled "The River Buster" in yellow. I hurried through the standing water and joined the crowd around the machine. It was almost exactly the same. The hinges in the foot pedal were a little different but ours might have even been better.

To cap it all off Justin Bullough came roaring into the

lot driving his old farm tractor outfitted with a bucket that ran off the PTO. That was what the snickers and the early lunch had been about. The hour lunch was probably only to let the paint set.

We broke into our teams and got ready to fill the first bags. Bullough ran the old tractor and filled the hopper to capacity. Then as we filled the bags he waited with the bucked lowered for us to throw the finished product in. This load was then carried to the far end of the berm and was dumped for Jack's team to place. It was a smooth operation, although with another tractor there would have been no pauses. No one complained though as these breaks gave you a chance to stretch your back.

The old, the infirmed and the female were sent back inside to their regular jobs. The middle line was eliminated. Only fifteen of us remained in the weather. The rain never ceased and the river was reported to be rising by one inch every two hours.

We worked until it got too dark to see. The generator powered light pole could either illuminate the fillers or the stackers but not both. We knocked off at 7:45. It was only then that I realized that I had forgotten to punch in. The payroll ladies would search me out later before payday. I would square it with them then.

34

It wasn't until I was pointed back home that I remembered that I was returning to an empty house. The thought erased my sense of accomplishment. Our fight with the river disappeared and sadness returned. Luckily, I was tired. I was bone worn and ready for a shower and bed.

Ginger's half-emptied bowl stabbed me over and over again until I felt drained of all my blood. I had made it up the stairs without looking at her chain tied to the old willow. I ignored that she didn't push past me as I opened the door. But as I closed that door and looked at her dish I was done. The full weight of my sadness returned.

I went to the kitchen and poured a water glass half full of bourbon and drank it down in three gulps. I had to tense every muscle in my body to make the whiskey settle. The pain subsided into a burn and I kicked off my boots and stripped as I walked towards the shower. As I waited for the water to turn hot I thought of taking another drink but decided against it. I didn't want to get drunk. I wanted to get to bed.

I let the water run over my head and neck and felt the whiskey grab hold of my insides. Warm inside and out. I wished for a chair. I could have spent hours in that steam but finally I felt the water change and knew it would soon be cold. After toweling off I pulled a red one-piece union suit and wool socks before racing around the house and turning off all the lights.

As I lay under the blankets finally warm and dry I realized that it was not even half past nine. There was only one thing that would have made me feel better and I didn't know where that was to be found. I fell asleep in the silence.

35

The phone woke me and for a moment I didn't know where I was, what time it was or even what day. I shuffled my wool socks over to the phone and picked it up. I did this all without thinking who might be calling. Of course it was Emily.

"Hello?" I said, but it was answered only by silence. "Hello?" I said again.

"What are you doing?" she finally said in a quiet voice.

"I was sleeping but now I'm not."

"Alone?" she asked. That made me angry.

"What do you want?" I demanded.

"I need a book I left out there, for school. It's on the coffee table."

I looked. It was. I told her to come out and then hung up. I unlocked the back door and then went back to bed but sleep wouldn't return. Thoughts of Ginger came by to see if they were still potent. A little of the sharpness was already beginning to dull. The fading of the sadness made me feel worse than better. Was I forgetting, or was I just callous?

I wondered what had happened with Emily. Her bitterness didn't seem explainable. I wondered if it was a young woman's trick. The possibility made me angry and I had to talk myself out of it so I wasn't furious when she finally climbed the stairs.

Slowly the warmth of the bed returned and soothed me to a near sleep. I doubted she was even going to come. Maybe I had been too rude. It was possible. I didn't like being woke up and when tired I could be mean. I thought back but discounted the idea. Who knew what guided that woman? I doubt even she did.

I was almost asleep when her wheels touched the gravel. I heard each step as she climbed the stairs. I heard her try the knob and then creak the door as she pushed it open.

"Why is it so dark in here?" Emily called. "Where are you?"

I didn't say anything and I heard her pick up the book from the coffee table. Her footsteps continued on to the door of my bedroom.

"Are you asleep?" she asked.

"No," I said.

She came into the room and sat on the foot of the bed. Her shoulders slumped forward. I could just see her from the light coming through the window. She must be looking at her shoes, I thought. I doubted she could see anything yet. Not enough time for her eyes to adjust. Then she straightened up.

"There's some other things I should get," she said. And then, "Where's Ginger?"

"She died this morning," I said from underneath the blankets. "Congestive heart failure. That was why she had been so tired, so winded lately. She was drowning in her own blood. We watched some movies last night and then she died. I took her to the vet's this morning to be cremated."

Silence. And then a little sob. Why is she crying? I wondered. Emily didn't say anything and didn't make a show of her emotions. She just sat at the end of the bed and I could see her shoulders move up and down. I watched her. And then she laid back and hugged me through my blankets. I looked at her through the corner of my eye but I doubted she could see me do that. Emily pressed her face against my cheek and I could feel the warm wetness. “I’m sorry,” she said. I wondered, for what?

Emily lay holding me that way for a while and then asked if she could join me under the blankets. I said that she didn’t need to ask permission but she didn’t say anything in return. She slid under with all her clothes on and soon it was too hot. She laughed at my long johns but followed the buttons down from my neck to my dick. She let her hand lie on it.

I hoped for something that did not come so I undressed her and then I undressed myself. Emily gave me sympathy. She gave me tenderness. She gave me what she would have wanted in the same situation.

36

I woke at a little past three. Emily slept with her ass to me in a pile of her hair. I petted her hips and pressed against her but I new something wasn’t there. Something was gone. I got out of bed, dressed and pulled the door shut behind me.

Rain still, heavy. I drove to town and as I crossed the bridge it looked as if I could drag my hand through the river water over the side. It was high and fast.

I stopped at the gas station and bought some coffee that could have been from yesterday. The lady behind the counter must have thought I was ending my night instead of beginning my day. I bought a second coffee. Back in my truck, I turned right into the neighborhood instead of left toward the factory.

Driving down the street I looked both ways, at every house until I spotted the one I wanted and then pulled to the curb in front of it. It was a small one-story house, the kind built in the fifties from a catalogue plan, a forerunner of the modular. The house didn't fit with the other Craftsmans on the block but must have been built on a sold off double lot. Sure enough to the right was a Victorian. Poor bastards must have run out of money and had to sell off their yard.

I didn't go to the front door but guessed windows by their curtains. Finally I pounded on the window with the Buffalo Bill design. It took a moment but the lights came on and then the curtains parted. Adam's face, eyes puffed to slits, a wedge of hair standing on end, peered out through the window. He struggled with the pane and then raised it.

"What's wrong?" he asked.

"You don't owe anyone money, do you?"

"What are you talking about?"

"You just opened the curtains. I could have been anyone." I took a sip from the Styrofoam cup in my hand and looked around for assassins.

"Warrell, what do you want? What time is it?"

I lit up my watch and said, "Three-thirty. Time to go to work."

Adam sighed. "Oh, you've got to be kidding me." He walked back to his bed and sat on the edge. He wasn't much of a sight in his underwear and t-shirt.

I looked down and saw a spigot. I stood on it, grabbed the windowsill and raised my chin above it. "Come on. I need your help." Adam was obviously disgruntled. He picked up his watch off the table next to his bed and checked the time for himself and then told me to go around back but to be quiet so as not to wake his mother.

"You live with your mom?" I asked with a broad smile.

"Do you want my help or not?"

I wasn't in a position to argue so I did as I was told. The back porch light came on and then the door opened. I handed Adam the coffee I had bought him and he said thanks. I sat at the kitchen table while he got dressed. The kitchen looked like someone had decorated decades ago and decided to let it ride. Yellow paint and green glass. I liked it. It had tenderness to it. And then I heard another voice.

"Adam? What are you doing?" It was his mother's voice coming from behind a closed door, from her bedroom. I laughed to myself. "But hun it's not even four," she protested. That's where he gets it, I thought to myself.

Adam went to her door and explained about the flood and the dike we were making and the old woman sounded like it was the first she had heard of any of this. Adam told her that a "co-worker" was here to pick him up. "Well, just a minute," she said and I knew that she was getting out of bed. And sure enough a minute later Adam's mom came into the kitchen wrapped in a quilted robe with flower print. She was a large woman but seemed happy to have visitors even at that hour.

I rose and introduced myself. "Actually, I'm Adam's

boss," I said.

"Oh, I see," she said but I didn't know what she meant. "Well do you boys want something to eat? I have some biscuits I could warm up. Gravy, too."

Adam came into the kitchen dressed for the weather. He looked at me and I smiled as wide as I could. He took off his raincoat and sat down. No wonder his ass was big, I thought.

Mrs. Smith whipped us up a splendid breakfast, four biscuits apiece and coffee refills before we left the house. I thanked myself that I hadn't tried to stir Mario. I thanked Mrs. Smith for the hospitality and then we left into the rain.

As we walked across the lawn Adam turned to me and said, "That's my mom."

"She's nice," I said.

"I suppose," he said. We got in the truck and drove for work. "Since my dad died I couldn't imagine moving out. I want to but I'm all she's got." I didn't say anything. We drove on and then pulled into the dark factory lot. "No one's here?" Adam said, his voice rising.

"We must be the first," I said as I parked against the pressroom wall.

Adam protested but it was too late for him to go back to bed and I wasn't going to drive him home. He should have thought about all that before he got out of bed, I said. But you knocked on my window, he peeled. You didn't have to answer. When he got used to the idea of actually being at work he started worrying about getting paid. He wouldn't take my word that I would pass our times on to the girls in payroll. To soothe him, I unlocked the door to the locker room and shut off the alarm. Adam was impressed that I had a key and the code. We punched in and he was appeased.

37

First I started the generator and gave us light over the sand bag machine. The foot pedals were closed all night and a foot of water had gathered in the hopper. I pushed the pedal and released it. More water. Justin Bullough's tractor was parked under the awning of the shipping dock and I went and got it started. While I did all this Adam stood in the middle of the great parking lot puddle and waited. You could only wake this man so much. The old tractor rumbled into the rain and soon we were tying ties and stacking bags.

I liked driving Bullough's tractor. It was similar to my father's. We never had a bucket although we talked often about getting one. A blade dragged from the three-point hitch was good enough for pushing and pulling snow, my dad thought. But using that bucket I realized what we had been missing. It was simple to operate. One control raised and lowered the arm while another tilted the bucket forward and back. I tried not to let Adam see how much fun I was having as he stood hands to his sides in the pouring rain.

After I filled the hopper we loaded the bucket with new sandbags. The early morning is hard on thought and we didn't see our fault until I raised the bucket and take the load to the wall. Instead of raising the bags the hydraulics whined and raised the back wheels. "Whoa Nellie!" I shouted. It seemed like the thing to say. Adam's mouth slacked open and I worried he might drown. As I hung there pressed against the steering wheel I had a moment of memory, of blood history. My uncle Tom died in a tractor accident. Actually he was my father's cousin but I called him uncle. He was dragging a plow when he hooked a rock, a big rock, and rode the tractor right over on himself. The power kept moving but the wheels stopped so the tractor moved, like closing a stapler.

But my problem was just too much weight up front. I lowered the wheels back to the earth and water. I gave her one more try with a little more engine just to hear the old tractor snort but to no avail. Weight was weight. Adam was still staring at me with his mouth open.

"She's real close," I said. "Let's just take off a few bags."

We unloaded ten, then with Adam riding along on the rear we made our way into the darkness and rain to the wall. I tried raising the bucket higher to drop the bags up the berm but the wheels came up again. Adam screamed like a girl and I set the wheels back down. I tilted the bucket down and shook out a dozen bags and then was able to set the rest in a pile at the top. Adam and I then loaded the dropped portion back into the bucket and I set them with the rest.

It was still too dark to work without the generator powered light so we left our staged pile and went back to fill more bags. I refilled the hopper. Adam and I then set back to filling the bucket with completed bags.

Just before five Turnbull's pickup came through the water towards us. We were almost ready for another shuttle to the wall. This time we weren't loading so many. Turnbull parked his truck and got out. He walked toward us but we kept working as if we hadn't noticed a thing. Adam and I didn't have to say anything to each other. We knew what the other was thinking.

"What do you guys think you're doing?" Turnbull asked.

"Filling sand bags," Adam said. I smiled down at the bag I was swinging towards the bucket. Turnbull looked out towards the river. I stood and stretched my back.

"We already put a mess of bags on the wall. It was too dark to see so we didn't place them," I said.

"What time did you get here?"

"I don't know… we had breakfast and coffee. Shit, I don't know but we punched in when we got here and been working since."

Adam stopped bagging to look at Turnbull. The light was just coming over the land. The gray of the day came slowly out of the black. The sound of the generator seemed isolated.

"Well, nice work," Turnbull said, slogging off to park his truck. The regular five o'clock shift began to fill what remained of our lot. Half the people went inside to work their usual jobs while the other half came out to help us fend off the river. The light now changed fast and soon faces were seen and groups broke off to stack and place without being told to do so. It was into six o'clock before Adam came over to me and thanked me for waking him up. I just smiled back at him. We both knew it was a victory best not relished.

38

I hadn't thought of United Tracked Truck or their needs for three straight days. Maybe I didn't have a brain for management. With Ginger's death and the sandbagging I just pushed thoughts of military spec door jambs and frame struts out of my head. I still thought of Emily and unfortunately I even thought of Rochelle. And when the truck pulled in through the water I didn't even think of it then.

The sandbag machine was working so well that three separate crews were at work stacking the supply of bags. Adam and I and two other guys from the press floor were forming a lower edge on the inside of the wall. Water would seep through the bank no matter what we did. We knew that so we were just trying to keep the wall in the same place where we started it. By afternoon the first four rows of the outside edge were beneath the river and watching them disappear renewed our determination.

The weather forecasted a chance for another storm. We were on the tail end of the third and we doubted the possibility of a forth. It had to quit sometime and the numbers were beginning to work against the clouds. Probability is probability even in nature. Not even a storm off Lake Michigan can flip seven tails in a row. But despite this we planned for all possibilities. We could continue building the wall for two or three more days. We had five feet of free board and felt confident that would outpace the creeping brown water.

Looking over the wall, it was impressive to see how much we had done. I was impressed we could work so efficiently on this new job. It felt good. Not enough to give your walk a swagger but enough to make a steak and a beer taste better.

Everything felt real. I can't remember when things felt unreal, maybe when I was young, but sometimes things feel more real. Colors become more vivid and you can hear all the sounds. You can hear an angry jay chasing off the other birds and the exhaust fan at the end of the building. You can taste the metal from the tap in your beer and smell the woman who passed five minutes before. You finally notice all the colors in the plaid shirt you've been wearing for years.

39

Dirt. Of all the things to run out of during a flood, we ran out of dirt. We no longer had enough earth to fill our bags and keep the water out. The gravel had long been scraped from out of the parking lots down to the riverbank clay and only the soggy sod was left around the sidewalks and the detached office building. I would find out later that it wasn't a shortage of dirt in Defiance county but a shortage of trucks to bring it in. All the dump trucks for a hundred miles were busy in similar operations. There was the fight to save the hospital, the middle school and even the library. This last struggle I didn't find out about until it was too late.

The rain was still coming down and the river was still coming up. We weren't in a position to have a pause in production. But we couldn't fill bags with air. When the last were tied and stacked there was a great stretching of backs. People stood smoking cigarettes in the rain. Finally Turnbull came down the line and told two out of three to return to the shop. Neither Adam nor I was picked. As Turnbull came by again I walked over to him.

"How long you think it's going to take to get more dirt?" I asked him.

"If I knew I probably would have told you."

Adam walked up to us. "You want us to go inside and do our thing?" he asked.

Turnbull looked at his watch. "You boys are taking an early lunch, I wouldn't worry about going inside." He looked over the distance of the berm. "Why don't you make sure everything is in place before you break for dinner." And then Turnbull walked away from us and toward the shipping building.

"He seems angry," Adam said. "You think he's pissed at us?"

"No," I said. "Not at us but something."

"What did he mean by, everything in place?"

"I think he gave us permission to fuck off until we were hungry. I think that early dinner comment was meant that our hunger would come sooner than later," I said.

Adam looked at his watch. "I'm hungry right now," he said.

I looked at my watch. It was only ten-thirty. "It's too early. If we break right now the afternoon is going to seem like forever and a day. But those biscuits and gravy sure were good. Your Mom serve lunch?"

"Maybe," he said and we climbed up to the top of the

wall and walked it to the south. It wouldn't take much for the river to bypass our effort and come in through the neighborhoods. Then our wall would only hold in the water. On that far edge we sat down and Adam had a smoke. I borrowed one because what else was there to do? A guilt reached us because we were visible from the factory doors. I tried to sit down on the riverside of the wall but you could only get low enough to hide your body. Heads would still stick above the sand bags and then it would look like we were trying to hide, which was the truth but unpleasant nonetheless. To really hide we would have to get waist deep in the river. Anyway sitting on those bags was like sitting on wet rocks, not pleasant.

"You'd think Turnbull would want us to pump out a hundred or so pieces in this down time," Adam said.

"Yeah. I wonder how much back stock we have left." I looked at Adam and he had found our grail. We had found the answer for an empty half hour. We stood, took our last drags, flipped the butts into the river and then slogged our way towards the shipping building.

40

We walked down to the dock to see what they were loading in the truck. Low and behold it was our parts. They were loading our complete back stock into his truck.

"What the fuck?" I cried and then stopped the next forklift that passed. "What's going on?" I asked the operator.

"Carlson told us to load all the United Tracked parts we had. But I don't think they'll all fit… Maybe, we'll see." He pushed past me with his load and entered the trailer. Adam stood on his toes as it passed and looked into the box.

"What do you make of this?" Adam asked me pointing at the box as it disappeared into the trailer.

"I don't know, but I can't see it being good." I tried to reason out why the factory over in Indianapolis would want all our parts at once instead of at a steady flow. They would have to store all that aluminum somewhere. Why not let us store it? I hadn't been close to the truth. I wasn't thinking correctly.

Maybe it was the rain. Maybe I had finally had enough. Or maybe it was my dead dog. All things considered I really didn't mourn the passing of my best friend. Hell, maybe it was Emily. I sure was pissed that we, us, hadn't worked out the way I hoped. But that wasn't it. Work. It always went back to work. I was pissed that this truck driver was going to cart off all my hard work and I couldn't see why he should be doing that. Hearing that Carlson was involved made me more suspicious.

Another loaded forklift drove by and I hurried over to stop him. I grabbed the roll cage but the operator cut me off saying that he was just doing his job and didn't know anything about it. I let him go and then checked my watch. We had wasted enough time. It was the regular dinner break time. I turned my watch toward Adam.

"All right!" he said. "We'll go to Mae's."

41

We continued speculating. It made no sense to ship off all our backstock. We didn't know that our dies were also on the Bill of Lading. Life was confusing and life was simple. We worked and then we needed food. Again, anything and everything was possible with a full stomach.

In that world of men, aluminum, and water it was nice to be reminded of the other side. And Rochelle was enough reminder for a hundred men. She was serving a table in the far corner, a table of two sheriffs and a statie. She was wearing one of my old western shirts and a pair of tight fitting cords. Her hair stuck out at medusa angles and was only subdued by the half-dozen pens she had stuck in it.

Eventually, Rochelle made her way to our table. She came over to my side and put her hip against me and her hand on my opposite shoulder.

"What do you boys want?" she asked.

"That's my shirt," I said and pulled at the untucked front.

"And you're not getting it back." And then like we were the only two people in the room, a talent she had and I've never seen replicated, Rochelle turned to me and said, "it was nice being with you. I miss the good times."

I don't know if she meant what she said or was putting on a show for Adam but it felt honest. I wanted to ask her about the other times but instead said, "me too."

And then she turned back to the world and was back in control. She was never out of control. Maybe she controlled only herself but it seemed like so much.

After we finished eating and were giving Rochelle our money she turned to me and said, "It's a shame about the library."

"What's a shame?"

"The basement. It flooded, all those books got ruined." She cocked her head at me in mock astonishment. "Surely your girlfriend must have told you."

There it was. Real life had returned. When I pushed the door open it was still raining. I was pissed again. I just drove the truck back to the mud and the water and the future that was changing like the river.

BOOK SIX

1

We were held up at the stop sign before turning into the plant by three dump trucks. "That's a good sign," Adam said. My wipers flopped but I remained silent. We followed them into the lot hoping for one of the few parking spots. The trucks created a stockpile next to the sandbag machine. It wasn't fill dirt. It was lighter in color. Later I would learn that the trucks weren't bringing fill because it was faster to load good sand and gravel at the concrete plant on the edge of town. The final rows would be filled with this gourmet sand.

Turnbull sat in his yellow rain suit on Bullough's tractor and waited to load the hopper. There was no parking, so I let Adam out and went into the neighborhood to find a spot. Adam and I worked the filling station through the afternoon. All the flood workers took the afternoon break inside because Turnbull wanted to talk to us.

The wall crew crowded into the break room and we steamed with our wet rain gear still on. The coffee machine ran constantly as each man tried to warm his insides. Jack sat in the far corner with two cups of the machine brew, one in each hand. Adam and I pushed over towards him. Jack told us that he had heard they would be asking us to stay and work through the night. As we tried to digest the scuttlebutt Turnbull walked to the coffee machine, the focus of the room and addressed the crowd. The news was both good and bad. What we had noticed pouring down our necks was the forth storm but the river was finally predicted to crest.

"The best information we can get says the river should reach its maximum height early next morning, around five. So between now and daylight the river is expected to rise another eighteen inches. We're hoping that the wall is tall enough at the middle but the upriver side may have to be extended into the first block of the neighborhood, past the RV park. So I talked with the Bulloughs and we would like a work crew to stay through the night to extend the wall and watch for and if need be patch any leaks that may occur."

Turnbull gave us a few seconds to moan and make remarks out of the sides of our mouths. I just looked into my coffee.

"Now we should have enough fill to make bags through the night. I'll be here to run the loader, and if I'm not Warrell will be." Adam nudged me in the ribs but the statement didn't come as a surprise. The only thing I found odd was that Turnbull had used my first name in front of other people. It sounded odd. Turnbull continued, "So I'm figuring that we'll need ten or a dozen men throughout the night. That's roughly half of you so I'll let you guys figure out who wants to stay. If you want to split the time that's fine but make sure everyone isn't on the one side of the clock. If you're going to split the night find a buddy that will do the other half."

Turnbull took a few steps toward the door but stopped. "Oh yeah, and don't worry about food. We'll have it brought in. And don't get punch drunk. We don't want twenty zombies standing around watching water come over the wall. If you get tired take a nap in your car or in here. Just don't leave the others hanging." He took two more steps. "But punch out if you're napping." A few men laughed but most were already figuring time slots in their heads.

Sean McClelland stood up. He had a clipboard in his hand. "Okay, who's in for the whole night?" Without looking up he started writing on the pad. "Me, Swanson… Smith. How 'bout you? Don't want to miss anything." Adam groaned and put his hand over his eyes.

Jim Wright spoke up. "I'll take the second half," he said. Slowly, piece-by-piece the roster was filled out. Adam and I turned toward Jack and tried to peer pressure him into spending the night. It was a team effort. He didn't want to leave us in the lurch, did he? But Jack hung tough and signed on only as a morning replacement.

I thought it odd that Sean had a clipboard in his hand as Turnbull left the room. He must have known what Turnbull was going to ask. Turnbull had probably gone to him first and asked Sean to organize the work parties. I was still thinking of this and the whys that surrounded the facts when everyone got up to leave. I drained my coffee and flipped the paper cup over to check my hidden card, an ace. I looked at my two showing cards. Both aces! "Fuck me," I moaned.

Sean was still writing on his pad. "What's up Swanson?" he asked.

"Three aces," I said showing him my cup. "Timing," I said. "I could have taken Smith for his whole paycheck."

"No one would bet you with two aces showing," Sean said, already looking back down at his paper.

But the cards weren't my point. I was upset about the timing. I thought of explaining that to Sean. But maybe he knew more about timing than I did. Maybe he had learned about timing before he turned thirty. We returned to the rain in time to see the truck carrying our parts pull out of the yard. I thought of all our work leaving at once and what it might have meant. Weren't they still on strike? It was another example of timing. I don't know what Adam was thinking about. Probably his mother.

2

An hour later Mario pulled into the yard driving one of the company stake beds, the blue one-ton. He towed a pump and another one was secured on the bed. Mario had to weave around the people and equipment. The wheels made wakes that went out through the rain smashing themselves against the factory wall and the sandbags. I walked down the dike to where he parallel parked the truck. He had been gone all day.

"What'd you bring us?" I shouted through the rain and noise of the tractor and generator.

"Pumps," Mario said and then waved for me to come down off my mountain and help.

I looked in the bed at coils of large hose. We removed the stake fences and leaned them in the front of the bed against the cab.

"Trash pumps," Mario finally continued. "I had to drive all the way to Bowling Green to find a rental shop that had them in stock. It kills me when those fuckers say they can get you a pump in three days. What do they think I want it for? It's like saying I'll sandbag after the flood. I'll get to it later. 'Hey baby, I'll put the condom on later'."

I laughed. "Where do you want to set these up?" I asked.

"The six-inch can stay here. We'll leave the two-inch on the truck and run it there," Mario pointed farther down the wall. "We'll have to dig a sump for the intake." I went for my shovel. Adam came over and started stretching out hose. Everyone just worked.

"I think these pumps will have to be primed to get the suction going." Mario was looking at one of the machines, into a hole beneath a cap on the top. "Can you imagine needing water in the middle of all this shit? Go inside and get a couple five gallon buckets."

I did as he told me and when I returned we got the first pump going and then the second. I was amazed at the volume of water they moved. The two discharge hoses sprayed their brown water into the air and then into the passing river. Let someone else down river worry about it. We've had all we can take.

"It's just like a boat," Mario said waving his hand across our pond. "Leaks are okay as long as your pumps push out more water than comes in. Keep the water on the outside. The first time I was on a ship I was terrified. First of all I'm not the best swimmer and then I'm watching them load on all our tanks and shit. Tanks, for Christ's sake! I kept waiting for the ship to just disappear underneath the water. A Navy guy must have seen the fear in my face and he described how boats work, but shit, it took me a long time to be able to sleep when we were underway. And then the rocking! Shit, no thanks man. A bass boat is big enough for me.

So anyway, one day I was on deck and looking over the rail as we went along and here's these two giant holes spewing water. Twice as much as that." He pointed at the streams from the trash pumps. "And I don't know what I thought. That's a lot of water to be coming from the toilets and showers, the heads. Something like that. And this other navy guy told me that water was coming up from the engine room. I thought he was fucking with me. A lot of that goes on. But another buddy of mine told me it was the truth. I almost had a second panic attack. And what good would that of done me? We were a thousand miles from land. So I got to love those pumps. And they had back up pumps and back ups for the back ups. I can't say I ever grew to like being on board, but finally I could sleep."

"That sounds like fun," I said.

Mario looked at me, his face screwed up. "Did you hear anything I said?" he asked.

"No, I mean yeah I did, but the adventure. Sounds like a lot of fun. I wish I would have stuck with it."

"Oh, shit. You've got to get over it, man. There's nothing fun about being a slave and that's what you are. Someone else owns you! I don't know about the officer side but I suspect it was similar. Different owner but the same effect."

"What about all this," now I waived my hand over the pond and people and buildings and machines. "Don't the Bullough's own us? Aren't we chained to this place?"

"I think you have water on your brain. Maybe you need ear plugs." Mario gently knocked my head with his fist. "You don't have to be here. You can walk away right now. The only thing that binds you is your need for money, that's it. But shit, go find another job if you don't like it. Even in the depression the Joads were free to starve anywhere they wanted."

I thought of my being volunteered to spend the night watching the river, and now the pumps. But Mario was right. I could have told Sean to fuck off and walked. But I didn't. The only chains that held me to this place were in my head. A sense of gratitude towards the Bulloughs for the thousands they had given me over the years. I had earned the money, that's true. But nothing I did was too difficult. It was easy. Just showing up everyday was the challenge. Routine. The chains were in my head, that was true. I had only one mouth to feed, now that Ginger was dead.

3

Afternoon rained on and the light finally began to change. The sky had been a dark gray all day and soon the generator would be needed for light. The pumps kept running and our wall was racing the water toward the neighborhood.

The men were organized into shifts. Some men went home to get a few hours sleep before returning at midnight to relieve those that would work straight through a double shift. Supervisors weren't given the choice of leaving. We were supposed to stay until we either dropped or the threat had diminished.

The factory went silent as the last day shift cars drove away. Small leaks were now popping up on a fairly consistent basis. The whole wall leaked a bit and walking it you would see water flowing out from the bags, through the cracks between them and know that it was the start of something much worse. The tractor brought loads of sandbags and a team would quickly stack a second wall over the leaking area. Soon our great wall was festooned with parapets, although they were not as neat as I imagined they should be.

4

At six, Justin Bullough drove his truck through the water to the wall. We thought that he was there merely to make sure we were adequately protecting his wealth. At least that was the thought that went through my head. The fatigue was already causing me to become irritated.

Instead he brought us ten pizzas and two large Thermoses of hot chocolate. It seemed a strange combination but proved excellent considering the setting. We crowded around and ate the pizzas off paper plates in the rain under the light from the generators. He thanked us and wished us good luck and then drove off. We stood where the boss's truck had been and cradled Styrofoam cups of hot chocolate in our hands. A few paper plates floated in the pond. The crowd was small enough that everyone could almost be part of the same conversation.

I stood on the edge of the group and listened to the topic change from the river to baseball. Jack held the Thermos and refilled my cup. I listened to more of the words but was distant. I thought of Emily. I wanted her. I wanted her to stay. I wanted her to love me with a passion at least close to mine. I might as well have wished for the river not to flood.

5

The wall grew formidable and our sense of panic retreated. The top was now four bags across and it made a pleasant walkway. I liked looking down the line and seeing all the bags in a row, all the ties to the left. I saw Sean standing atop the wall near the hook in the J where it turned into the neighborhood. I walked for him. When he saw me coming toward him he bent down and messed with a bag but when I got close he stood back up.

"I got to leave for fifteen," I said.

"Make sure you punch out," he said.

"Fuck you." I climbed down the wall, walked straight to my truck, got in and drove toward the library. Although it was after eight the lights were still on. Emily's car was in the lot along with Mrs. White's and some others. I parked and made my way across the wet asphalt my boots clop clopping my arrival. The library didn't look flooded. The lawn out to the guns was still above the river. The river was below the railing and wall. Everything was wet, but not flooded. I took off my hat and ran my fingers through my wet hair. My arms and shoulders were tired from lifting. My legs and ass were tired from lifting. My clothes hung on me and even the insides of my pockets were soaked. My money was wet. I put my hands to my lower back and stretched, rain falling in my open mouth.

"I thought we could count on you to help us, but you're too late." Emily had come up the side stairs behind me carrying a file box. She wore rubber boots but her clothes were dry. Her hair was stacked up high out of purpose rather that effect. I followed her to the dumpster and opened the lid for her. She pitched the box in. "You should have been here. I told Mrs. White that you would be and you made me look foolish." Emily turned and walked back to the library. I shut the lid gently so it wouldn't bang and followed in silence. I stared at her boots. They were the same as mine. Smaller, but the same. I wondered if Sean had made a sales call here, too.

The basement was flooded and the women carried box after box of wet files up the stairs. Mrs. White looked as if she'd been crying. "It's horrible," she said, unable to say more. I looked at it all but couldn't bring myself to pitch in. It seemed too late, too hopeless. Maybe I feared being mired in two tragedies. Two-front wars don't work out. Mrs. White was deciding what was to be saved and what was junk. Depending on her ruling the box would either go upstairs or to the trash.

"Do you worry about this electricity?" I asked. The lights were still on. The ladies stopped and looked at me, eyes wide with a sudden fear.

"Should we?" Mrs. White asked.

I said I didn't know. It was just a question. But it was good that they all had rubber boots on. The women didn't look reassured but they went back to their sorting and carrying. Emily brushed past me and made another trip up the stairs with ruined and useless knowledge, mostly local archives.

I went up the inside stair and thought about taking my box from beneath the counter but didn't. I walked back into the history section and looked out the window at the river in the failing light. I could see the far shore and most of the troubled brown water between. The warmth of the library let me feel how cold and wet my clothes were. I shivered and touched the cool glass then felt the wood grain of the sill. My body became a fire and I thought steam was rising from me and that my clothes might dry in minutes. I heard Emily's voice from the stair well and knew that she was the cause, that she was the lighter that had torched my blood.

She called my name. I put my hand in my pocket to cover my hard on. I didn't want to show my cards too soon. She called my name and her boots rose on the stairs. I crouched back behind a shelf my nose pressed against Lawrence's history of the desert war. She called my name again. But there was bitterness in her voice. It was short and sharp. She needed help lifting something or prying something. She didn't need a wet man pressed against a wall of books with an erection that felt like it would split the skin. Her boots descended and I exhaled. What life was missed hiding in these books. I should have taken her. No, I couldn't. Possibly I could have struck a bargain in exchange for muscle. No, she wouldn't bargain her body. These thoughts made me angry and I fell back into the Ohio rain and reality. I decided to make a break for it. I would leave these sad women and their wet paper memories. I tucked my penis under my belt and took long strides towards the door to minimize footfalls.

Their shoes were piled at the top of the sand stone stairs leading to the main door. I saw Emily's shoe in the pile. I loved the foot that wore the shoe. I thought of her foot and of her knee, her magnificent thigh and her heavenly ass.

I picked up the shoe and ran out the door and down the steps towards the river. A tree floated by its branches scraping the railing on the retaining wall. I tossed the shoe a few inches from my palm, like weighing a baseball, and then pointed my front foot and cocked back to throw. I grunted out a "fuck" as my throwing arm came through but my grip was only on the toe and when I released the shoe it flew like a German potato masher grenade end over end, up and to the right. That was stupid, I thought as I watched the shoe hit the oak tree next to the guns. Instinctively my shoulders came up as when I over throw the first baseman turning the dugout into a pachinko machine. A body takes a brain. Emily's shoe fell to earth and lay in the wet Ohio grass.

I groaned and spun on one toe, a pirouette. Through the slits in my eyelids I saw Mrs. White watching me from the top of the side stairs. It was a look I had never seen before, tight-lipped, stern and silent. She turned and went down the stairs.

I walked over and picked up the shoe. I was beaten. There was no denying it. I carried the shoe back to the pile and wondered why I didn't throw myself in the river. Why did I keep going forward with the hope and expectation that some victory awaited? It wasn't so and that I knew. Yet I would drive back to our sand bag wall and laugh at Adam and taunt Mario. Somehow I even thought that Emily and Rochelle would end up loving me. Possibly they weren't able to express their love but deep in their souls and late at night they whispered my name. In short, I was a fool.

7

As night fell, we placed the last bags on the finger that extended into the neighborhood. The river was a foot below the wall and we started to feel pretty good. We made a good supply of sand bags and placed them on pallets along the wall. We started to stand up straight and stretch our backs but Sean wanted a few more. He wanted to fill the tractor bucket. No one argued we just kept on working. It was too easy now.

Eventually even Sean was satisfied and we took shelter from the rain under the shipping dock awning. Spirits were up and we lounged around like we were at a hunt camp. I didn't notice Adam and Mario sneak away. They ran up the street to the corner store and bought a couple of cases of beer. They returned to cheers. The night was really looking up. A couple of guys thought we should have a fire and went out in the rain to scavenge a burn barrel but by the time they returned it was decided that a fire would be too dangerous underneath the awning. We couldn't imagine burning down the shipping building in the middle of a flood. I voted against it out of a feeling of guilt. We were on the clock after all and sitting around drinking beer and watching the rain come down was bad enough. The barrel was kept nearby all the same.

An old station wagon weaved its way through the lot and came over to where we were camped. I was sitting on the far end of the dock leaning against one of the posts. At first I thought it was Turnbull's pickup and I hid my beer behind my back. I noticed a couple others do this also. But the car was driven by Gladys Westerhoven, a press operator.

"I thought yous mighta been warshed away," she said up to Sean when she got out of her car. Gladys opened the passenger door of her car and pulled a heavy cardboard box out. She handed it up to him.

"What do you have here?" he asked and all the men started to crowd in a little. I saw some grease marks on the box. Gladys went into her car again and pulled out two large thermoses. Sean was already opening the box.

"Fried chicken and coffee. Got to feed the horses, eh? I sees you got beer already. I put some whiskey in the coffee to keep you boys strong. Yous the horses."

I peered in at the box. Layer upon layer of chicken separated my newspaper and paper towels. I looked over at Mario and he was smiling wide. I had never liked Gladys but I didn't know her. To me she just smoked cigarettes and fed her press. Now I wanted to hug that big woman. She must have started cooking right after work. We were here getting wet but at least we were getting paid.

"Gladys, can we pay you for this?" Mario asked.

"No need. Mr. Bullough already done that," she said. "Just make sure I get my coffee pots back."

Everyone started reaching for pieces, legs and breasts and wings. I saw Adam pull out of the crowd a leg in each hand. Gladys didn't stay long. She delivered her gifts and then moved back out into the rain towards her car. We all shouted "thank you" and "God bless."

There was enough chicken that each man got four pieces, a considerable amount. After the meal we laid around the best we could. Adam went into shipping and found some cardboard for us to sit on. If I had a blanket I might have fallen asleep. It was dark.

8

Sean organized patrols of the wall. Every fifteen minutes someone would walk the length of the wall and make sure the water, for the most part, stayed on the other side. The rest of us lay there listening to the sound of the rain beating on the corrugated tin above and the sound of the generator and pumps. Once, around midnight the pumps started to falter and Mario went and filled all the fuel tanks.

The rain quit about one.

9

I wasn't asleep. I was just laying on the loading dock with my eyes closed, listening to the quiet. Sean pushed my foot.

"Hey Warrell, wake up."

"I'm not asleep," I said.

"The wall is leaking pretty bad near the new section. Think we should double it up."

I looked around. A few of the men were sleeping. Mario and Adam sat at the shipping desk playing two handed euchre. "Alright," I said and rolled to my side and then stood. I was still wet. I couldn't remember being dry. I scratched my head. "You get the tractor and I'll bring the guys," I said to Sean. I lit my watch. It was 3:47.

I woke the sleepers and then broke up the card game. We left the shipping dock and sloshed through the eight inches of standing water, past the pumps and past the light plant.

Brown, muddy flood water seeped through every seam where the new extension joined our original wall. Sean was right. It didn't look good. "The pumps are keeping up but we'll just throw another layer over it to be safe," I shouted to Sean loud enough for everyone to hear.

I pulled a bag from the tractor bucket and thought that the weak spot in the wall was where the dirt cored wall joined the pure sandbag hook. Of course it was weak. It was like trying to weld dissimilar metals. We were tired. I was tired and a little silly from the lack of sleep. The beer wasn't a good idea. I handed the bag to Adam who was half way up the wall. He dropped it on the far side and a three-foot wide section of the wall instantly disappeared underneath the water. The river took a hard right and rushed through the new gap. Adam fell back on his ass. He landed on the remaining wall. I watched another bag get peeled away by the rapids. Everyone watched, disbelieving.

We ran toward the breach but it was like running up a creek bed. Muddy water spilled in and bags still hanging on the edges fell into the water. There was a couple of foot difference between the water levels and rapids were forming. Sean throttled the tractor forward and dumped the load of bags in the hole but they were swallowed by this new branch of the Maumee. I worried about how much of the wall had already washed. If the gap was down to the gravel we were beat. But as I made my way to the edge I started kicking fallen bags. I reached down for one and struggled to pick it up. Once I had it clear of the water I threw it into the gap. It disappeared with a splash. It was demoralizing. Across the rapids Mario was doing the same and behind him was Adam, next to him was Jack. Each man shot putting water logged sand bags against an angry river. When had Jack arrived? I reached for another and pulled it up to my waist but when I stepped forward I rolled my ankle on a submerged bag and fell over to the side into the brown water. I went under, dunked, baptized. When I got to my knees I was facing away from the river, looking at the factory.

Sean came racing through the water with another load of bags and dumped them into the gap. The last bags stuck out of the rushing water. We had salvaged most of the fallen bags and now a line of men stretched out away from the hole towards the nearest pallet of spares. We bucket brigaded that pallet clean and Sean brought another load from one of the far stockpiles. The wall rose again from the water and we kept piling the bags on. The sky turned and when I looked up at the purple blue of the early morning there wasn't a cloud.

10

I didn't see Mario go down. When I heard the commotion I looked over and saw Sean holding Mario by his collars against the sandbag wall. It looked like Sean was threatening Mario or just getting done kicking his ass. But Sean was yelling over his shoulder. I heard him say "ambulance," then I heard him call my name. I ran through the water toward them. Turnbull took off towards the factory. Sean was talking to Mario and shaking him.

"Mario… Mario!," he said.

"What's going on," I asked, fear already running through me.

"Mario just fell over. He's not breathing."

"Oh shit, Mario," I said as I grabbed his arm and together we pulled him up the wall. Mario's eyes were half open. "Mario!" I yelled in his face. Sean fell to his knees as we tried to lift the heavier man. "Seven to one?" I asked Sean. Sean had Mario's wrist and I felt his neck.

"Nothing," Sean said. "Five," he answered me.

I couldn't feel a pulse either. We pulled on Mario's armpits again trying to reach the relative flat of the top of the wall.

"This isn't going to work," I said.

Sean fell against the wall. "Time clock," he said. "It's still dry in there." I nodded and we pulled Mario forward and started dragging him face down through the water in the parking lot towards the open door. Everyone else had noticed our panic by then and two men ran over to grab Mario's legs. I thought we were doing something wrong but couldn't remember what. Immobilization was for trauma victims. That was probably it but Mario hadn't been in a car accident. I looked at his neck and the color had already faded.

"Airway," I said between steps.

"Doesn't matter, he's not breathing," Sean said.

We had to switch around to fit through the door and then we laid Mario on the concrete floor. I pushed his forehead back to clear his throat and looked into his face. His eyes were cold and one pupil was fully blown but at the time I didn't know what that meant. I then put my mouth to his and watched his chest rise with my full breath.

"One, two, three, four, five," Sean counted as he pumped on Mario's chest.

I breathed into him again. Sean continued pumping. After a few sets we paused and both looked for a pulse but didn't find one. We kept pumping blood and breathing for our friend. Sweat began falling off Sean's nose onto Mario.

"Switch?" I asked during one of our checks. Sean nodded and we switched positions. A crowd had formed around us and I heard Turnbull say that the ambulance was on the way.

People were still trying to clock in. What a sight. Standing water, pumps, the broken and fixed wall, the river and a dead man under the time clock. The siren in the distance grew closer then stopped. Outside the ambulance was blocked by water. Adam flagged the driver over to the breezeway entrance and they brought the stretcher through the pressroom. The two paramedics asked Sean and I what we knew which was very little. Fell over, not breathing, no pulse. They took Mario away, continuing CPR. Sean and Adam and I and a few others followed the stretcher through the factory and out into the sunlight. The light hurt my eyes and I shaded them.

Turnbull and Bullough were at the ambulance and Turnbull shut the doors after Mario was loaded. Bullough walked over to us and shook everyone's hand. But what could you do?

11

It was Monday morning but we didn't clock out or tell anyone anything. Adam walked away and Sean and I got into my truck and drove to the hospital in silence. We sat in the waiting room and saw Jill walk by red eyed in her nurse's uniform. Two other nurses followed her and none of them said a thing. I noticed that Sean and I smelled bad, like a swamp, black dirt and stale water.

I had known Mario was dead for a while before the doctor told us. I continued hoping but I knew he was dead. It was almost ten by the time I dropped Sean off at his car.

"I better go in and tell them," he said to me. I stayed silent. Sean walked off and into the factory. I stayed put. I might have been too tired to put my truck in gear. Maybe I didn't know what I should do. I wasn't going to go to work, although it was a Monday. I didn't even consider that. I merely stared straight ahead and didn't think. Some time later Sean returned with two cups of coffee from the machine. He handed me one.

"They already knew," he said. "Turnbull said the river is already down five inches. He thanked us." Sean looked at me. "You look like shit. You'd better catch some zees."

I nodded and pulled down on the handle putting the truck in first. But truth is I had passed the tired moment and now I was awake although not fully conscious. I turned right and then left and headed to the grocery store. The coffee was tearing up my guts so I poured it out on the street. A couple of blocks from the river the town looked fine. It was wet and clean but definitely not troubled. I pulled in the lot and parked. I staggered in, my socks sloshing in my boots. I grabbed a six-pack before wandering over to the deli case. I put my hand against the glass and felt the warmth. Only the fried chicken was ready. It didn't look as good as Gladys' from the night before. Was that really last night? It seemed like two days ago. Trying to figure the time actually hurt my brain and I knew I really was tired even if my eyes didn't feel heavy. A couple beers and some chicken aught to equal half a bottle of sleeping pills, I thought. I ordered two breasts.

"I saw your truck in the lot," Rochelle said behind me.

I turned and she put her arms around my waist and her head against my chest. "I heard about Mario," she said and almost squeezed the air out of me. I put my empty hand around her. I could feel her breasts against me and the edge of her pelvis against my leg. I got a hard on. It was one of those tired beyond all thought, loss of rationality and return to primeval hard ons.

If she had let me I would have fucked her right there against the warm glass of the deli case. The lady behind it handed me my chicken.

"Come home with me," I said. Rochelle looked up at me and then after a moment nodded. She might have expected me to talk about the river or about Mario but she also might have expected the exact words that came out of my mouth.

12

Rochelle followed me in her car and I opened a can of beer and ate the first chicken breast. I took long pulls off the can and started to feel more human. I continued eating and drinking as I drove through downtown. Who would think of pulling me over at eleven in the morning I thought and as I passed the courthouse Ian was coming out of the parking lot in his cruiser. I waved a piece of chicken at him but he just stared back. Fuck you Ian, I thought. He pulled out behind Rochelle and I didn't drink any beer until he turned off to the right before the bridge.

13

As I parked my truck I realized that fall had finally come. The air had changed. I walked back to look at the river behind my house. It was high on the bank but still a couple of feet below the willow. Ginger's chain lay there but I was too tired to have a break down. Rochelle came up behind me and tugged on my belt loops.

"Doesn't look like much of anything from here," I said. We went up the stairs and I opened all the windows. Fresh clean air blew through the house. Rochelle was wandering around looking at things so I grabbed her and pulled her close to me.

But I felt dirty. It had been three long and dirty days since I had showered and when she started kissing my ears and neck I was embarrassed. "I need a shower," I said. Rochelle ran her hands down my arms and agreed with me, which felt like an insult and felt like the truth.

The hot water loosened something inside me and the full weight of my fatigue came upon me. I turned the showerhead and leaned against the tile letting the water run down the back of my neck. With so much to think about I didn't think about anything. I felt eyes and turned to see Rochelle watching me through the parted curtain. She passed a can of beer in to me. "Here, drink this," she said. I took it, did as I was told and then leaned again on the wall. It took awhile but she finally undressed and got in with me, which is what I wanted. Rochelle made some half-hearted protests and complaints of the "if you want a job done right" variety. She grabbed the soap and worked me over. She told me to "spread 'em" and worked over the nether regions, which I found very pleasurable. It's a nice thing to have your ass washed by a naked woman. Things got even better and as I was finishing the can of beer my knees buckled or I passed out. I fell back and in my panic pulled the curtain off the rings. I fell hard and hit my head against the wall. When I looked up Rochelle was standing, naked in the running water with her hand over her mouth. When she determined that I wasn't dead she laughed like it was the funniest thing she had ever seen. We gathered up the curtain and threw it in the tub.

Rochelle dried me off with two towels and several kisses. She moved me towards my bed and drew back the covers. The room reeked of Emily's presence, I thought, although she hadn't been there for five days. The waste basket held condoms full of sperm brought out by that other woman's hips.

I wanted to say something again but the words wouldn't come. Rochelle just muttered "no, no," and pushed me down into the bed covers. I worried a little more but quickly found the sleep that I needed. Sounds of cooking followed me into me dreams.

14

"Hungry?" she asked.

I woke to her open eyes looking at me. Her body was presses against mine, naked. She held me as I liked to be held.

"Are you hungry?" she asked.

"Famished," I said.

"Good," she said and then moved away and got out of the bed and then pulled my robe from the back of the door. It was such a natural act.

Rochelle returned with two plates of lasagna. I was amazed. I asked how this was possible and she laughed. She had bought the noodles months ago. "You just need to look," she said. We ate and then made love with an unusual amount of tenderness. I almost started crying and Rochelle saw this in my eyes. She put her arms and legs around me and rocked me back into sanity.

After a while we were tired of being tired and got up. It was only six in the evening but my sleep was so confused that it felt like morning. I wanted coffee.

A quietness came over Rochelle that I couldn't fix. And

then the phone rang and I wished I had turned the ringer and the answering machine off. It rang again and again. Rochelle looked at me and I tried to look back at her with absolutely no expression at all which is really another expression. After the sixth ring the machine picked it up. My message played and Emily's voice came through the little speaker. Rochelle and I continued looking at each other.

"What the fuck was that?" the voice asked loudly. "First you don't help us and then you try to throw my shoe in the river? Were you going to throw all the shoes? You're fucked up and don't blame it on the rain or the river. You can just hide out there and play with your little battleships. I don't need your antics. I thought you were a man. I was wrong." Hang up and then silence.

Rochelle raised an eyebrow at me. "She was just looking for an excuse," I said.

The silence returned. I didn't know what to say. It all seemed too hopeless.

"I think it's good that you're finally going to finish the Bismarck," Rochelle said pointed to the naked hull on my bookshelf. I shrugged my shoulders and then Rochelle got up and grabbed her purse making for the door. "Listen, this was what you needed. That's all. I'm not coming back. I'm not going to be around," Rochelle said. She stood next to the open screen door. The evening light washed in on her.

I stood up. I felt kicked. I felt desperate. "Don't say such things," I protested.

"It's the truth," she said.

"Maybe, but don't say it." Why did she want to make things ugly?

"I need to say it. Both for you and me. Goodbye, Warrell," she said and walked out the door.

I followed her down the steps dressed in only my boxers. "Wait," I pleaded. "What the fuck?" The gravel hurt my feet. A car passed and honked. It was obvious what was happening in my driveway. I gave them the bird. Rochelle got into her car and I quit protesting. I just watched her back around then drive off towards town. When I saw her tail lights blink that last time before making the turn a panic seized me. It was the final realization of how alone I was. A man without a woman, friend or dog. Alone in a foreign land. As I made my way back up the stairs I thought this wasn't much different than when I came down here. But it was. Ten years ago it was a choice to be alone out by the river. Now everything just seemed to wash away and I was the same, except alone.

I drank two beers fast. Oh God, how I wanted to talk to my dog. I went over to the calendar and put my hand on the month of October and tried to locate myself. To my surprise it was Monday the 18th. Opening day of bird season.

15

That night I tried to walk the woods in a vain effort to hunt. The field to the right was submerged and completely impassible. The low center of the woods was swamped. I walked the edge of the wood but kept listening for Ginger's bell. I reached the outside edge of the birch stand as darkness fell. My seat had disappeared. I unloaded my gun and walked home.

I finished the Bismarck. I worked on it until five in the morning. I was waiting to grow tired and just as the light changed I finally felt the ability to sleep. I did. I knew in the back of my mind that it was Tuesday and that I should be at work but I didn't give it any serious thought. Maybe I thought that they owed me a weekend.

16

When the phone rang I knew who it was. It was work. I walked slowly over to the machine and picked it up before the sixth ring.

"The dies are gone," Adam said. I had expected the voice of management. I had expected Turnbull or Justin Bullough or even Sean. But it was Adam and there was panic in his voice. "The dies are gone and no one will give me a straight answer. Turnbull said go back to the pressroom. I haven't found Sean yet but I thought I'd call you. Where are you?"

"I'm at home. You called me," I said.

"What do you make of this?"

I told Adam that I didn't make anything of it and I would be in as soon as possible. I took a shower and shaved and put on a fresh set of greens. Looking in the mirror as I put gel in my hair, I realized I looked ten years older. I finally looked like a man. Damn, I thought, so this is how it happens.

I parked against the sand bag wall and it already looked old and dirty. Only the small pump still ran and it sucked air. I walked through the plant with my hands in my pockets. The dies were gone. Adam wasn't crazy. I checked the rack outside of tooling. Every UTT die was gone. I knew that they were on the same truck with our back stock. I didn't need to ask any more questions. Turnbull was in his office.

"I was wondering if you were going to come back to work," Turnbull said when he noticed me leaning against his doorjamb.

"I was wondering the same thing. What the fuck?"

Turnbull took off his glasses and rubbed his face. "Do you want to be laid off or fired? It's up to you."

"That's how it is, huh. Thanks for the years, now get out."

"Like I said, it's your choice," Turnbull was looking at me now. He didn't flinch from anything and I admired him for that. I started to feel sorry for him. I'm sure this wasn't his idea. It was probably that bitch in Personnel. Fire me and hire someone new for ten grand less a year. Brilliant. I should slit her tires, I thought.

"No, I'm laid off. It's ok. Adam gets to stay right?"

"Yeah. He'll go back to his old job." Turnbull turned away from me. He turned towards the papers on his desk and I knew that our time was over. "Mario's funeral is Thursday at one-thirty."

I nodded and walked away. I left the plant without saying anything to anyone. I didn't want any backslaps or handshakes. Maybe it was callous, but this loss didn't sadden me. I drove back out to my house and gathered up all my uniforms, including the one I was wearing, put them in a laundry bag, then drove back to the plant. It was still before the dinner break and I managed to walk into the time clock room and throw my bag into the hamper without running into anyone. Wednesday was laundry day and my new uniforms would stay on the pole and then everyone would know I was gone.

I went for a drive. There was still much standing water but the sun was out. I cut back and forth and finally made it over to Bryan. There was a plant there that made concrete mixer trucks. I looked at it from the parking lot. It seemed like interesting work. I took to the road again and passed truck after truck. Maybe I should get my license, I thought. I stopped for lunch and then bought a pint of whiskey and started my wander back to Defiance. It was the afternoon when I came back into town from the west side. I was feeling better due to the sun and whiskey. I thought I should stop by Emily's and try to sort things out.

As I walked up to her door a confidence came into my feet. I felt good. Rarely in my life have I ever felt a genuine confidence. I had faked a confidence to fool officers and NCOs but that was faked. And this wasn't a nothing-left-to-lose sensation. I wasn't at the bottom and still had plenty to lose. There was no desperation in my walk. I didn't want to take anyone else with me. No.

My strength came from a pride that I could take it. I could take life. I could endure the floods and deaths and layoffs and injuries. All my life I had liked losing a fight more than winning it. And if I was on the road to victory I might pull a little off and take a few punches to remind me what that felt like. I could take it. I could take not ever touching Rochelle again, not ever hearing her or tasting her again. And now I needed to know about Emily. Was she done with it? I could take it but that didn't make it any more pleasant. I knocked on her door and she answered.

"My friend Mario died Sunday. It was an aneurysm. We thought it was a heart attack because we were working on the wall. Mario liked his bacon so we thought it was a heart attack. Me and Sean gave him CPR for a long time. Worked up quite a sweat pumping his blood and kissing him. It's funny because Mario and I talked of aneurysms before. He called them 'God's snipers'. He liked the idea of living and then dying with no in-between time, no decline or fall. How you live is how you live. It's odd that he said that. I don't think it was any sort of premonition, just something we talked about at lunch over beers. His wife wanted kids but Mario couldn't get her pregnant. I think that's lucky now. She's young and pretty and will be alright."

Emily was holding the door open and when I ran out of words she invited me in with politeness but without warmth. I stood in her kitchen and accepted her beer. She wandered around straightening things and I could tell what she was thinking. She thought that I had come over to fuck. She thought that I wanted to fuck because my friend was dead. She also thought this repellant because death never made her want to make love. It was the opposite. She was right of course. About me I mean. Just being near her made me want her but I knew she was cold. She didn't need to be let down slowly. She just switched it off and it was over. That was what a woman like her was truly capable of. The coldness was so accessible. The warmth was forced. I drained the beer and said, "ok I'm going to go." And I did without saying anything else.

17

The morning of Mario's funeral I sat around and drank coffee while reading the paper in my underwear and t-shirt. I was shaved and my hair was done and I moved gingerly so as not to disturb or dirty anything. Adam called at eleven and said that everyone was meeting at Mae's beforehand. That was the tradition and I expected it. I put on a grey flannel suit I had bought in a second-hand store in Toledo years ago and never worn. I headed into town. The water was retreating in the streets but still stood in ponds around houses and in fields. My hair got a little messed up because I drove with the windows down but I still looked sharp as I pulled into the restaurant parking lot.

Inside there was the whole range of funeral outfits from those who seemed barely out of work to the three-piece wedding suits. Adam had a blue blazer on with tan pants and that seemed to be the most popular. I sat down with Jack and Adam and when Rochelle came over I ordered whiskey instead of beer. What did I have to pace myself for? When Rochelle returned she said I looked nice and I thanked her. As she walked away I noticed that she had a skirt and blouse on, dressed up. Everyone was going. I looked around the bar and everyone looked a part of the process. We were all going to pay respects to Mario. I thought of how well liked he was and it swelled my throat. I was envious. Rochelle kept bringing me drinks and I finally said that she looked good but it was too late. It was time for us to move to the funeral home and Jack and Adam rode with me. We took hits off the bottle that I had brought, steeling ourselves for what was to come.

Jill was greeting people in the foyer and I realized that this is what I most dreaded. The wife of a dead friend. A wife who didn't like me when the husband was alive. She couldn't hold me responsible for weak blood vessels in Mario's brain but in times of need and desperation we all hate things that are convenient and that I was. I tried not to make eye contact until I was upon her.

"I'm sorry, Jill," I said.

And she said, "I know you are." And that was that.

We moved on into the room with Mario's coffin and took our seats. The bosses were there, the workers, the friends and the families. Around these people I realized that I was more than a little drunk. It was barely the afternoon. But what did I care? These people had let me go. I looked over at Turnbull in his ill-fitting suit. I looked over at the Bulloughs. Jean from Personnel was sitting with them and although I blamed her for my sudden unemployment I couldn't hate her. I find it impossible to hate women for any reason except love. More and more people filed in and took their seats. A section of nurses. A section of family. Co-workers and then some people I couldn't peg. Rochelle came in and sat in the row behind us. She rubbed my shoulders and it made me feel worse. The crowd quieted and Father Mike made his way to the podium. I thought that Emily should be there but then couldn't figure out why.

Father Mike talked about how Mario was beautiful and a peacemaker. I laughed to myself and thought "haymaker, maybe." Then Mario's father talked and when he cried, I cried. Everyone cried. I wanted a drink badly. Rochelle rubbed my shoulders again and I couldn't look at anything except my feet. My right shoe was discolored from vomit after a graduation party almost fifteen years before. I elbowed Adam without looking up and he elbowed me back. Father Mike spoke again and then it was over. The family would stay for some prayers before the cremation but the rest of us filed out.

18

We co-workers, neighbors and friends walked out in that uncomfortable silence following expressed grief. Not ashamed, but humbled. Several people were going to go back to Mae's. Rochelle asked if I was coming. I said no.

I wanted some silence. I thought of driving out to see my grandmother's grave, to see how it weathered the flood. I realized I could start driving for New Orleans or Denver. I was a free man. I would have to make a budget, I thought, as I got into my truck. Adam stood at my window.

"You sure you don't want to come?" he asked.

"No, but I'll give you guys a ride," I said.

"Tom and me are going to walk, build up a thirst."

I laughed at his joke on Jack and then backed right into Sean's car. Even if I had looked I could barely see the roof of Sean's little car over my tailgate. The noise of breaking glass and plastic attracted everyone's attention. Sean threw his car in park where it stood instead of pulling to the side, blocking the parking lot. He got out and rushed to the point of impact. I got out somewhat slower.

"Aw, Swanson. Look what you did," he moaned.

The passenger side headlight assembly was crushed. My

bumper had cleared his bumper and killed his light. The sheet metal looked straight. That was what concerned me.

Sean continued. "Look what you've done…"

I was looking. "Sorry," I said again. "Hey it doesn't look too bad. I'll take care of it, buy you a new light without my insurance." I shouldn't have said that. Sean's head turned. He smelled blood. "Don't worry. I have insurance if you want it that way," I reassured him.

Sean shook his head and looked back at the light. A small crowd had gathered. "I don't know, maybe we should call the cops," Sean said.

"It didn't happen on the street," Adam interjected. Adam should have been a lawyer, I thought. He could still live with his mom and be a lawyer. But who would pay the bills while he went to school. Some things were just too difficult. Maybe night school.

"I think I should call the cops," Sean repeated.

"Ian's a cop," Adam said pointing to the policeman in full uniform with his wife at his side coming out of the funeral home. We were all looking at him and Ian came over to the scene without being called. I kept my eyes down, away from Lisa. I pretended anguish for the broken light.

"Are we going to have a rematch or are you guys just going to take the loss?" Ian asked in the loudest voice of the day. I thought of Mario and his five home runs in the game last year. Adam said that we would beat the cops if we had to play in the snow. I liked that he said that.

"Does Warrell need a ticket for this?" Sean asked pointing at the broken plastic and glass.

"Swanson needs more than a ticket," Ian said. They were talking like I wasn't five feet away leaning on the box of my truck. "Swanson needs a life." And if I wasn't so tired Ian's comment might have forced tears. But I stayed silent and stayed away. I felt a little drunk and didn't need to be baited into Sean's trap. I wanted to tell Sean that he already won and to take some things with magnanimity but it was a lesson that he would never learn. Rochelle waved at Lisa and went over to talk to her. They put their heads together and whispered. I didn't even know that they knew each other. Bizarre. And what were they talking about? Could it be me? I doubted it. I turned my gaze back on the men out of tact and fear.

"Just exchange information and stop blocking traffic," Ian decreed. I nodded but Sean didn't seem satisfied. He wanted to win all the time. I smiled and nodded at Ian. Jack and Adam walked off towards Mae's. Ian and Lisa towards his cruiser. Rochelle went to her car. Pete Smith was in the first car behind Sean in the jam. He honked at the resolution and Sean turned, got in his car and then drove off the glass and plastic crunching under his tires. I put my hand up to Pete and then grabbed the broom from the bed of my truck. I swept the broken pieces into a pile away from the passing cars.

"Better luck, Swanson," Pete said through his open window. I waved.

19

It was turning out to be a perfect fall day, cool and sunny. I drove out to the cemetery. The low spots were filled with water and the ground was too soft to walk on so I sat on the rail of my truck bed. Two robins were jumping from headstone to headstone. Through the pines I could hear traffic pass. I thought I ought to be sad but the smell of the wet earth baking off in the October sun was too much, too beautiful for the sadness I required. Tears welled in my eyes but they were tears of joy. I looked to my grandmother's grave and knew I would leave this place. How could I leave her here? She was with Fred and that was enough. She had found love and she should sleep in that comfort despite a foreign blanket. The devil was there looking plain and stumpish. I was surrounded by a subtlety overwhelming and irritating. It was time to move on.

20

I drove to the edge of the water, to where the road disappeared beneath the pond. There was now a couple hundred feet of water between myself and the gate. To the left and right were scattered headstones like poorly planted rice. The pond had grown since the last time I had forded it and I worried about a slow passage. If I had to cross the river Styx, I'd do it in a rocket car.

I backed in high whiney reverse past the devil and my grandmother. I should have backed all the way out, but I didn't. I poured on the gas slowly at first but grabbed second before the curve and was high into it when I hit the water. You can bend metal with water I thought as I watched the great tsunami of corpse water sail straight up from my grill. The front tires came off the ground and were useless, but they settled and I pulled straight. Water arced up to my left and right. But power faded and the truck quickly came to a stop. The engine died. I hadn't rolled up the windows and my shoulder was damp.

I sat there with both hands still on the wheel and listened to the waves lap against the frame and body. The engine turned over by the key so I knew I hadn't thrown the battery from its perch. I looked down at the water. I was fairly sure what had killed the engine. Water in the distributor. No spark. I had been meaning to switch from points to an electronic ignition but I wasn't sure that would make any difference. I needed a better truck. A newer one, at least a four-wheel drive. But it was no use dreaming of such things. I had no job.

The water calmed. I didn't like the idea of wading around in the dead people water and it was a shame to step out into it in my good suit. I might need this suit to get my next job. My baseball uniform was still in my toolbox and I could have put on those pants but I decided against it. That would be sacrificing something that was rare and that I was currently hoarding. I thought I could climb out the window and crawl across the hood and then stand on the front bumper but eventually I would have to step into it. I couldn't walk on water. Human, all too human. Who wrote that? Nietzsche. How he used to soothe my soul, I thought. I was to be the officer with quiet dignity and strength, not fearless, but accepting. An unsuperstitious officer of Marines comfortable with the weight of history on his shoulders. How had that boy turned into this man? Stuck, broken down in corpse water in a thirty-year-old truck, in an old suit with no woman, job, dog, Mario. It was an absurdity that tasted of Truth.

21

I stepped out into the water with a purposeful stride. Gritted teeth held the squeamishness down. After getting a screwdriver out of the toolbox I popped the hood and knelt on the fan shroud while I pulled off the wires and then freed the distributor cap. My wires were all numbered so I didn't need to worry about replacement. Cap in hand I stepped back down into the water.

My shirttails wouldn't dry the contacts. Fifty-fifty blend is many things but not absorbent. I knew what I needed and I knew where to find it. I walked out to the road and headed north towards town. Cars passed but I didn't follow their faces. I stepped across the fog line and let them pass but I continued walking straight ahead, neck and back straight, ears in line with my hips. My shoes squished and then squeaked and then wore on my feet. It may have been a crime of vanity to buy suede wingtips but I loved those shoes and grieved their passing. You have served me well boys, I said to them. I was wet from the knee down and my cuffs wrapped around my ankles. To free them I would discreetly shake my feet every eighth step. If a car was passing I might wait sixteen. I walked and eventually neared Emily's apartment. Her car was in the lot.

What would she say if I knocked on her door? I didn't want to find out. I didn't want Emily to see me in my nicest clothes. She wasn't worthy of that. When she thought of me, if she thought of me, let her remember dirt and grime. Let her feel the soot on her teeth when she leaves this town. I wish I had humiliated her a little. It would have been good for her. I should have slapped her ass more and made her crawl around the floor naked. Her beauty was overpowering and it made you overlook that her pride was without foundation. It was an act copied from a book or a movie.

22

Rochelle's car was not in her lot. I turned her doorknob but it was locked. It wasn't past five and she would still be at Mae's. I stepped over the shrubs and went to Rochelle's bathroom window. It didn't have a lock and was Rochelle's spare key. I slid it to the side. The opening was small, more suitable to Rochelle's body than mine. I put my elbows inside the sill and then made a little jump to clear my chest. A door opened behind me and then a voice.

"Hey!" the voice said.

I backed out the window and turned. Through a cracked door I could see Ed's face. His hands weren't visible and that worried me for a moment. Asthmatic and alcoholic, Ed spent his days drinking and smoking and watching TV. He watched too much TV. I never liked Ed. But Rochelle was always kind to him. She made sure he was still breathing and didn't light himself on fire. Rochelle had a kindness of heart and a depth of soul that was incomprehensible. To me, some people just weren't worthy of sympathy.

"What do you want Ed?" I asked, exasperated.

"I ask the questions," Ed snapped back. More TV cop talk followed by silence and his sickening stare.

"Well?" I asked.

"Where's Rochelle?" he asked.

"At work."

"What's that?" he asked, nodding towards the cap on the curb.

"A distributor cap," I said.

"Why are you climbing through her window?"

"I don't have the key."

"Where's Rochelle?"

"At work."

"Why are you climbing through the window?"

"I need her hair dryer."

"Your hair is too short."

"No shit Ed. For the distributor cap." I pointed at the curb.

"I thought you two were broke up," he said.

Rochelle shares her private life with this man? I was getting angry. It seemed that I had something to do. My suit was ruined and my truck was stuck in a pond.

"Friends don't climb through windows," Ed said.

"Call the cops Ed. If that makes you feel better, call the cops. Or call the restaurant and tell Rochelle I'm about burglar her home. Shit Ed, do whatever you want." I went back to the window. Ed's door closed and I wedged myself through the window and came down on the bathroom floor headfirst. I walked around and opened the front door. When I brought in the distributor cap it was almost dry, so I used the hair dryer on my pants, shoes and socks. I went to Rochelle's closet and rifled through it until I found a pair of cut off fatigues that I had given her. I put them on and it was then that I realized how foreign Rochelle's apartment seemed to me. I felt like an intruder. I looked around and realized I hadn't been there for months. I had no claim there. Her answering machine blinked and I knew none of the messages were my voice. I packed my suit into a grocery bag and made for the door. I wanted to leave her a note but could not think of anything to say.

The robins and the jays and the chickadees were out and as I walked down the asphalt I grasped the possibility of life. It was odd and amusing that I was alive and whole. My shorts and dress shoes weren't absurd or even silly. Things just were and I kept on walking confident that I could restart my truck and move on.

Made in the USA
Lexington, KY
22 March 2019